The Winter Widow

AnneMarie Brear

Print ISBN 978-0-6450339-9-1

The Winter Widow

AnneMarie Brear

Chapter One

Springwood Farm
North Yorkshire, England
September 1852

Caroline Lawson opened the gate leading from the milking shed to the field beyond and stepped aside to allow her two cows, Buttercup and Clover, to slowly wander from cobbles to grass.

Clover bellowed loudly in the still dawn air and, satisfied she'd made her presence known, decided to rub her neck on the fence post.

'Go on, girl.' Caroline pushed her away. 'Let me shut the gate or you and Buttercup will be in the yard eating the last of my flowers.'

With the gate secured, Caroline leaned her elbows on top of it and stared out over the fields to the rising sun in a pink and orange sky. Summer weather had lingered into the first week of September and she was grateful for it. Her days were sad enough without bad weather to add to it.

Sighing deeply, she turned and went into the milking shed and collected the full bucket of milk. Roger, the rooster, crowed from the dung heap behind the stable, shattering the quietness of the morning.

Crossing the dirt yard, she entered the dairy shed and placed the bucket into a large stone sink filled with cold water to keep the milk cool until she could come back to it later to begin the strength-snapping task of churning the milk into butter.

In the barn next to the dairy shed, she grabbed a bowl of grain and went to feed the chickens on the other side of the yard near the low-walled kitchen garden she tended to so happily.

'Good morning, ladies,' Caroline sang to the hens, opening the door to their pen. Some hens eagerly rushed for the open space of the yard, while some waited, knowing she'd feed them, and two hens stayed on their nests, sitting on eggs.

She tutted. 'What have I told you two?' She brushed them off their eggs. 'You're not having chicks at this time of the year.' Carefully placing the half dozen eggs into her apron pockets, she sprinkled a handful of grain inside the pen before going out to scatter more over the yard.

Such mundane jobs usually brought her joy, but happiness had vanished from her and the farm since her husband died four weeks ago.

A rusty nail piercing his boot, days of agony and fever, and a week of her caring for her darling Hugh and finally his painful death were the contents of her nightmares. She still couldn't believe it had happened. How could a strapping man in his prime, strong and powerful, cheerful and loving, be taken from her after only two years of marriage? They had their whole lives ahead of them, plans and dreams forged in midnight talks cuddled in bed beneath a mountain of blankets.

Tears burned behind her eyes, begging to be released, but she shook her head, determined not to give in to the grief that formed a hard knot in her chest. She had cried enough over the last four weeks. Crying didn't help her, it just made her feel more miserable, more alone.

She had no time to wallow. Marching into the farmhouse scullery, she pulled off her boots and replaced them with house slippers. A loaf of bread in a tin was proving on the window ledge, basking in the early sunlight. Another half an hour and she'd pop that into the oven. She'd been up before dawn to make the dough, unable to find sleep. The bed seemed so cold and empty without Hugh in it. Their bedroom upstairs, only one of two, held all his clothes and she found it difficult to be in there. Instead, she preferred to nap in the big chair in front of the fire in the small parlour at the front of the house.

Caroline added seasoned apple wood to the fire in the large shining black range and placed the kettle on to boil. Since Hugh's death, food meant little to her, but she knew she had to eat for strength to work on the farm. The harvest was in, brought in by Hugo the week before he trod on the nail. But the piglets needed to be taken to market tomorrow and she'd have to put the cart to their horse, Barney. The old shire was no trouble and patiently did as he was bid, but the cart was heavy, and it took her a good hour to drag the cart in place and get it and Barney harnessed.

Of course, she could ask Howard, her father-in-law, to help her, but he lived five miles away and by the time she walked there, she could have done the task herself. Anyway, to go to Hopewood Farm where her in-laws lived would mean having to see and talk to her brother-in-law Leo and his awful wife, Lisette and she would rather do a week's worth of deeply stained washing than be in their company for a single moment.

Cooking two eggs for her breakfast, she mashed a pot of tea and buttered the last of the bread she'd made two days ago. To-morrow she'd go to the village and place fresh flowers on Hugh's grave, and his mother's, who rested beside him. Although Hugh's mother had died before Caroline married Hugh, placing flowers on his mother's grave was something they had done each Sunday after church, and she would continue to do so.

She ate her breakfast quickly, wanting to wash the stone-flagged floor before it got any later, but the sound of a horse and cart coming into the yard had her glancing out the window. She groaned on seeing Howard, Leo and Lisette climbing down from the Lawson family cart.

Taking off her apron, Caroline faced the back door, knowing they'd come in that way for no one but strangers used the cottage's front door.

'Good morning, daughter,' Howard said, entering the room first, taking his hat off and giving her cheek a kiss. 'How do you fare?'

'Well, Father,' she answered. She liked her father-in-law. He was a kind man, and Hugh had been his image in looks and manners.

'Caroline.' Leo nodded to her as he entered, Lisette on his heels and with a strained smile in Caroline's direction. A small bird-like woman with plain features, Lisette's gaze roamed about the kitchen as though she'd never seen it before.

'This is an early call.' Caroline went to the table and lifted the teapot. 'Tea?'

'Aye, lass, that'll be grand,' Howard said.

'We just had one before we left,' Lisette whined at him. 'We should just get this over with.'

Caroline frowned at her sister-in-law. They'd never got along. Lisette felt Caroline had taken some of the attention off her when she married Hugh. Before then, Lisette had been the sole woman at Hopewood Farm to care for Howard and his two sons. Lisette had shown Caroline no warmth or offers of friendship.

Now though, Lisette wouldn't meet Caroline's gaze. A stirring of anxiety churned the breakfast Caroline had just eaten. 'Get what over with?'

'Now lass...' Howard gripped his hat in both hands, his grey eyes softening with worry. 'There's been a bit of a development.'

'Oh?' Caroline gave Howard her full attention.

'We're to have this farm,' Lisette blurted out.

'Lisette!' Howard barked. 'I'll handle this, not you.'

Caroline carefully placed the teapot back on the table, trying not to become emotional. 'What do you mean?'

ANNEMARIE BREAR

His expression tense, Leo stepped forward, an older and larger version of Hugh but without the good looks and easy character of his brother. 'We've been up to the big house and spoken with Mr Craven, the estate steward, and he's spoken with Lord Stockton-Lee. They give their consent for us to have this farm.'

'I don't understand.' Caroline felt breathless. 'We already have the farm.'

'No, not you, not now Hugh is dead,' Leo said bluntly. 'The lease has been granted to me.'

Caroline's legs felt unstable. What were they saying? 'Do you mean you'll be farming the land?'

'Aye, lass,' Howard said. 'Springwood joins Hopewood's boundaries, so we'll have both farms.'

'But we have that now.' Why were they making an issue of this? She didn't understand.

Leo coughed into his hand. 'Hugh had the lease for this farm and Father has the lease for Hopewood. Now *I* have the lease for *this* farm.'

'Which means *we'll* be moving in here,' Lisette stated, a greedy gleam in her eyes. She folded her arms and eyed the room once more.

'But you live at Hopewood.' Caroline looked from one to the other.

'Not anymore. We will live here from now on.' Lisette raised her chin as if in challenge. 'You're a widow. This is no longer your farm.'

'But you're welcome to come to Hopewood and live with me,' Howard hurriedly put in, his tone earnest.

'With him and his soon-to-be wife,' Lisette crowed.

'Wife?' Caroline's head spun.

'Aye, lass. I'm getting married.' Howard's cheeks flushed scarlet. 'To Mrs Aspall from the village. You know the widow who has the candle stall at the market?'

She knew who Mrs Aspall was. She'd bought candles from her stall. But that information wasn't important, at least not to Caroline. Howard could marry the woman who seemed nice enough. However, this farm, her *home*, was the only thing to concern her. 'Why has my farm been given to you?' she accused Leo.

'Because Hugh is dead.'

'I know he is dead!' she shouted, frustrated.

'Lass...' Howard put his hands out to her.

'What I want to know is why you've taken this farm from me? I can manage this place just as Hugh had.'

'But you're a widow now,' Leo said matter-of-factly. 'This farm needs a man to run it.'

'You and Howard could help me when I needed it.' She tried to keep the begging tone out of her voice. Working the land had been something she'd thought about. Hugh had spent long hours behind the plough. Could she do it?

Leo shrugged. 'Both Mr Craven and Lord Stockton-Lee want a family in here, someone they can trust to make a go of it and pay the rent. They don't trust you can do it as a woman alone.'

'You can come to me though, lass,' Howard added, as though it was an enticing reward for giving up her home.

Lisette tutted. 'As if she'd want to live with you and your new wife. No, Caroline will have to move away, start her life again somewhere else.'

Like a knife was slicing through her organs, Caroline gasped and staggered. 'Leave?'

'What option do you have?' Lisette inspected the shelf of the large dresser by the door. 'You're bound to get a position as a maid somewhere.'

'Lass, just come and live with me,' Howard said gently. 'We get along fine, don't we?'

Leo turned for the door. 'We'll be back in the morning with our things. See that you're packed up and ready to go.'

'Don't I get a say in any of this?' Caroline wanted to throw something at his retreating back.

'Widows can't farm the land alone, Caroline. Be sensible.' Lisette gave her a sly grin as she left the kitchen.

Howard came to her and rubbed her upper arms. 'I'm sorry, lass. I couldn't stop him from going up to the big house. He wanted a farm of his own, especially when I started courting Mrs Aspall. Leo's always coveted this place and hated it when Hugh was successful in getting the lease.'

'This is my home.' She clasped his hands. 'Can you not change Leo's mind, please? This was Hugh's farm. He worked so hard to get it into shape after old man Yates died. We both put everything we had into turning this farm into a comfortable home and profitable, you know we have!'

Tears gathered in the old man's eyes. 'Aye, I know, lass, and my heart is broken with the loss of my dear boy, but I can't do anything about Leo's plans now. It's all settled. Them up at the big house don't want a widow here. They think you'll not be able to pay the rent.'

'But I will!' she defended fiercely. 'They need to just give me a chance to show them I can do it. I'll plough and sow seed. I'll raise the beasts and take them to market. I can do all that Hugh did. I can prove it to them.'

'The decision is made, lass. They won't change their minds now.'

'How could they have decided without talking to me?' Her voice broke.

'They listened to Leo. He pleaded his case to take over his brother's farm.'

She turned away, anger burning like a fire in her chest. 'I can imagine Leo would have told them a suitable story that I couldn't cope.'

'Lass, you wouldn't have been able to do it all,' Howard murmured. 'Farming is tough. I've been doing it all my life and I still find it hard going.'

'I would have tried. With your help, I might have managed. At least I deserved to be given a chance.'

'I'm sorry, lass, truly I am. Leo and Lisette have wanted this farm for years. They wouldn't listen to me.'

'What about me?' Fear choked her words. 'Where will I go?'

'To me, lass, come and live with me.'

She stepped back, away from him. 'No. That would never work, and it wouldn't be fair to Mrs Aspall.'

'Then what will you do?' He looked as wretched as she felt.

'I'll have to go away and find work...'

Leo called for his father from outside and, reluctantly, Howard put on his hat. 'Tomorrow, come to Hopewood and stay a few nights until you've sorted out what you'll do. Promise me you will?'

She nodded and received his kiss on her forehead.

When the door closed behind him and she heard the cart rattle away out of the yard, she sank onto a chair and buried her face in her hands. Sobs erupted from her. She sobbed for the husband she loved and now the home she'd lost.

Chapter Two

Standing in the morning sunshine, Caroline surveyed the yard. All was in order. The two sweet cows were milked, and they grazed in the field with their calves. The hens were fed and released to peck about the barns. Her heart twisted at the thought of never seeing them again, but she quashed the emotions that clogged her throat. She'd cried most of the night until exhausted, and she'd only slept for a few hours. Before dawn, she'd woken hungry and thirsty and purposely eaten all the food that was left before packing two carpet bags of her clothes and personal belongings.

Unable to cope with being inside the cottage any longer, for it was not her home anymore, she'd dressed in her best clothes, a dark blue dress and black bonnet, gathered her things outside and stood to wait for Howard's cart. Only it wasn't Howard who came alone, as she expected. Beside him sat Leo. Lisette was seated on a crate in the back of the cart, surrounded by other crates and chests.

Caroline clenched her jaw at Lisette's triumphant glare as they halted. Howard climbed down and came straight to Caroline. 'You're all set, then?'

She nodded. Words seemed impossible now the time had come.

'Is this all you have?' Lisette asked, pointing to the two carpet bags by the door.

Caroline nodded again. 'I can hardly take my furniture, can I?'

'Right, let's get this unpacked so we can be off,' Howard said to Leo, going to the back of the cart.

Without moving, Caroline watched them unpack the cart. She jumped when Lisette's spoiled tabby cat meowed from a small crate. It hissed from within, and Caroline shuddered, knowing the dratted thing would soon be scratching at the furniture she had lovingly polished every week since her marriage.

Lisette came alongside of her, a cunning smile on her face. 'Have you had a thought about what you'll do? Maybe you could get a position at the big house?'

The last thing she wanted to do was chat to her awful sister-in-law as if it was simply a normal day and they were passing time over a cup of tea. Caroline's world had crashed around her and at that moment she couldn't see a future.

'You know,' Lisette continued, 'I heard the kitchens are enormous up at the big house. I bet there's plenty of work there. A scullery maid, or if you're lucky, maybe work as a chambermaid upstairs. Wouldn't that be interesting?'

Caroline glared at her.

'Or you could always get work at the haberdashery in the village. I heard Mrs McFee was looking for someone to help her now her arthritis is so bad. Or what about working at the pit? Larkson's Pit is always putting on women to work on the slag heaps. It's only three miles away from Hopewood.'

Her hands itched to slap Lisette's face. She knew the horrid woman was riling her, wanting to break her and put her in her place.

'We're done, lass.' Howard took Caroline's elbow. 'I've put your things in the cart. Was there anything else?'

Shaking her head, Caroline walked to the cart on legs that shook, but she kept her head held high. She refused to look at Leo and Lisette as Howard clicked his tongue for the horse to move on.

Tears hovered on the edge of her lashes as she left the yard. Back straight and her gloved fingers clenching her velvet reticule that Hugh had bought her for her last birthday, Caroline stared straight ahead even though her heart was splintering.

'A nice cup of tea when we get home, hey lass?' Howard patted her arm.

'No.' She swallowed. Any idea of going to stay at Hopewood fled. She couldn't live there, not with a new woman coming into the house and also because she knew Lisette would call often and talk of the changes she'd made in the cottage and what not, and Caroline couldn't stomach it not now, not ever.

She turned in the seat. 'I'm sorry, Father, but could you take me to York?'

'York?' Howard's eyes widened. '*York?*'

'I know it's a long way, but it's best for me to start somewhere new. In the city, I have more chances of finding work.'

'It's fifteen miles away, lass,' Howard spoke in surprise.

York was a once-a-year trip in spring for the whole family when the snow had melted, and the narrow dirt roads were usable again.

He glanced at her. 'I said you can stay with me for as long as you want.'

'I know and I'm grateful., but I need a fresh start. You understand, don't you?'

'What will you do though, lass? Have you got any money?'

'A bit.' She tapped her reticule. 'Twenty-one shillings and nine pence and a farthing.' It was all the money she had found in the cottage since Hugh's death.

'That won't last you long. You've nowhere to stay, no job...' Howard shook his head. 'Let's talk about it over a cup of tea and give it a few days.'

'If you don't want to take me, I'll walk.' She would not budge on her decision. She had to go.

'Lass, you're being hasty.' Howard slowed the horse at the road junction that led to the village on the left or to York on the right. 'There's no rush for you to go off anywhere for a bit. Take some time to think things through.'

'I don't have time, Father. Leo saw to that. I have no home and no money coming in now.' It grated on her that Leo would benefit from the hard work she and Hugh had done on the farm.

'If you go to York, I'll not see you often, lass.' Howard rubbed his eyes. 'I can't lose you, too.'

'I'll write.' Caroline embraced him and then prepared to climb down.

'No, don't get down. I'll take you, then I know you've got there safe.' He flicked the reins and turned the horse right. Ahead stretched the long dirt track to York and her unknown future.

Three hours later, they tiredly rumbled into the western edge of the city. From the quiet country lanes, they merged onto Holgate Lane and rows of tidy houses began to appear. After crossing the railway line, Howard encouraged the horse to turn left onto Blossom Street, a wide, tree-lined street of large, elegant houses with pretty gardens. From her previous two visits, Caroline knew this was the best part of York and perhaps she could work in one of those houses as a maid. Down the gentle hill of grand residences, the street narrowed into Mickelgate and headed for the River Ouse.

'Where shall we stop?' Howard looked worried as he controlled the horse, who wasn't used to so many vehicles vying for space on the cobbled bridge. Water flowed underneath, carrying with it boats of varying sizes, from little skiffs to long barges.

'On the other side of the bridge will be fine.' Caroline suggested, but had no real idea of where to go or what to do.

'I need a drink,' Howard muttered as a dog ran out in front of the horse, causing it to throw its head up and skitter sideways. 'Whoa there, Dossy. You're fine, girl,' he soothed the horse.

'Over there is a pub,' Caroline pointed to a corner building proclaiming itself to be the Coach Inn.

Fortunately, Howard was able to pull up the cart in front of it and tie the horse's reins to a post.

'You can't leave that here,' a fellow shouted, passing by, pushing a wheelbarrow full of potatoes.

'I'll do what I damn like,' Howard answered.

Caroline glanced at him, for it was unlike Howard to be sharply spoken, but the tight expression on his face showed his concerns. He helped Caroline from the cart and they stood on the corner of a busy thoroughfare. The Yorkshire Bank was across from them, and on the other side of the street was St Michael's Church.

'I'll not stay long, but Dossy needs food and a drink and a rest and so do I.' Howard patted the horse's nose.

'They might have stabling behind?' She glanced down an alley to the side of the pub, but it seemed too narrow to lead a horse down it.

'I've a feed bag I keep in the back of the cart for emergencies.' Howard sorted out Dossy with her nose bag of grain. 'I'll fetch us a drink from inside the pub. You stay here and mind the cart.'

Caroline waited by the cart and received a sullen glare from the wheelbarrow man on his return journey.

'Didn't you hear me?' the man said. 'You can't stop here. The brewery dray will be along any minute.'

'We won't be long. We just need to rest the horse.'

'Do it somewhere else!' the man snapped and pushed his barrow down the road towards the river.

Caroline shrank into herself at the confrontation. Was this how people spoke to each other in the city? Weren't there any pleasantries?

Finally, Howard returned carrying two glasses of water. He gave one to Caroline and kept one for himself. 'They wouldn't let me bring my beer outside, so I had to swig it down quickly and ask for water. I hate cities.' He scowled at the people hurrying by.

'It's very different to the farm,' Caroline whispered, suddenly afraid of being left here alone.

'Dirty, filthy places, rife with disease,' Howard muttered. 'Not a friendly face to be seen.' Then his shoulders slumped. 'Lass, will you not change your mind and come home?'

She was so tempted, but she didn't have a home, not now. Howard was the only person who cared about her in the world, and soon he'd be getting married. No, she had to find a new path. 'I'll be fine, Father. I'll soon settle.'

'I don't want to leave you, but I need to be getting back. It'll be dark before I'm home.'

'Yes, of course. You go.' She steeled herself for his departure.

He took down her bags from the back of the cart. 'You'll write and let me know how you fare?'

'I will.' Tears filled her eyes.

'I want you to have this.' He gave her a handful of coins. 'It's all I have on me. If I'd known, I would have given you more that I have hidden away at home.'

'That's so kind of you.' She didn't count the coins but added them to her reticule, knowing she'd need them.

Howard embraced her and she held him tight.

'And you promise to come home if it doesn't go well here?' he murmured.

She nodded, swallowing back her tears. 'Take care and thank you for accepting me into your family. You've been the father I never had.'

'And you, the daughter I never had.' He cleared his throat and, with a final pat on her shoulder, he mounted the cart and flicked the reins to guide Dossy into the road.

Heart thumping, she watched him until he was lost to the buildings and horse-drawn vehicles that filled her teary vision.

Sucking in a deep breath, she grabbed the handles of her two carpet bags and, back straight, walked around the corner of the pub and along High Ousegate.

From living in the countryside, the noise of so many people and industry assaulted her ears. The smell of sewers and waste lining the streets filled her nose. Caroline turned her head away from a man urinating in a side alley and quickened her step.

Turning into Parliament Street, market stallholders were packing away their unsold goods. The afternoon was becoming cool, and the crowds of shoppers were thinning out as Caroline strolled along, not knowing where to go or what to do.

She needed lodging for the night, but in the centre of the city, all she found were shops and businesses. She needed to wander into the side streets, but was worried about getting lost and nightfall arriving.

Her bags weighed heavily in her hands with each step she took. She jumped when the large bells of York Minster boomed across the city. Time was running out to find somewhere before darkness descended. With a spurt of energy, Caroline dashed across a street and up a small lane which took her into The Shambles, a narrow, cobbled street filled with butcher shops. The buildings were old, painted white with black wooden beams, so old the top stories leaned towards each other blocking out the light.

A butcher threw a bucket of bloody water onto the cobbles right in front of her and she skidded to a halt with a gasp.

'Sorry, duckie.' He grinned.

She wasn't sure if he was or not, but he was the first person she'd spoken to in over an hour. 'Could you help me, please?'

'Aye, lass. What are you needing?'

'Lodging for the night.'

'You're new to the area, then?'

'Yes. I'm looking for work.'

The butcher, bald and with a large stomach, rubbed his chin. 'I don't know about work, but me and the missus can put you up for the night. We've a spare bed now our Simon has gone into the army.'

Unsure whether to be relieved or wary, Caroline dithered. 'You have a room?'

'Aye.' He stuck his head back inside the doorway of the shop. 'Judith!' he hollered. 'The missus will sort you out. I need to get on with shutting up the shop for the night.'

'Thank you.' She waited a few moments, watching other butchers pack away their hanging pieces of meat and swill down the cobbles with pails of bloody water. Eventually, a tall thin woman came out of the shop door, drying her hands on her grubby apron.

'What do you want, Charles?' Her expression was hard and unfriendly. 'I'm busy.'

The butcher, taking down braces of rabbits on hooks in front of the shop, smiled at his wife. 'This here lass needs a bed for the night. I said we could put her up.'

'Well, you said wrong, Charles Bent.' His wife scowled at him. 'Have you got rocks for brains? I've enough to do looking after you and this shop without taking on a lodger as well.'

Embarrassed by the scene, Caroline took a step back. 'I understand. Please don't worry about it. I'll look somewhere else.'

'Get along to Fossgate. There's lodging houses down there and in Goodramgate, too. We ain't one!' The woman turned and slammed the door on Caroline.

'Sorry, lass.' The butcher shrugged. 'It was worth a try.'

Quickly grabbing her bags, Caroline smiled her thanks to him and hurried down the cobbles to escape the embarrassing scene.

At the end of the Shambles was St Criux's Church, a small stone building unadorned by any carvings or towers to give it some beauty. Yet, the quaintness of the church called to her and the urge to go inside and sit in the calmness of quiet was difficult to resist, but she had to keep going and find a room for the night.

In the next street along, she found Fossgate, a narrow, cobbled street lined with shops on either side. Tiredly, she walked along looking for signs of any lodging houses. She reached the stone bridge over the River Foss, a waterway that led to the bigger River Ouse. The smell of the putrid water made Caroline's stomach churn. Feeling light-headed, she avoided looking down at the disgusting dark water clogged with refuse and pollution from the sawmills and tanners. She could smell the tang of blood from a slaughterhouse nearby and the further she walked, the stink of a tannery became prominent. She kept walking, even though the sign on a building said Walmgate. She was no longer on Fossgate, but what did it matter as long as she found a boarding house?

Two children, dressed in clothes fit for rags, came running towards her, shouting and hollering, waving sticks in the air like soldiers on a charge. Behind them a dog ran barking, while from a window of an upper story a woman threw out the contents of a chamber pot, narrowly missing Caroline's head. The splash hit the ground and bounced onto Caroline's polished boots and the hem of her skirt.

Disgusted, shocked and totally fed up, Caroline leaned against a building. What had she done? Had she been foolish to leave Howard and reject his offer of a home with him? Her pride and her grief mixed together to muddle her brain.

'You all right?'

Caroline looked at the old man hobbling towards her. 'I'm looking for a lodging house.'

'Ah, head to Beryl Overton's place, just down a bit further. She runs a good establishment.'

Relief gave her hope. 'Thank you, sir.'

He nodded and continued slowly on his way, and she realised he had a peg leg.

Confidence returned, Caroline carried on down the road and saw the sign for Overton's Lodging House. The building was three stories tall, made of red brick, and each window showed white curtains. She glanced at the front step and noted it was clean and swept. Taking courage that it was a suitable place to stay, Caroline rang the brass bell beside the black door.

A grey-hair woman with spectacles answered, wearing all grey except for the white lacy cap on her head. 'Good afternoon.'

'Good afternoon,' Caroline repeated. 'I was wondering if you have a room for the night, please?'

'I do, yes.' The woman didn't move. 'I'm Mrs Overton. I run an excellent establishment despite being on this street. So, I expect my guests to conduct sensible and respectable behaviour.'

'Of course.'

The woman sniffed and looked Caroline up and down. 'You seem a reasonable sort or person.'

'I am.' She tightened her grip on her two bags. 'I'm recently widowed and came to York to look for work.'

Mrs Overton raised an eyebrow. 'It's one shilling and nine pence per night, which includes an evening meal and breakfast of porridge and tea. Can you pay for the room? It must be paid in advance.'

'I can, yes.'

'Very well, you may come inside.' Mrs Overton opened the door wider and took one of the bags from Caroline. 'What's your name?'

'Mrs Caroline Lawson.'

'Go on up. Top of the stairs and then it's the third door on the right. You'll have the front bedroom.'

Inside the bedroom, Caroline was grateful to see a clean but sparsely decorated room. A single iron bed made with crisp sheets and a patterned blanket jutted out from one wall. A chest of drawers stood near the door and a wash table was placed under the window. Heavy burgundy drapes and white lace curtains hung at the window, and against the side wall was a narrow wardrobe in plain dark wood.

'There's no fire in this room. I had them all boarded up because people can be careless, and I didn't wish for my business to be burnt to the ground. So, you'll have access to a stone water bottle which are kept in the scullery downstairs to warm your bed each night. The dining room below is well-heated and that heat rises to the rooms above. Is this suitable for you?'

'It is, thank you.' Caroline counted out the required coins and handed them to her.

'The evening meal is served at seven o'clock sharp. It'll be beef stew and suet dumplings tonight. There is no late supper.'

'I'll look forward to the meal.'

'I'll bring you up some hot water to wash the dust off you.' Mrs Overton closed the door behind her.

Slumping onto the bed, Caroline closed her eyes as tiredness enveloped her like a heavy weight. What a day it had been. Untying her bonnet, she hung it on the bedpost and pulled off her gloves. She stared at the gold band on her finger and ached for Hugh.

She laid back on the mattress and let the tension ease from her body only for it to be replaced with sadness. Everything she had loved was gone, ripped away so quickly without time for her to adjust. Last night she had laid in her own bed, the one she had lovingly shared with Hugh. Tonight, she would be in a strange bed, in a strange city. How had it happened? To be so happy and content one moment and then lost and tossed aside the next?

A tap on the door had her sitting up just in time for Mrs Overton to come in carrying a jug in one hand and a piece of paper in the another. 'I've brought you some warm water and your receipt.'

Caroline stood and took the receipt.

'If there is anything else you require, just let me know.' Mrs Overton tugged the white towel hanging on the end of the wash table straight. 'My rule is no visitors to your room at any time.'

'There won't be. I don't know anyone here,' Caroline answered.

Mrs Overton sniffed, her posture stiff, her face serious. 'Right, well, just so you know. I run a respectable establishment.'

'I'm pleased to hear it.' She met the woman's stare. Did the landlady think she was someone of ill repute?

'So, you're not from around here then?'

'No, I came from a village, Melliton, in the northwest. Fifteen miles away. Have you heard of it?'

'No.'

Caroline smiled. 'Not many people have. It's in the middle of nowhere, really.'

'I've never left the city.' Mrs Overton went to the door. 'You are my only guest at the moment. If you prefer, you can have your meal on a tray in your room? I don't normally allow it, but it'll save me setting a table just for one.'

'Oh, yes, of course. I don't mind.'

At the door, the landlady turned, her gaze direct behind her glasses. 'What kind of work are you looking for?'

'Any I can get.' Caroline said, tipping water from the jug into the porcelain basin. 'Do you know of anything?'

'No.' Mrs Overton closed the door behind her.

Rebuffed by the woman's coldness, Caroline washed her hands and face. She wouldn't be getting any friendship from Mrs Overton it seemed. She stared out of the window as she got dried. Directly opposite was The Black Horse public house. Two little boys were throwing stones at the sign above the front door. One stone hit the picture of the black horse and the boys cheered until a man dashed out of the pub and yelled at them. The boys ran off hollering while a cat slinked along the gutter. A woman with a baby strapped to her chest in a shawl plodded slowly past, lugging a sack of coal.

She wasn't used to having strangers living and working so close. The noise of the busy street, the clanging and banging sounds from the surrounding factories boomed in her ears. Would she ever become used to it? Did she have a choice? The city would have more opportunities for work, but already she was missing the quiet of the countryside, the greenness, and the space, the peacefulness.

Tiredly, she unpacked some of her clothes, her bible, given to her from the convent where she grew up, and her hairbrush and combs. Tomorrow, she would find a job, she was sure of it and with a job she could find a proper long-term room to rent and make it her home.

Lifting a skirt from her bag, she saw beneath it the blue woollen scarf that she'd knitted for Hugh last Christmas. Her heart twisted with love and longing. She couldn't leave that behind as she had with all his other belongings.

Pressing the scarf to her face, Caroline let the tears flow.

Chapter Three

Letting herself out of the lodging house, Caroline put a hand to her bonnet as the wind gusted down the narrow street. Leaves and papers were swept along the cobbles. The morning sun cast long shadows and she shivered in her coat.

Head down, she crossed the bridge, careful not to bump into the flock of people heading to work or to do their shopping. Caroline had a mental list of places to visit, those she'd not been to in the last three days of searching.

Mrs Overton, in her blunt way, told her to try the houses on The Mount or Blossom Street. Caroline was doubtful one of the elegant houses would give her a position when she didn't have a reference, but it was worth a try. She'd spent money on her room for the week and was conscious of the amount dwindling. She had to secure a wage soon.

Walking past the beginning of Parliament Street, Caroline looked at the market filled with early shoppers. She wished she could stop and browse the stalls, but she couldn't afford to waste the morning and she had a fair walk yet.

So far, she hadn't crossed the River Ouse to look for work on the other side, instead concentrating on the city centre, but having no luck finding any paid work, she knew she'd have to search further afield.

The river glinted silver in the sunshine, the breeze rippling its surface and causing it to lap gently along the banks. Walking across Ouse Bridge, Caroline watched the men working on the docks, the cranes lifting cargo nets to the order of different whistles. Howard had once told her how the larger ships plied the river from York to the River Humber and the port of Hull. The busy wharves were interesting to watch, but she couldn't linger and hurried to the other side.

Micklegate Bar, the old medieval gate to that part of the city loomed above her. She had ridden in the cart beneath it but never stood next to the tall stone tower. The city's walls continued left and right, huge stone structures that had guarded York for centuries. Once through the arch, Caroline would be out in the wide residential streets and beyond that the open countryside... and the road home.

No. She mustn't think like that. Home was gone. She had to shake it from her mind and think of the future here in the city.

It didn't take her long to reach Blossom Street and she slowed as the hill rose ahead. Did she have the courage to knock on the shining doors of such refined houses and ask for work?

Gathering her courage, she opened the first wrought-iron gate and stepped into a neatly tended garden. The path led to the front door, but Caroline knew she'd not be received and so went along the drive beside the house and looked for a service entrance.

'Can I help you?' A young woman in uniform and apron held a basket of clothes on her hip.

Caroline glanced about the small yard. 'I'm wondering if there's a position available?'

'For in the house?' The girl hitched the basket higher on her hip. 'I doubt it but knock on the door there and ask for Mrs Malloy, she's the housekeeper.'

Caroline did as the girl suggested. Smiling kindly at the young lad who led her into the wide kitchen. Several girls working in the room stared at her.

'Good morning.' A woman rose from a small desk in the corner of the room. 'I'm Mrs Newcombe, the cook.'

'Good morning. I'm sorry to disturb you but I'm looking for work, any work.'

'Of course, you are. I didn't think you'd come to attend a dinner party.' Mrs Newcombe grinned. 'Unfortunately, there's nothing going.'

'Is Mrs Malloy here who I can speak to?' Caroline didn't want to give up too easily.

'Aye, she is, but she's with the mistress at the minute and can't be disturbed.'

'Oh.'

'Do you have a reference?'

Caroline flinched. 'No.'

'You'll be hard pressed to get a position without a reference.' Mrs Newcombe took a piece of paper from her desk and a pencil. 'Can you write?'

'Yes.'

'Then put your name down here and where we can write to you. If Mrs Malloy wants to see you, she'll send a note, but I wouldn't hold your breath.'

'Thank you.' Caroline wrote well, having been taught by the nuns in the convent. She gave the paper to the cook. 'Thank you for your time.'

'Try Stanton House further up the street. They might have something.' Mrs Newcombe put the paper in her apron pocket. 'Good luck.'

'I appreciate your kindness.' Caroline left the house and waved to the girl who hung out clothes on a line at the bottom of the long garden.

Feeling more confident, Caroline walked with a lighter step as she went up the street. However, at Stanton House she received the same reception. No work available and a look of disbelief that she didn't have a reference.

For the rest of the day, she knocked on nearly every door along The Mount, Blossom Street and down into Micklegate. The result was the same for each of her enquiries. No positions and, without a reference, she was never likely to get one.

Walking the streets as the sun sent long shadows across the cobbles, Caroline tried not to be despondent, but it was difficult.

How could she obtain a reference when she'd never worked for anyone before?

She'd left the convent in Harrogate at sixteen and went to live with an aging distant great uncle, Emery Ponting, a relative of her late mother's. He brought her to the small village of Melliton and she kept house for him and his third wife who was in ill health. Although content to look after her uncle, she found his rules as strict as those in the convent. Her world shrank to a life of drudgery within his house and the garden. A retired church warden living off an inheritance, Emery gave her little money or freedom.

When her great uncle and his wife died within a year of each other, Caroline was twenty-two. At last, she had independence and in his will Uncle Emery left her some money, enough to pay the rent on his house for a further three months. For those three months she did exactly as she pleased for the first time in her life. She went for long walks beyond the village to learn about the area she lived in, and she attended her first ever harvest dance. There, she met Hugh Lawson and fell in love with his cheeky smile, the way he swung her around the dance floor, and his attentive nature. When he asked to see her again the next day, she agreed.

For the next two months they spent every day together and when the time came for Caroline to give up her uncle's house, she accepted Hugh's marriage proposal. Three weeks later they were married. She never regretted her hasty acceptance to wed a man she'd only known for the length of a winter. Hugh showed her love in tiny ways every day and she knew, for the first time, what it was to have someone care for her deeply. Never did she think their idyllic life would be cut so terribly short.

Letting herself into the lodging house, she met Mrs Overton at the bottom of the stairs.

'Any luck?' the landlady asked.

'No. I've walked up and down The Mount and Blossom Street, even went along Micklegate down to the bridge.'

'It'll be the lack of a reference.' Mrs Overton shook her head, as though Caroline was a fool to think any differently.

'Yes, it seems so.' Caroline stepped past her to go upstairs. She wanted to take off her boots and have a good wash.

'I've another guest staying. A regular. A gentleman named, Mr Casey, an inspector for the gas works. He has the room next to you.'

'I wonder if he'll give me a job?' Caroline joked.

'Don't be so ridiculous!' Mrs Overton snapped. 'He's an educated man. Don't be annoying him with your begging!'

Shocked by the rebuke, she frowned at the other woman. 'I was jesting.'

'Huh. I've no time for fooling about and neither does Mr Casey!' Mrs Overton marched down the hallway.

Climbing the steep staircase, Caroline paused at the top. Humming could be heard from behind the closed door next to her own room. At least Mr Casey seemed a cheerier sort than their landlady.

Suddenly the door opened and a tall, thin man with a large moustache stood there. 'Why, good evening. This is a pleasant surprise. Have you come to turn my bed down, miss?'

Caroline reddened. 'I think not. I am a guest.'

He wore a grey striped suit and a bright red cravat and held a top hat in his hand and gloves. 'Ah, Mrs Lawson I presume? Mrs Overton did mention you.' He held out his hand for her to shake. 'Mr Septimus Casey, which sounds decidedly formal for a fellow guest, does it not? My friends call me Mussy.'

'How do you do?' She shook his hand and then stepped towards her own door. He seemed a friendly sort. 'I shall see you downstairs for the evening meal?'

'No, not tonight. I have plans.' He tilted his head at her. 'A recent widow I hear?'

She stiffened. Their landlady had spoken about her. 'I am.'

'I'm sorry for your loss, madam.' He bowed slightly. 'To lose not only the man you love but your home as well must be rather difficult.'

Annoyed that Mrs Overton had told this stranger all about her, Caroline simply nodded and retrieved her key from her reticule and opened the door.

'Should you need someone to talk to, I'm all ears,' Mr Casey told her. 'I know how it feels to lose someone close.' His sad expression appeared genuine.

'Good evening, Mr Casey.' She closed the door on him, not wanting to talk about Hugh and her home to a strange man. She didn't want to hear about his loss, it was hard enough to deal with her own.

Sitting on the bed, she unbuttoned her boots and slipped them off and rubbed her feet, noticing that her stockings needed darning. A hole was forming on the right big toe and the heels were threadbare. She'd have to dip into her precious hoard of coins to buy a needle and thread or could she wait a little longer until she secured a position and had a wage coming in?

Later, alone in the dining room, Caroline ate her meal of fish pie. The heavy drapes had been drawn shutting out the dark and the passing people. A small fire flickered in the fireplace, the coals burning red. Two gas wall lights lit the room and although comfortable, Caroline wished she'd had a tray in her room. Sitting here by herself deepened her loneliness.

'Are you finished?' Mrs Overton asked, coming into the room with a tray. 'I have your rice pudding.'

'Yes, thank you.'

'I bet you're early to bed tonight? You'll have another busy day tomorrow walking the streets looking for work.'

'I don't know where to go next.' The very thought of roaming the city again depressed her.

'You need to aim lower. Without a reference you'll not be employed in a nice house. Best you try the market, or one of the factories. Terry's chocolate factory or Rowntree's. Or you could try cleaning at one of the hotels near the railway station. You'll find something if you look hard enough and aren't too picky.'

'Yes, I'm sure you're right.' Half-heartedly, she ate the rice pudding, not eager to endure another day of begging for a job.

The following morning, Caroline left the lodging house, determined to find work. She spent an hour asking the market stall holders if they needed an extra hand, but they shook their heads. She enquired at a press shop, to be told they only employed men.

By noon she had blisters on her heels as she trudged alongside streets and lanes, enquiring at shops and anywhere half decent. She loathed to work in a dirty factory, but perhaps one of the better ones would be willing to give her a chance?

Walking along the Shambles, Caroline was thirsty and wincing with every step she took.

'Hey there, lass. I remember you.' The butcher she met on her first day in the city leaned out of his doorway. 'Did you find some lodgings?'

'I did, yes.' She glanced up at the painted sign and read Bent's Butchery. She remembered his name, Charles Bent. 'Overton's Lodging House, past Foss Bridge.'

'Grand.' His apron was covered in grime and blood stains. 'You off to do some shopping?'

'I'm looking for work.'

'Oh, aye?' He stepped out onto the damp cobbles. The narrow lane was shadowed by the overhanging roofs above.

'And without much success. I don't have a reference, you see. I was married and worked on our farm. I've never held a position before.'

Mr Bent scratched his chin. 'Hmm. Tricky, yes.'

Another butcher opposite came out to hang up a side of beef in his open window. 'Who's this then, Charles? A new face.'

'A country blow in, Kel,' Mr Bent replied. 'Looking for work.'

'Aren't they always?' The butcher named Kel was a huge man with arms as thick as his legs and a stomach as round as a barrel. 'Are you Irish?' he asked with a sneer. 'The Irish plague this city as much as rats. They take all the jobs and will do owt that earns them a penny. It leaves no work for the English folk.'

'No, I'm not Irish.' Caroline defended.

Charles grunted. 'Leave the Irish be, Kel. If they earn money with which to buy my meat, then I'm fine with that.'

'Steal it more like the minute your back is turned.' Kel glared at the people walking by as though every one of them was a thieving Irishman.

'Charles Bent!' Mrs Bent came to the door, her face pinched in fury. 'If you spent as much time cutting up beasts as you did jabbering away out here, we'd be rich!'

'Coming, my little flower.' Mr Bent gave Caroline a cheeky wink before following his wife back inside the shop.

Circling back into the market, Caroline headed for St Samson's Square and Terry's chocolate factory. She would take any work now, even if it meant long hours in a crowded noisy factory.

'You, lass!' A man hollered out to her as she passed his stall of leather goods. 'You came by earlier, didn't you, looking for a bit of work?'

'Yes!' She hurried over to the side of his stall.

'Give me a hand to pack this lot away and you'll earn yourself a few pence.'

A few pence wasn't much, but it was more than anything she'd been offered so far. 'What can I do?'

'Start packing away the goods on the table into those crates I've stacked up. Me back went this morning and I've been in agony all day.'

'That's a shame.' Caroline stepped behind his stall and pulled a crate closer to the display table. The sharp tang of leather filled her nose as she packed away small leather purses, larger satchels and bags.

'Walt Miller is me name.' The old man groaned as he bent to untie a crate lid.

'Let me do that. Sit down.' She ushered him to a stool near the table. 'Just rest. I can pack it all away for you.'

'What's your name, lass?'

'Caroline.' She smiled, collecting a few belts which hung from the top of the stall's awning.

'I'm glad I saw you, Caroline. I could have asked Mrs Gainsborough.' He inclined his head to the stall directly behind him. 'But she's a right snarky woman, always complaining she's too busy to help other stallholders when we need to duck away for a few minutes. So, I didn't want to trouble her.' He sighed heavily and winced. 'Me backs been playing up for a few days now. I'm getting too old for this business, but what else can a man do at my age to earn a few bob?'

'I understand,' she replied, curling more belts into the crate. 'You have some lovely things.'

'Aye, working with leather has been my life.' He held up fingers bent with arthritis. 'For how much longer I can go on I don't know. I hate the thought up ending up in an alms house or worse still, the workhouse.'

Caroline shuddered at the mention of the workhouse. The threat of entering one of those dismal places played on her mind. 'Do you know of any work going, Mr Miller?'

'I don't, lass, sorry. But if you help me well enough this evening, and you can meet me tomorrow morning at dawn and work on the stall all day tomorrow, I'll pay you two bob. What do you say?'

'I say yes.' Caroline could have embraced the old fellow. Two shillings! That would pay for another night at the lodging house without dipping into her money.

Feeling much lighter in spirit, Caroline packed away the leather goods in quick time. Mr Miller was impressed that she could lift the crates onto his handcart.

'I lived on a farm. Lifting heavy things was something I did often to help my husband. It was just the two of us,' she told the old man.

'Right, well, if you can push that handcart over to the passage-way beside The Crown pub over there, we'll take it down to me lock up.'

Concentrating on not tipping the cart over while dodging shoppers, children and the odd dog, she manhandled the cart down the passageway to behind the pub and into the yard where Mr Miller unlocked a small shed. They transferred the crates into it, and he locked it up again.

'Meet me here at six.'

'I will.' She nodded vigorously. 'I'll be here.'

That night she wrote to Howard and told him she where she was staying and that she'd found a day's work on a stall in the market. She believed it was a start of her new future. Perhaps Mr Miller could give her more days working his stall if he was happy with her. She had to make sure she sold as much as she could tomorrow to impress him.

Taking her letter downstairs, she asked Mrs Overton if she'd post it for her tomorrow if she was going out.

'I suppose I can.' Mrs Overton stood in the kitchen doorway. 'I'm off to the shops in the morning, though not anywhere near the post office but I can make a special trip for you.' She made it sound as though Caroline had asked her to walk to London and back.

'Thank you. I appreciate it.'

'Who is the letter for?' Mrs Overton wanted to know. 'I thought you didn't have any family?'

'It's to my father-in-law. He's the only family I have. He'll be worried about how I'm getting on and so I wanted to let him know I'm here and I have a bit of work.'

'A day on a stall isn't a bit of work,' the landlady scoffed. 'I doubt old Mr Miller will give you any more than that. He couldn't afford to.'

'One day is better than none and it might lead to something else,' Caroline said hopefully.

'Your head is in the clouds. You need to find something permanent, or you'll not be able to afford to stay here for much longer, and I don't rent rooms on credit either.' With that Mrs Overton turned away and shut the kitchen door on Caroline.

Unperturbed by the other woman's negative words, Caroline walked up the hallway. At the bottom of the stairs the front door opened, and Mr Casey stepped in, his head bowed, his hat pulled down low.

'Good evening, Mr Casey,' she said, climbing the stairs. When he didn't answer, she turned to find him immediately behind her on the stairs.

'Excuse me,' he mumbled, trying to overtake her. His hand reached for the banister and Caroline gasped. It was covered in blood.

'Mr Casey, you're bleeding.'

'I'm fine.' He pulled his hand back and stumbled a bit.

Instinctively, Caroline held onto his arm. 'Mr Casey?'

He glanced up at her and then quickly down again but not before she saw his battered face.

'Oh, dear heavens. You need a doctor.'

'No!' he snapped. 'I just need to get to my room. Don't make a fuss.'

'Let me help you.' Broking no argument. She gripped his upper arm and helped him up the stairs into his room and to the chair in front of the dressing table. 'What happened?'

'Close the door,' he barked. 'I cannot have *her* seeing me like this.'

Caroline hurried to close the door. She stared as he took off his hat and revealed the damage to his face. 'You need a doctor.'

'No, I don't. It's just cuts and bruises. A bit of blood. I'll be fine.'

She poured some water from the jug into the basin and found a cloth hanging from a hook. 'Let me clean you up.'

'Be gentle,' he whispered.

Carefully, dabbing and wiping his face lightly, she managed to clear away most of the blood, to reveal a split lip, a cut above his swelling left eye and bruising on his cheek bones. 'Are you in much pain?'

'Some,' he croaked. He closed his tear-filled eyes. 'I should be used to it by now.'

'What do you mean?'

'Nothing.' Abruptly, he stood and took the blood-stained cloth from her. 'I can manage now. You've been brilliant, Mrs Lawson.'

'Please, call me Caroline.'

He smiled and then winced. 'Caroline it is, and I'm Mussy.'

'Is there anything I can do for you?' She felt so sad for him for he looked forlorn and broken.

'No, you've done so much already, and I thank you, but please don't mention a word of this to our landlady.'

'I don't see how you can keep it from her.'

'I'll stay in my room for a few days.' He shrugged.

'She'll come knocking when you don't appear for breakfast.'

'I'll talk to her through the door and say I'm unwell and for her to leave a tray outside the door.'

'Have you eaten this evening?'

'No, but I'm not hungry.'

'Can I fetch you a cup of tea?'

'Would you?' His voice broke.

'Of course, but first let's get rid of this lot.' She pulled aside the curtains and opened the window, letting in the night's cool breeze. She looked down to the street and seeing it clear for once, emptied the contents of the basin onto the cobbles below. 'I'll fetch you my water jug and I'll refill this one. Mrs Overton won't know.'

'What about this?' He held up the bloodied cloth.

'Give it here. I'll toss it on the fire downstairs after she's gone to bed.'

'Mrs Overton will know it's missing.' He frowned. 'You know what she's like. Nothing gets past her.'

'Let us worry about that tomorrow.' Caroline went to the door. 'I'll go down and ask for a cup of tea and I'll say you've returned and not feeling well. A cold on the chest and want an early night.'

'Lay the seeds so to speak.' He nodded.

'Exactly. I'll be back soon.'

Mrs Overton put up a performance about making tea trays, but relented when Caroline mentioned Mr Casey was feeling unwell. Eventually, she was able to take the tray up to him without the landlady insisting she go as well.

'She'll be up to check on you in the morning, so make sure the door is locked,' Caroline joked.

Mussy took the tray from Caroline. 'What a strange woman Overton is. One minute as cold as ice and so abrupt, and the next needing to know everything about you.'

'Yes. I was annoyed she had told you all about me.'

'I gathered that.' He looked kindly down at her. 'I wasn't asking though. I understand the need for privacy.'

'I know. Forgive my rudeness when we first met.'

'Nothing to forgive.' He poured the tea from the pot with hands that shook slightly.

'Are you certain you don't need a doctor?'

'Completely.'

She hesitated to leave, wanting to help him. 'Is there anything else I can do for you?'

'You've been an angel, truly.' His broken smile matched the sadness in his eyes.

'Very well. I'll leave you to rest.'

'Caroline?' His voice stopped her at the door. 'You haven't asked what happened to me.'

'I assumed you'd tell me if you wanted me to know. If not, then it's none of my business.'

Mussy's tall thin frame sagged a little. 'How refreshing that is to hear.'

'Good night, Mr Casey.'

'Good night, my new friend.'

Closing the door, Caroline smiled a little. She had made a new friend. It was a lovely feeling, and tomorrow she'd be employed for a day. Things were looking up.

Chapter Four

In the crisp light of a pink dawn, Caroline waited for Mr Miller at the lockup. She shivered in her coat. Behind the pub it was eerily quiet with long shadows hiding the ugliness of the yard littered with empty barrels, broken chairs and several heaps of kitchen waste. She imagined that at night the place would be a haven for rats and mice.

'You made it then?' Mr Miller hobbled through the gate, back bent, wheezing heavily.

'I said I would. I'm true to my word.'

He gave her the key and she unlocked the door to the small lockup. Without speaking, they packed the handcart with the crates and once more Caroline pushed it up the passageway and into Parliament Street to the market.

'I'm allus last down the end, lass.' Mr Miller instructed. 'Fruit and vegetables have the main share of the space. They've allowed me to tuck on at the end of the row all these years because I don't make a fuss of where I am.'

Caroline focused on listening to his instructions as they set up the stall. Other stallholders greeted them. Everyone working quickly to have their goods arranged for display before the shoppers arrived.

She hung the belts up, marvelling at Mr Miller's craftmanship and tooling of the soft leather. Portmanteaus were stacked in front of the table and small leather seat stools were placed beside them.

'Now, lass. Here's a few pence. Run along to Jubbergate and fetch us two pork pies to start us off for the day.' He gave her the coins and shooed her away.

With a pork pie to satisfy her hunger, Caroline listened and learned when Mr Miller spoke of serving customers and of the different grades of leather. She took it all in, wondering if she'd remember it all. Her first test came when a woman asked to buy a belt for her husband. Caroline served her politely and with a smile, she even encouraged the woman to buy a small purse, which she did.

Grinning, Mr Miller slapped Caroline on the back. 'Well done, lass. I think you're a natural at selling.'

Beaming with the praise, Caroline spent the morning talking to customers, serving a few and enjoying every minute of it.

By midafternoon, grey clouds scudded over the sun and without warning a deluge of rain battered the awning above their heads.

'Bloody weather,' Mr Miller mumbled, watching as the shoppers fled the market, eager to be out of the downpour. 'We might as well pack up, lass. The rains looks set in for the afternoon and we'll have few customers now.'

'That's such a shame.'

'It's the market world, lass. That's why none of us who have a stall are rich.' Miller grumbled as they packed away, and some items got wet. They threw a canvas sheet over the cart, but Caroline had no covering but her coat and bonnet, which was soaked by the time she lumbered into the lockup.

'Here's your money, lass. Thanks for everything. I'm grateful for you helping me while me back was bad.'

'Can I come back tomorrow?'

With sadness in his eyes, Mr Miller shook his head. 'I can't afford you, lass. I barely make enough for me stall rent and to buy more leather. I'm lucky to have money left over to keep a roof over me head in the filthy cellar where I live and a bit of food.'

Disheartened, she clenched the money. 'I understand.'

'Look lass, get yourself a proper position somewhere nice. You're too pretty to be roaming the streets.'

'I've tried.'

'Keep trying.' He patted her shoulder and sent her on her way.

The drizzling rain accompanied her all the way back to the lodging house. Mrs Overton was carrying fresh linen in her arms as Caroline came through the front door.

'I've clean sheets for you here, and your washing is done and ironed. That'll be one shilling and three pence for the washing, please.'

Reluctantly, Caroline handed over the money and was given the folded bedsheets in return. 'Thank you.'

'What's wrong?' the landlady asked.

'I can't work on the stall anymore. I'm not needed.'

'Did you think it would be a long-term thing, a stall on the market? More fool you.'

Caroline mounted the stairs. She didn't want to listen to the other woman's cutting remarks.

'Oh, and Mr Casey is unwell, so I expect you to be quiet in your room and not disturb him,' Mrs Overton said as a parting shot before disappearing down the hallway.

In her room, Caroline made her bed with the clean sheets and put away her washing. She couldn't afford to have Mrs Overton do her washing and ironing, not at those prices. Her money was dwindling at a rapid rate and if she didn't find work soon, she'd have to leave and look for somewhere cheaper to stay that wasn't so clean and pleasant.

A knock on the wall between her room and Mr Casey's had her going out into the hallway to check for the presence of Mrs Overton and seeing it was clear, Caroline knocked softly on Mussy's door. 'It's only me.'

'Come in only me,' was the reply.

Caroline closed the door quietly behind her. 'How are you feeling?'

'How bad do I look?' he grimaced.

'Terrible.' She grinned. His face was a mixture of coloured bruising and a swollen eye with a cracked lip to add to the tally.

Mussy snorted as he lay on his unmade bed. He wore a white and blue striped nightshirt over trousers. 'I need a drink.' He nodded to the empty whiskey bottle on the floor. 'I've had to work hard to keep old *nosey drawers* out of my room all day. Constant tapping at the door, trays being left that I didn't ask for. She's driven me mad.'

Caroline picked up a newspaper from the floor and folded it. The bedroom was a mess of discarded clothes, tea trays, the curtains half opened, books on the dressing table and piled on the end of his bed. 'She obviously cares that you are unwell.'

'Huh! She wants to know what's going on.' He swung his legs over the side of the bed and walked to the window to stare out at the grey skies and the wet street below. 'How was your day at the market?'

'Good until the rain came. Mr Miller doesn't need me anymore so I've no work. I'll have to go out and look again in the morning.' She sighed heavily and, moving a shirt from a chair, sat down.

'You will find something.'

'I need to and soon or I'll be out on my ear.'

He came and put his hand on her shoulder. 'If you need money, I'm your man. I can give you some to tide you over.'

'Thank you, that's kind, but I have to face it, without a job, staying in a nice lodging house is not possible.'

'If my face wasn't all the colours of a rainbow, I would take you out for a drink somewhere,' he said in his cultured accent.

'I don't drink.'

His eyebrows shot up into his hairline. 'Don't drink? At all?'

'A sherry at Christmas.'

'Girl, you have not lived until you have felt that warm fussy glow of a good drinking session at a party.'

'No, I don't think I have lived, really.' A party. Goodness she couldn't remember the last party she attended. She and Hugh went to the harvest dance each year, and the Christmas carols church service and in summer they'd have picnics in the field when Hugh was ploughing, but parties? No.

'You really are a country girl, aren't you?' He shook his head slightly as if in awe. 'You are so innocent. Lovely, but innocent. I can scarcely believe you were married. I've never met anyone like you before.'

'Maybe that's because you've always lived in a city. The countryside is different to cities.'

'True. I was born in Manchester, you know. I've moved about a lot, always to other big cities. Sometimes, I travel to other places just to be somewhere new, but York is a place that I keep coming back to.' He scratched at his stubble for he'd not shaved that day. 'I am not terribly keen on the countryside... Too many smells...'

She grinned. 'And where will you go after your time in York?'

'Wherever my fancy takes me.'

'You don't ever want to stay in one spot and settle?'

He roamed the room like a caged tiger, his long legs eating up the space. 'Settle. It's a loaded word, don't you think? Settle for what exactly?'

'A home, a wife, children...'

'You talk of family.'

'Yes.'

Mussy went back to the window and ran a finger down the glass following a raindrop. 'I'll never have a family, Caro.'

His words were said softly, regrettably and with a finality about them. They made her sad.

'Look at us. What a pair we are!' he announced suddenly. 'Let us go for a drink. We'll sneak out. I'll wear a scarf around my face.'

'Mrs Overton is expecting us downstairs to eat soon.'

'She's not our keeper, Caro.'

'I've never been called Caro in my life.' She laughed.

'It is what I'll always call you,' he said flippantly with a wave of his hand.

'You talk as if we will always be friends.'

'Won't we be?' He frowned as if the thought was ridiculous.

'I hope so, but you'll move on, and so will I, probably sooner than you.' She stood, knowing she needed to wash and change before going downstairs. 'Do you want a tray bringing up or are you coming down to eat?'

'I'm not hungry. That woman has been feeding me all day.' He flung himself onto his bed. 'Come back after the meal and we'll talk.'

'Very well,' she agreed happily, for spending each evening alone in her room was becoming depressing. She missed Hugh terribly, and the farm, and most nights she went to sleep early just to put an end to another day without either of them.

As promised, Caroline returned to his room after the meal of a pork chop and boiled vegetables with a gooseberry fool to finish. She knocked on Mussy's door and waited but no sound came from inside. She knocked again lightly, not wanting to draw attention from Mrs Overton, who seemed to appear like a ghost whenever Caroline was out of her room.

Hearing nothing, Caroline turned the handle, but the door was locked. 'Mussy.'

No reply. Believing he might be asleep, she went to her room feeling a little disappointed that she'd spend more hours alone. This was a lesson. She'd started relying on Mussy for company and that wouldn't do. As friendly as he was, soon they'd be moving on, especially if she found a live-in position, which she desperately needed. The cost of living in a lodging house was not beneficial on a low wage.

Feeling low, she did her nightly wash routine and climbed into bed. Snuggling into the pillows she allowed tears to fall for Hugh. She missed him so much. He'd be furious that she was in this position, evicted from their farm, and alone.

Banging woke her, then singing. Sitting up in bed, Caroline tried to make sense of what had woken her. A loud crash had her up out of bed and dragging on her dressing gown. She paused at the door and listened. More singing and then Mrs Overton's stern voice.

Hurrying down the staircase, Caroline stared as Mussy swayed at the bottom of the stairs, the hall table lamp smashed on the floor.

'Mr Casey!' Mrs Overton stood fuming, hands on hips, in her nightwear. 'You are drunk.'

'Decidedly so, madam.' He bowed gallantly with a chuckle and almost toppled over.

'This is shameful behaviour!'

Caroline quickly went to Mussy and grabbed his arm. 'Come up to bed,' she urged.

His blood-shot eyes were unfocused. 'Caro?'

'Yes, now come up, for heaven's sake.' She pulled him up two steps, but he swayed dangerously backwards.

'This is entirely inappropriate!' Mrs Overton glared at them both in suppressed rage.

'Help me get him up and into bed,' Caroline said through gritted teeth as she pulled Mussy's tall frame upwards.

With much grumbling from Mrs Overton and the odd line from a song from Mussy, they manhandled him up the stairs and across the landing. Reaching in his coat pocket, Caroline found his room key and unlocked the door.

Mussy turned a shade of green and Mrs Overton gasped as he vomited all over her carpet rug.

'How disgraceful! My carpet!' She fled the room.

Caroline, taking Mussy's weight, pushed him towards the bed and let him fall onto it. 'Oh, Mussy.' Shaking her head, she pulled off his boots as Mrs Overton came in with a bucket and scrubbing brush.

'I'll not stand for this,' the landlady muttered, on her hands and knees cleaning up the mess. 'I'm shocked, I tell you. Shocked! Look at the state of him, his face! Fighting, no doubt. Drinking. I'll not have it.'

'He was attacked, Mrs Overton,' Caroline told her, seeing no point in hiding the fact anymore. 'He wasn't ill, but had been attacked, beaten.'

'Why wasn't I informed?'

'He didn't want you to worry,' she said lamely, not knowing if that was the case at all.

'Worry?' Mrs Overton scrubbed harder on the carpet. 'One of my lodgers getting beaten *is* a cause for worry.'

'Mussy, er, Mr Casey just wanted to hide in his room and recover.'

'Hide?' Mrs Overton scowled at Caroline. 'Going out drinking is hardly hiding now, is it? I'll not stand for this at all. My reputation will be in tatters.'

'I'm certain it won't be.'

'An expert on gossip are we now?' Mrs Overton got to her feet, her face red from the exertion and anger. 'Well, Mr Casey can find somewhere else to stay. In the morning he is out!'

The door slammed behind her, and Caroline glanced at Mussy, who lay sprawled sideways on the bed snoring. Carefully covering him with a blanket, she placed the water basin by the side of the bed in the hope that if he was sick again, he'd aim for it.

There'd be a reckoning in the morning.

As she predicted, early the next morning, it wasn't the sounds of the street which woke Caroline but the banging and slamming coming from within the house.

Dressing quickly, Caroline went to Mussy's room, assuming she'd find him still asleep sideways across his bed, but he was curled up in a lanky ball. The smell of vomit was thick in the air.

'Mussy, wake up.' She shook his shoulder. 'Wake up.'

Murmuring, groaning, Mussy opened one eye. 'What are you doing?' he slurred.

'Get up, get washed, quickly.' She pulled the blanket off him. 'Mrs Overton is in a rage after last night.'

'Last night?'

Caroline dragged the curtains apart and opened the window to another rainy day. A weak light and dampness filled the room.

'Urgh.' Mussy squinted against the light. 'Are you trying to kill me?'

'Mrs Overton will! Now get up. Wash.'

'Why?'

'Don't you remember?' Caroline started to tidy his chaotic room. 'You came back drunk. You woke us up by smashing into the hall table. You've broken the lamp.'

Mussy swore. 'Please tell me this is all a dream.'

'I wish it was. Mrs Overton is livid. You were sick all over her carpet.'

A wave of green washed over Mussy's face. 'I don't feel that great now.'

'Oh, hell. In the basin!'

Thankfully, his aim at the basin was successful as he retched and retched.

'So, we start as we left last night,' Mrs Overton snapped from the doorway.

'Forgive me...' Mussy groaned.

'Not likely, Mr Casey. You have an hour to leave.'

Caroline closed her eyes, not wanting to lose the only friend she had. 'Give him another chance, please.'

'Are you mad, girl? Do you think I want a repeat of this?'

'There'll be no repeat,' she pleaded. 'Will there, Mussy?'

For an answer he rolled over and retched again.

Mrs Overton's lips became a thin angry line. 'Out! I want you gone in an hour. And you being a gentleman! You should be ashamed of yourself, Mr Casey.' She tutted at Mussy before turning to Caroline. 'Not anther word, Mrs Lawson, not another word.'

After Mrs Overton stomped from the room, Caroline poured a glass of water for Mussy to sip, while she continued to tidy the room. 'Where will you go?'

'Another boarding house,' he murmured, swinging his legs over the side of the bed with a moan. 'I shall be fine.'

'I'll miss you.' She stacked four books on the bedside table. She was always saying goodbye to people.

'I will miss you, too.' His unhappy expression only heightened his bruised face. 'I am such a fool.' Shoulders bowed, he pulled on his boots. 'When will I learn to control myself?'

Caroline knew he didn't need an answer from her and folded his clothes while he took his case down from the top of the wardrobe and began to pack. They worked in silence until his room was devoid of any personal items.

'Let us meet up,' Mussy abruptly said, knotting a purple cravat over his white shirt.

'Meet up?'

'Yes. We are friends, aren't we? We should still meet and learn more about each other. Good and true friends are hard to come by, I know that for a fact. I would hate for us to part and not see each other again for I believe you and I are meant to be the very best of friends, don't you agree?'

'I do.' She smiled, relieved this wasn't a final goodbye. 'I'd like to see you again.'

'How about every Friday evening we meet at the Malt Shovel pub on Newgate?' Excitement lightened his mood. 'They have a snug in the back, and the food is decent. The landlord is a not a bad fellow and he knows me. We can eat and have a chat each Friday evening.'

'Perfect. I'm so lonely in this city and meeting you has been the only highlight of my stay so far.'

He grinned, standing to his full height again, his head up. 'That's settled then.'

Caroline walked with him downstairs where Mrs Overton came into the hallway to see him off.

Mussy bent to kiss Caroline's cheek. 'Friday,' he whispered. Straightening, he nodded to Mrs Overton. 'Please accept my full apologies.' He placed money on the hall table. 'That is for the damaged lamp.'

Mrs Overton inclined her head, her eyes narrow with contempt.

With a wink at Caroline, Mussy left the building and with him went her last remaining bit of cheerfulness.

'Your breakfast is waiting,' Mrs Overton stated.

Caroline went into the dining room, determined to find work today, no matter what it was.

Chapter Five

Plunging her hands into hot water, Caroline winced as the heat and soda irritated the cracks on her fingers. Using her wrists, she wiped the sweat off her forehead. Despite it being cold outside and that morning the first frost had arrived, inside the scullery it was humid with steam fogging the high windows, which were at ground level.

Four days after Mussy left the lodging house Caroline received a letter from Mrs Claymore, the housekeeper at Greenleigh House on The Mount. After a short interview, which, citing she held no references, was conducted in only a few minutes, Caroline was told to start the following morning at five o'clock sharp. She was the new scullery maid, the lowest rank in the house.

For two weeks now she'd woken at half four in the morning and quietly left the lodging house to make the twenty-minute walk to Greenleigh House. Each evening, exhausted, she made the return journey and collapsed into bed. She had Sundays off. Something she had negotiated with Mrs Claymore, who agreed simply because Pammie, the other scullery maid, was a live-in servant and could wash whatever pots were used on Sundays, but as Caroline found out, Pammie was lazy and tended to leave Sunday's dishes and pots soaking in the large stone sinks for her to do on Monday morning.

'Lawson, get a move on with those frying pans, Mrs Townsend wants them today not next week.' Lena, one of the kitchen maids, and Pammie's older sister stood in the doorway to the scullery, arms folded, happy to be giving orders.

'I'm going as quick as I can,' Caroline answered, head down, scrubbing with salt and lemon on the baked-on grease that coated the copper frying pans.

'Not quick enough.'

'Where's Pammie? She's meant to be helping,' Caroline snapped, knowing full well Pammie was out in the kitchen talking to the other maids as she pretended to collect used dishes from the preparation table.

'Never you mind what others are doing. Just get on with what you've got to do and be quick about it.' Lena strolled back into the kitchen and a moment later, Caroline heard some of the girls laugh. It irked her that she was older than most of the girls working downstairs. She'd be twenty-five next week and most of them were barely twenty. Yet, they'd been in the job since small girls of twelve and thirteen years old. Those kitchen girls had spent years refining their skills, moving up in the staff hierarchy. Whereas Caroline had been a wife, working in her own house and had little to show for it now.

For hours she soaked, scrubbed, rinsed and dried the large iron pots and the shiny copper pans as well as any cooking utensils and items used in the busy kitchen. The glassware and china was washed separately by Pammie, having earned her one rung up the domestic ladder once Caroline was employed to take her spot. The silverware was done by the butler's team and stored in a locked room near the butler's pantry.

Caroline had been given a tour of only the kitchen and scullery when she first started. The rest of the house was out of bounds to Caroline, who had no reason whatsoever to venture beyond the kitchen door to the corridor that led to the other service rooms and what happened upstairs in the house was a complete mystery to her.

Greenleigh House was owned by a banker, Mr Greenleigh, and he lived with his wife and three grown-up daughters. A family that Caroline had yet to see. In fact, she rarely saw the upstairs staff unless they were all in the staff dining room to eat and Caroline had to bring something to them. Otherwise, Caroline's world consisted of the scullery, the kitchen and the back door which led out into the small yard. Even the stables and buildings beyond the yard were unknown to her. She had no reason to wander. At five o'clock each morning she walked through the back door into the scullery and left whenever Mrs Townsend dismissed her for the evening.

Mrs Townsend, the cook, seemed a kind enough woman, but she ran the kitchen and her staff with a rod of iron and had no time for those who didn't work hard. So, Caroline kept her head down, and ignored the whispers and the laughter of the other girls as she washed and cleaned pots in a monotonous routine that broke her back and slowly her spirit.

Pammie sauntered in with two heavy pots and plonked them into the stone sink, splashing Caroline in the process. 'Get these done next. Mrs Townsend needs them.'

'What about the frying pans? I've the last one to do and they all need drying.' She wiped a thick towel around the pan she'd just finished scrubbing, her fingers crack and raw from the lemon and salt.

'Then you'd best hurry up, hadn't you?' Pammie, thin and small with sly looking features gave her a filthy glare. 'You need to work faster.'

'I'm going as fast as I can. Why can't you help?'

'Because I've my own work to do.' Pammie sneered. '*You* help *me,* not the other way around.'

Teeth clenched in frustration, Caroline started scrubbing the black iron pots with lemon-soaked salt. The pain of the salt seeping into the cracks on her fingers was nearly unbearable, but she refused to show any discomfort in front of Pammie and the others. Her hope when she started here was to make friends. She'd never had any female friends and longed for one or even two, but mainly she simply wished to have another woman to talk to, to confide in and share things with. The kitchen maids had shown her no inkling of friendship, the opposite in fact, as though they were a closed circle, and she was an outsider who would never be admitted into their friendship ring.

She had Mussy of course, but that was different. He was a man, and a little strange, not that she was bothered by his odd ways. They had met at the Malt Shovel twice since his disgraceful exit from Mrs Overton's. They laughed about it now. Comfortable in the little snug at the back of the pub, they would order stew and chunks of bread, a whiskey for Mussy and an elderberry cordial for Caroline.

For the last two Fridays they had spent a few hours getting to know each other even better. They ate and laughed and talked of their pasts, even cried a little when they spoke of loved ones. She'd told Mussy all about Hugh and the farm. In return, he mentioned a little of his brother, who he'd been close to until his brother died of fever when they were youths. She noticed Mussy never spoke of his father or mother.

Friday evenings with Mussy were her favourite time and she'd spend all week waiting for the hours to go by until she could ask Mrs Townsend to leave after the dinner pots were washed, dried and put away and she could make her way to the Malt Shovel on Newgate. Mussy would be waiting in the snug, cradling a beer in his hands and would have bought her a small sherry or a cordial. They'd talk for hours about so many things. Mussy adored talking about books and theatre, about his university days and his dear friend Douglas who died. From their time together Caroline realised Mussy came from a wealthy background. She didn't believe he really was a gas inspector as he said, but she never asked him outright. If he was hiding something from her, then he obviously had a good reason for it. Maybe one day he would confide in her, but until then, they grew closer, and she came to care for him.

After a tiresome day, Caroline left Greenleigh to walk back to Fossgate in the cold darkness of October. Winter seemed to be in a hurry to arrive, the trees becoming barer each day, the temperature icier each morning when she woke. Gas streetlights glowed against a moonless night, and she shivered in her coat, which had seen better days. Her wages were low, only enough to cover her lodging, but at least she had a roof over her head. She'd have to make her clothes last, though her boots were showing signs of wear.

Crossing over the bridge, she gazed at the river, the inky blackness dancing with spots of light from the boat lanterns. A cool breeze blew off the water. Head down, she hurried on, eager for the warmth of her bed. She'd asked Mrs Overton for a stone hot water bottle for her feet each night for her bedroom was becoming chilly now.

The relationship with Mrs Overton had soured since she found out about her friendship with Mussy. The older woman rarely spoke to Caroline and now that Caroline ate her meals at Greenleigh House, she had no reason to sit in the dining room. She'd told Mrs Overton she needed a reduction in her rent because her board no longer included food. Mrs Overton grumbled and mumbled about ungrateful people and turned her back on her when Caroline gave her only three shillings a week.

At the front door of the lodging house, the light from the hall spilled out on to the steps. Caroline frowned as she neared and saw her carpet bags on the top step. Mrs Overton stood just inside the door.

'What is all this?' Caroline asked, shocked.

'Your things.'

'But why?'

'You're not staying here any longer.' Mrs Overton looked down her nose at her, pushing her glasses up at the same time. 'Everything is there. I've cleared out your room.'

'Can I ask why?' she asked, panic creeping into her voice.

'Ask your friend, Mr Casey.'

'Mr Casey? I don't understand. That incident was weeks ago.'

'It's not just about that time, but you've been meeting him since.'

'So? Why is that a concern for you?'

'Because of whom he is! I'll have no one staying in my residence who associates with the likes of *him*.'

'Please, Mrs Overton, it's late. I have nowhere to go.'

'That's not my problem.' The door shut with a slam.

Stunned, Caroline stood for several moments trying to understand it all. A tabby cat slinked against her legs making her jump. She grabbed her bags and walked down the steps full of fear. The coldness of the night caught her breath as she breathed. Where could she go? She knew of a lodging house down near the river, but it was close to the Water Lanes, the slums, and she didn't want to be around that area at this time of night.

She wished she knew where Mussy stayed, but he'd only said he'd found rooms close to St William's College and she wasn't sure exactly where.

Retracing her steps back along Fossgate and then across The Pavement, she looked up to see the Shambles was in darkness, the butcher shops closed for the night. A small part of hoped to see Mr Bent so she could ask for his help, but the narrow, cobbled lane was frightening when no light penetrated down from the rooms above. She didn't want to be walking in the shadows carrying everything she owned. Who knew what could be lurking in the darkness.

A dog prowled around the side of St Criux Church. He growled at her, prompting her to keep walking. Two men came along the street, hands in pockets, talking quietly. One smoked a pipe and tangy tobacco smell filled her nose. They glanced at Caroline but kept walking and she quickened her pace.

Where was she to go? She didn't know. Looking at the signs on buildings, she searched for a lodging house, trawling streets she'd not visited since she looked for work in those first few days of arriving in York.

Hours later, she couldn't walk another step. Her feet ached and her fingers cramped from carrying the bags. She paused before another large house that read Dolan's Lodging House. She'd knocked on lodging house doors four times in the last few hours and each place had no vacancies. Although not a heavily praying person, despite her convent education, Caroline prayed for a room now. She was so exhausted she was considering sleeping under a shop awning.

She rang the bell and waited. It felt like forever but must have only been minutes before the front door opened. A man stood there, his face thrown into shadow by the light behind him. 'Yes?'

'I need a room for the night, please.'

'We're full.'

Beaten, she slumped and dropped her bags. 'I'll take anything you've got, a cupboard if I have to.'

'Hmm...' He scratched his hair, which stood up on end. He turned and looked over his shoulder and the light caught his face.

Caroline shrank back in surprise as his unkempt appearance and pox-marked face.

'Are you on your own? No husband, babies?' he asked.

'No, just me.'

'I've a box room up in the attic.'

'How much?' She stalled for time, the stale odour coming from him turned her stomach.

'Two shillings.'

'Oh. I can't afford that.' She picked up her bags.

'Wait. We'll sort out the price in the morning. I'm not standing on a cold doorstep to haggle.' He opened the door wider and moved aside to let her in.

From somewhere above came a moan as Caroline entered the hall. Stairs went up before her and closed doors were numbered on either side of the hall.

'Straight up,' the man said. 'What's your name?'

'Caroline Lawson.'

'Pleased to meet yer.'

She noticed he didn't give her his name. Was he Dolan, the name on the sign?

Going in front of him, Caroline climbed the stairs conscious of him being close behind. He told her to go up again at the first landing and then again on the small second landing where a tight spiral set of iron steps led up to the attic.

'Up there.' He grabbed a lantern from a hall table and lit it with a match. The brightness of the lamp threw the shabbiness of the lodging into stark relief.

Once at the top of the stairs, he unlocked a door, smaller than average, and led the way into the attic space. A single bed was under the eaves and a mattress on the floor. Both were bare and stained. The attic held a few boxes and a set of drawers which were lopsided. The air was frigid and musty.

'This will do you. I've no bedding though,' he warned. 'You'll have to sleep in your coat. I'll not charge you much for the night.'

Caroline didn't care. She was dead on her feet and ready to cry from despair.

'I'll leave you to it.' He lumbered out, bending to keep his head from bashing on the sloped roof. He'd left the lantern and by the glow of it, she pulled out of her luggage an extra petticoat and put it on, plus another pair of stockings. The iciness of the room wasn't helped by the cracked little window and looking up, she could see a slither of night sky between broken slates.

The iron bed creaked when she sat on it. The sound of something scampering in the corner by the boxes told her she had company, mice or rats or both. She shivered in revulsion. She took off her bonnet but kept her boots on for warmth. Gingerly she laid down, wrapping her scarf about her head, forecasting she'll be covered in bed bug bites and possibly lice by morning. Still, she was dry and off the streets. Tomorrow, after her shift, she'd look for better rooms, or even ask if she could become a live-in servant at Greenleigh House.

She woke from a deep sleep to something touching her face. She batted it away, hazy, unaware of time or place. Opening her eyes, she blinked away the sleep. Darkness enveloped her. The lantern had long gone out. She was so cold. Where was her coat? Abruptly, there was movement and pressure on her chest. Startled, panicked, she sat up only to bang her head against something hard.

A man grunted, then pushed her down onto the mattress. The acid smell of an unwashed body filled her nose. Someone was on her! She screamed. A hand clasped over her mouth, stifling any noise she made. Thrashing, she pushed at the man covering her body with his. The complete darkness was disorientating. The hand left her mouth and she screamed again.

'Shut up!' he snarled and punched her on the jaw. Her neck cracked and a pain so intense shot through her face and head, stunning her.

Whimpering in agony, Caroline took a moment to think straight. In the dim light, she could make out Dolan lunging for

71

her again. He tugged at her bodice and she lashed out. Working on the farm gave her a strength most city women didn't have. She fought with everything she had. Fear and anger gave her power.

Swearing, Dolan hit her again.

Dazed, Caroline rocked back, pain biting deep along her cheek. Enraged, she clawed at his face, scratching her nails deeply down his cheeks, drawing blood.

Dolan howled and backed away. 'You bitch!' He put his hands to his face, moaning. 'I'm bleeding. You'll pay for this!' He stumbled from the room, groaning in agony.

Chapter Six

Caroline woke up to a streak of weak sunlight piercing the space between the broken roof slates and blinding her eyes. Turning her head caused pain to throb along her jaw and up into her nose and cheek bone. The harrowing event of the night before came flooding back. Terrified, she didn't move, but looked around the dim attic, searching the gloomy corners. She was alone. Dolan hadn't come back. She'd stayed awake for hours, sitting in the darkness too scared to move, expecting him to return to beat her again, and worse.

In the dark hours after he left, she couldn't find her coat. She ached from cold and soreness. As the dawn light filtered into the attic, she saw her coat half under the bed and retrieved it. Her face throbbed from his punches. Her fingernails were torn with dried blood underneath them where she'd clawed at his face. Remembering his howl, his threats and the smell of his body, she gagged. Staggering from the bed, she fell on her knees onto the wooden floor.

Crying, fighting the absolute fear that blocked out all her senses, she scrambled up to her feet, using the bed as support. With fingers that shook violently, she pulled together her torn bodice, doing up the remaining buttons. Shivering with cold and shock, she kept glancing at the door. She needed to get out, get away from the madman who attacked her. Her face throbbed as she looked around for her bags. Where were they? The realisation they were gone hit her like a hammer in the chest. Everything she owned was in those bags.

She ran to the door, pulling at the handle but it wouldn't budge. The door was locked.

'Help!' she screamed as loud as she could, ignoring the pain of her cheek. Banging on the door, she screamed again, long high screams of desperation and panic. She had to get out, get away from the vile beast who'd hurt her.

Running to the little window, she stood on tiptoes but couldn't see out of it. Covered in cobwebs and years of dirt, it was nothing but a piece of small grimy glass. It didn't open and she fought the urge to smash it because it wouldn't do any good. The opening was too tight for her to climb through and out onto the roof which was too steep to be safe.

Going back to the door, she rattled the handle again. 'Help! Help me, please! Someone!'

She waited, ear to the door hoping there'd be movement of someone coming to let her out. Then she sprang back. What if *he* came back to torture her again?

Sobbing in terror, she searched the attic for a weapon. Upturning the boxes, she found they held old ledgers and papers, posters and books. Nothing to give her power over him. She went to the drawers and yanked them out. The top drawer was empty. She couldn't open the second jammed drawer and the third drawer came out in pieces.

Frustrated, anger building, she held up an end piece of the drawer. Could she use this? Would it be strong enough if she hit him over the head? Would it knock him out?

Caroline bent and looked under the bed, but it held only a chamber pot, which she promptly used to pee in. She closed her eyes at her torn stockings, the buttons missing off her coat and the rip of her bodice. Her hair, long and untidy, hung about her shoulders and down her back.

Suddenly, the fight left her. She sank to the floor and hugged her knees to her chest. She cried from fear and pain. She cried for what had happened to her. She cried for Hugh, the only man to have ever touched her until last night.

Eventually, she rose and tried the door again, knowing it was still locked but her brain refused to accept it. She held the piece of drawer and knew it wouldn't be enough. It needed to be broken, jagged, sharp, wounding. A sound downstairs stilled her movements. Voices.

'Help!' She banged on the door. 'I'm up here in the attic!'

She listened. Nothing. No sound. Had they gone? Was it him? Had he brought someone with him?

Shaking, she hurried to the drawers and rapidly started smashing pieces of wood over the end of the bed. It took several whacks to finally break a piece into something like a dagger. She held it to her chest and sat on the bed. She'd fight him with every ounce of strength she had.

She sat watching, cautious and anxious.

The daylight faded. Caroline grew hungry, then thirsty. Waiting, hours of being on edge, sapped her energy. She had to keep alert, but as the dusk threw long shadows across the attic, she grew weary. Every now and then, she'd pace the floor to keep herself focused, and then rattle the door handle and yell for help. But no one came and the hours ticked by.

As rain fell, tapping softly against the little window and dripping through the gap in the roof slates, the evening light faded to night. Standing under the dripping hole, Caroline opened her mouth and let it hit her tongue. She stood like that for a long time, letting the water trickle down her throat. Thunder rumbled in the distance. Forks of lightning flashed, illuminating the attic sporadically, so Caroline could see the door that she watched so intently.

She was terrified of falling asleep. She kept putting her face under the drips to refresh her. The room grew chilly, then even more freezing as the night wore on. She moved closer to the door, to hide behind it when it opened. She had to surprise him, attack him as he came in. A hit hard and fast and then flee.

Sliding down the wall next to the door, Caroline stayed that way until cramps in her calves forced her up to walk about. She heard voices again, but fainter than before. Outside in the street below the rain soothed the noises of passing traffic. The darkness overwhelmed her. She'd never been afraid of the dark before, she had no reason to be. But now, alone, caged in this awful room with her captor able to strike at any time, the darkness wasn't her friend. It hid the horrors of what he did to her, it hid him.

Covering her mouth with a hand, she tried so hard not to cry. Her head had throbbed all day, and the pain in her cheek ached if she touched it or opened her mouth too wide. She longed for the farm, the peaceful sounds of birds, the familiar routine of tasks she did every day. She wanted Hugh's arms around her and to sleep in her own bed, secure, loved.

When morning came again, Caroline felt weak with hunger, her mouth dry. She dozed on and off sitting behind the door. But no one came. Would he do so tonight? Could she last another day waiting, inert with fear at every sound beyond the door?

The rain continued, lighter showers and then heavy downpours throughout the morning and then into the afternoon. Caroline collected water in her cupped hands and drank little mouthfuls. It was better than nothing.

Today was Friday. This evening, she should be meeting Mussy. Would he worry when she didn't turn up? And her position at Greenleigh House... They would be angry that she'd not come in to work. Would she lose her position? Would they care to find out what was wrong with her? She doubted it. She'd given Mrs Claymore, the housekeeper, her address as Mrs Overton's Lodging House, but even that was no longer true.

Going to the window, she looked out at the rooftops, the grey sky. Abruptly, voices reached her from beyond the door. Caroline rushed to it and banged. 'Help!'

'There's someone in there,' a whisper came through the wood.

'Yes! I'm in here. The door's locked,' Caroline yelled. 'Please help me.'

'We can't open the door,' the voice, a female said.

'Smash the wood,' Caroline pleaded. 'Get a hammer, an axe, anything. Let me out.' She sobbed.

'We'll come back.'

Caroline panicked. 'No! No, don't leave me, please, no.'

'We'll be back. Stay quiet. I promise I'll be back to help you,' the voice spoke calmly.

Fear of abandonment rose sharply, but Caroline fought to control it. The woman said she'd come back, and she had to trust her. Wrapping her arms about her waist, Caroline paced the floor. The minutes ticked by, stretching as long as the weak shadows across the floor. The rain stopped, but the clouds she could see were low and heavy at times broken by the sun piercing through.

The waiting was torturous. She strained to listen to any sound. Hunger gripped her stomach. Her concentration blurred and she grew tired as dusk fell.

They weren't coming back. Tears trickled down her cheeks.

Going to the window, Caroline measured the width of it with her hands. A foot wide and high, perhaps? If she took off her clothes and wore only her chemise, could she squeeze through it? Desperate, she carried a box to place under the window and stood on it. She'd never fit through it with her dress on, but without the volume of her skirt and petticoats, maybe she could manage it. What choice did she have?

Using a piece of wood she'd smashed up earlier, she struck at the glass where it was cracked. On the second strike, the glass snapped in several places. Gently, using the end of her scarf to protect her hand, Caroline broke off the glass shards. The icy evening air hit her face. She shivered but stayed focused as she removed all the pieces of glass.

Concentrating so much to make sure she didn't cut herself, she didn't at first hear the sound at the door. A scraping of the lock. *He was back.* She froze, a shard of glass in her hand.

Instantly she was filled with rage. She'd kill him!

Caroline rushed to the door as it opened, hand raised ready to stab him with the glass.

'It's me!' A girl held up her hands.

Skidding to a halt, Caroline blinked in disbelief.

In the gloom, the girl glanced worriedly over her shoulder. 'We need to go. Hurry!'

Dropping the glass, Caroline crept behind the girl, who tip-toed down the spiral stairs and across the landing to the next staircase. Heart in her mouth, Caroline stayed right behind her, wincing every time a floorboard creaked.

'In here.' The girl opened a door to a room that held only a bed and a small table.

Caroline baulked. 'No, not another room. I need to get out of here.'

'I know, but you can't go out the front door, it's watched.' The girl beckoned.

Swallowing a moan of terror, Caroline followed her across the room to the open window. A cold breeze touched Caroline's face and she shivered from cold and the image of being caught by Dolan.

The girl pulled her scarf around her head, covering most of her face, and climbed through first to stand outside on an awning of slate tiles. Nervous of falling, Caroline climbed out, struggling to clear her skirts of the sill. Darkness had fallen suddenly as it did in October. A light shone from a window on the building opposite but, other than that, it was dark.

'We need to get over the wall and into the yard next door. Can you do that?' the girl asked, already squatting down to reach for the top of the high wall below them.

Caroline did exactly as the girl did, carefully placing her hands and feet on the wet brick wall and then shimmied down to the top of a small shed. A dog barked from a neighbouring yard and Caroline stilled, her gaze scanning the shadows.

'Come on.' Agile like a cat, the girl dropped down onto a water barrel and then to the ground.

Doing the same, Caroline landed beside her. The relief to be outside made her light-headed and she swayed.

The girl grabbed her arm to steady her. 'Do you have a home to go to?'

'No...'

'Right, I'll take you back to mine. Unless you want to go somewhere else?'

She tried to pull herself together but couldn't stop shaking. 'I have nowhere else. He took everything I had. I've no money, nothing.'

The dog continued to bark, and fat drops of rain began to fall.

'Let's go.' The girl dashed up the black alley between the two buildings.

Caroline kept up with her, running through the slippery wet streets, shocking the people they passed, but Caroline didn't care if they stopped and stared. The night hid them between gas streetlights and Caroline became a little confused as they wound their way through alleyways and lanes, across filthy stinking yards until finally they were down by the river. The girl didn't speak and didn't even seem breathless as Caroline was.

They followed the river, keeping tight to the sides of the buildings until the girl turned into a narrow, cobbled lane. Terraced tenement houses rising three and four stories high crowded over the lane, their top floors hanging over as though ready to lean against the opposite house. Rubbish and waste lined the bottom of the buildings while a filthy open drain flowed down the middle of the cobbles to dump waste into the river. Men gathered in doorways to each house, smoking pipes and even at this late hour children ran barefoot, chasing rats or each other. The smell of rotting matter and sewer was thick and cloying.

Hurrying into a doorway of an old stone and timber building halfway up the lane, the girl made for the steep staircase and went up to the first landing. She opened the second door and paused to let Caroline enter.

'This is my place,' the girl announced.

Caroline stood and stared. The room wasn't large. The walls were more grey than white and the smoke from the fire drifted back down the chimney in small puffs. A cooking pot hung over the small fire and in front of it on a ragged mat, sat two dirty children.

'You don't have to stay if you don't want to,' the girl said, going forward to add another piece of coal to the embers. 'But you'll be safe here. No one comes to the Water Lanes unless they live here.'

Caroline's gaze flittered to the double bed by the wall next to her. It held a striped mattress and a couple of grey blankets. The only window faced the lane, or more precisely looked into the window of the house opposite, a mere five foot away.

'Well?'

Blinking away the shock, the exhaustion, Caroline nodded, finding her voice. 'I would like to stay.'

The girl laughed. 'You really don't have much choice, do you?'

Caroline wished she could laugh, but tears formed instead and spilled over her lashes. She had lost everything, her bags, what small amount of money she owned and worst of all, she'd been held hostage and violated. Staying in this awful room couldn't be more horrific than what she just endured and escaped from.

'You'll be all right.' The girl rubbed Caroline's arm. 'Get some sleep. Tomorrow is a new day, and you'll face it better if you get some kip.' She waved to the bed. 'These two will likely jump in with you, down at your feet.'

Caroline stared again at the silent children.

The girl flapped out one of the threadbare blankets. 'They're my sisters. Our Elsie and our Bertha. They won't bother you, will you girls?'

'I'm Caroline, and thank you,' she mumbled, remembering her manners. Every part of her wanted to collapse and sob her heart out but she kept standing, kept dashing the tears from her cheeks.

'And I'm Trixie. Trixie Wilkes.' The girl had a name.

In the gloomy light Caroline looked at her properly. She was small, thin, with an elfin face, but huge hazel eyes, which were stunningly beautiful, and dark curly hair.

'I'll be back in a few hours,' Trixie told her, heading for the door. 'We don't have much, but there's a bit of tea in the caddy and some day-old bread in that tin box. Always keep the lid on the box or the rats will have anything inside.'

'You're going?' Caroline asked, surprised, not wanting to be left alone.

'Aye, I've got to work, haven't I? Behave you two.' Trixie smiled at her little sisters and closed the door behind her.

Devoid of all strength, Caroline crumbled onto the edge of the bed, the shaking returned.

'You can have my pillow,' the oldest-looking girl said. Like her sister, she wore a frayed nightgown, and each had an equally old shawl wrapped around their thin shoulders.

'Thank you,' Caroline murmured, the tears continuing to fall. 'What's your name again?'

'I'm Elsie and this is our Bertha.' Elsie pointed to the younger sibling on the mat. 'I'm seven and Bertha is five. I can make tea.' Without waiting for a reply, Elsie scrambled up and swung the black iron kettle, which hung from a hook, over the fire. Next, she grabbed a cup with a broken handle and put in a half teaspoon measure of tea leaves. 'We've bread and a bit of jam left.' She opened the tin box and took out the end of a bread loaf and cut it thinly before spreading a smear of some kind of dark jam on it. She proudly passed it to Caroline.

Biting into the slice, Caroline's mouth watered at the taste of plum jam. She ate the stale bread in a few bites, stuffing it into her mouth hungrily. The tea, black, weak and sugarless was warm and welcoming. 'You're very clever,' she told Elsie, wiping her eyes.

Elsie preened and went to sit on the rug again.

'I'm clever too,' Bertha piped up.

'No, you're not,' Elsie argued.

'I am too!' Bertha pouted.

Caroline felt the beginnings of a smile. 'I'm sure you both are very clever.'

Satisfied with that, the girls settled down again.

A wave of tiredness tumbled over Caroline so heavily she closed her eyes, ready to give in to it.

'You can go to sleep if you want,' Elsie's soft voice barely reached Caroline.

Without further encouragement, Caroline curled up into a ball at the bottom of the bed, fully dressed and wearing her boots. Elsie dragged a blanket over her, and she welcomed the blackness that claimed her.

Chapter Seven

When Caroline woke, she was warm and hazy. Rubbing her eyes, she noticed a little body tucked in beside her, Bertha. At the top of the bed slept Trixie and Elsie. Four people in a bed not much bigger than a single, but the warmth was embraced as her breath misted in the air.

She stirred, needing to pee and cautiously climbed over Bertha to stand by the bed. Looking under it, she noticed the pot and pulling it out found it half full already. Grimacing at the stale urine smell, Caroline hastily relieved herself. Opening the window, she threw out the contents onto the street below, then looked out to see if she'd hit anyone. Thankfully, no one received a shower of gold.

Another grey morning peeped between the rooftops. Not many people were up and about, and she wondered if that was because they had no work to go to. With daylight she could guess there were in the slums of the Water Lanes, an area Mrs Overton had warned her not to venture into. Caroline leaned out of the window and could see and smell the river close by. A boat's horn shattered the dawn quietness and from somewhere in the building a baby wailed.

Closing the window, she rubbed her arms. Cold penetrated her bones. She squatted in front of the winking embers that threw out no warmth.

A new day. A new start, yet again. Her heart ached for Hugh and the farm. She needed his solid embrace, his cheeky smile she'd first fallen in love with. She didn't know how to continue without him, it was all so hard, so terrifying. A widow at twenty-five years old, with nothing to her name except the clothes on her back. She never dreamt her life could turn out so dismal, so utterly devoid of hope or happiness. What had she done to deserve it?

Trixie stirred and stretched. Her black curls were a riot about her head as she sat up and smiled at Caroline. 'How are you feeling? Better than you look hopefully.'

Standing, Caroline gently touched her swollen cheek and the tenderness around her jaw. 'I don't know how I feel and that's the truth.' She shivered remembering the attic, the attack and the escape. It all seemed surreal yet also horrifyingly real. 'You saved me, and I can never thank you enough.'

Trixie reached for a large green shawl that had several holes in it and wrapped it around her. 'Well, it was only right to help you. Victor is an animal. We all know what he's like.'

'Victor?' She was confused.

'Victor Dolan.'

'He's the man who locked me in that attic and attacked me?' Caroline flinched. Victor Dolan. Once again, she saw the glazed look of desire in his eyes as he grabbed her, the pain of his fingers digging into her flesh. She hugged herself.

'Aye, but don't think of reporting him. He's got half the police in his pocket.' Trixie went to the fireplace and poked at the embers with a short iron poker.

Caroline had no intention of going to the police. To tell them what had happened to her filled her with shame. She couldn't face that, and would they even believe her? Why would a respectable woman, alone, enter a filthy attic and not question it as she had done? She'd acted foolishly, recklessly, and she'd paid the price.

Trixie added a few pieces of thin wood to the embers from a box in the corner and then small chunks of coal. 'I'll get dressed and then go out and buy some bread. I earned well last night.'

'I've no money to give you. I've nothing at all. He took everything, my bags...' Caroline thought of her job at Greenleigh House. They'd be wondering where she was. She should be there now, scrubbing the pans left to soak overnight.

'We'll work something out later, don't worry about it now. I can afford a loaf of bread, yesterday's mind, and I'll see what else I can stretch to.' Trixie got dressed in a brown skirt and bodice and pulled on boots without stockings.

The girls slept on, and Caroline wished she hadn't woken so early for she'd been warm in bed and now was freezing. The room was icy with moisture running down the walls and the window. She tended to the fire to coax more heat. The coal box was practically empty, and she didn't know if Trixie could afford to get more. She hunkered down in front of the tentative flames, holding her hands out to it. Her filthy fingernails reminded her again of the attack. She washed them in the bowl of water on the hearth, eager to be rid of any evidence of what had happened. What she wouldn't give to have a bath right now. Hugh had loved to wash her hair in the bath by the fire...

Caroline thrust those memories away. The past was gone. Her future needed her concentration, but the enormity of her situation was all too overwhelming.

She stared into the flames, reliving the attack, feeling sick at the image of Victor Dolan touching her intimate places where only Hugh had caressed. She flinched remembering Dolan's howl of pain when she raked her nails down his face. Caroline blinked away the tears that were always burning behind her eyes. She dared not give into the sobs that pressured her chest, aware of the girls sleeping behind her. As much as she wanted to howl out the hurt and grief, she couldn't. The hard knot of pain and anger would remain stuck in her chest.

When Trixie returned, she brought in a waft of cold air but also the smell of fresh bread. 'It's our lucky day.' From under her shawl, she brought out a loaf of fresh bread still warm. 'Old Penny gave it to me for the price of day-old bread because this loaf was smaller than the others. Penny also gave me this currant loaf as it was too old to sell.' Trixie held the two loaves in the air like trophies at a prize giving. 'Old Penny has a soft spot for me and my sisters as she used to know our mam. Oh, I also got a few ounces of tea.' Trixie sliced the currant loaf. 'We'll toast this, and it'll be smashing.'

Caroline was given a slice of the loaf on a fork, and she held it out to the flames of the little fire the same as Trixie. She nibbled at the dry toast, aware that her cheek and jaw ached when she chewed too much.

'What were you doing at Victor's?' Trixie asked, making tea in two cups, the broken handle one and a chipped one.

'I was looking for a lodging house for the night. I had to leave the one I'd been staying at.' A spurt of anger towards Mrs Overton caught her by surprise. If that evil witch had not thrown her out none of this would have happened.

'You didn't know the *lodging house* sign is a front for his brothel?'

'No!' How could she have possibly known that? 'I'm new to York.'

'As I say, the police are in his pocket, so he's able to do things like that, and more. Victor turns away families or men, but women are given a room, not knowing what might happen to them.' Trixie passed a cup to her. 'How many men did he bring into that attic to use you?'

'None,' Caroline whispered, the blood draining from her face at the notion of other men coming to harm her. She felt faint.

'You got off lucky then.' Frowning, Trixie blew on her black tea. 'Strange. For sure I would've thought he'd charge a string of men to go up and have their turn with you being fresh. He'd have made a packet because you're so pretty. Your hair is a lovely colour, tawny like a cat.'

Caroline's stomach churned. 'I fought him. Clawed at his face. He left me with blood running down his cheeks and didn't return.'

'Maybe he was planning something, but you escaped before he could make any of his plans happen. He's pure evil.' She lowered her voice. 'He provides women and young girls for men who pay him well for the service.'

'That could have been me...'

'Yes. He uses laudanum or opium to make the women senseless, they don't know what day it is, never mind what the men are doing to them. Victor is going to be livid that you've got away.' Trixie looked worried at the thought.

'Thanks to you.' How would she ever repay this young woman who only looked to be about eighteen, but had an old world look in her eyes?

'I don't need any thanks. Some girls walk into that line of work, for whatever reason, it's their choice, and that's fine, but I don't tolerate forcing a woman into it, as Victor would have done with you. He'd have worn you down, kept you locked up and used until you were nothing of the person you once were. I've seen it happen before and it's wrong.' Trixie stared into the fire.

'That's frightening.' Caroline had a lot to thank this girl for, probably her life.

Trixie ate more toast. 'Do you have a job?'

Amazed at the quick change of subject, Caroline nodded. 'I'm a scullery maid at Greenleigh House on The Mount.'

'Fancy.'

'Not really. It's hard work and long hours on my feet. Though I've not turned up for the last two days so I might not even have a position anymore. I should be there now.' As much as she wanted to keep her position, the idea of facing the kitchen girls at the house daunted her. She felt battered and bruised and wanted to hide away from everyone.

'Do you have any family?'

'No. My husband died in the summer and then my brother-in-law took over our farm. I came to York to find work.' Caroline felt another pang of loss for Hugh and for the farm.

'I've only got those two.' Trixie waved towards the sleeping girls. 'We lost our father four years ago and mam last December a few days before Christmas.'

Elsie woke and rolled over. 'I thought I smelled something.'

'Currant toast.' Trixie smiled. 'Isn't that a treat?'

Caroline watched as Trixie made toast for the girls and they shared her cup of tea. Bertha was quieter than Elsie, but she gave Caroline a small smile. After they'd eaten, Trixie told them to dress, which they did in little dresses of grey serge. Bertha's dress was stained at the back and when Trixie laced up their boots, Caroline noticed Elsie had a hole in the sole of one of them and Bertha's were too big and didn't match.

'Where are we going?' Elsie asked as Trixie combed her black hair with a comb that had more teeth missing than it held.

'We're going to walk with Caroline to see if she still has her job.'

Caroline glanced up at her. 'I am? You are?'

'You want to know if you've still got it, don't you? I thought we could keep you company.'

'Frankly, I don't feel up to it. I can't face it.'

'Look,' Trixie waved the comb at Caroline, 'you've a good position in a decent house. You can't give that up. Jobs are hard to come by. You need the money.'

'I know, but I'm tired and sore and I can't cope with all that's happened...'

Trixie softened a little. 'You've been through a rough time, but you can't hide away in this room forever. Life goes on. We can't afford to sit around all day crying and feeling sorry for ourselves.'

Caroline bristled. 'I was assaulted, held prisoner. I think I've earned the right to hide away for a bit.'

'Not here, you don't. If you lived in a fancy house and were a gentleman's daughter, perhaps. But you're not. You live in the Water Lanes now and we don't have time to wallow. To *survive,* we have to *fight* every day. We fight being poor, the filth, the sicknesses, having no decent jobs or nice homes. We fight to keep going. None of us can sit on our arses all day and moan how unfair it all is, otherwise, we'd throw ourselves into the river and be done with it!'

Caroline turned away from Trixie's anger. Tears once more flowed freely and she buried her face in her hands. At that moment, she could have easily jumped in the river and ended it all.

'Listen, don't be upset.' Trixie patted Caroline's back. 'I was harsh, but I spoke the truth. You've been through a lot, but you just have to get on with it. We have no choice. This is our life, and we have to make the best of it any way we can.'

'I was so happy and now...' A sob broke from Caroline and before she could stop it, another followed. She wailed deep with despair and grief for all she'd lost and the ugliness she'd experienced.

Trixie rubbed her back and let her cry it out until eventually, Caroline lifted her head and dried her eyes. Wrung out and exhausted, she sighed deeply.

'Feel better?' Trixie asked.

'Yes, sorry about that.' She smiled tentatively in apology, realising the girls weren't in the room.

'I sent them out,' Trixie supplied. 'Now, wash your face. We'll go to The Mount and see if you still have a job.'

Caroline sighed again. She really didn't want to see anyone at Greenleigh House, but she needed the money and to keep her position. She had some explaining to do and as much as she hated the notion of leaving this room, she knew she had to do it. She had to do it for Trixie, to repay her kindness and she had to do it for herself. Victor Dolan wouldn't win. He wouldn't reduce her to less than nothing, where her only choice was the workhouse or jumping into the river.

'Come on.' Trixie banked down the fire and placed a flimsy, wonky iron fireguard around it.

'I'm not tidy enough to go to Greenleigh.' Caroline brushed at her dark blue skirt and bodice, both creased terribly and the rip noticeable in the bodice. Her coat would have to cover it as best it could, but her hair was a mess and she had lost her bonnet. 'My face...'

Scowling in thought, Trixie took a small square mirror from the windowsill and gave it to Caroline with the comb. 'We could do with some powder, but I don't use it and I don't think the other women in this house do either. Margie in the next street does, but she'll be sleeping, and I'd hate to wake her as she doesn't get in until the sun rises.'

'I'll just have to explain I was harmed...' Could she? Could she explain what happened to her? Caroline took a handful of water from the bucket and washed her face, flinching at the coldness and the tenderness of her cheek.

'They'll be able to see the state of you and might let you keep your position. None of this was your fault,' Trixie said hopefully.

Combing out her hair and then braiding it, Caroline readied herself to face the ordeal ahead while Trixie called the girls in and tidied them up.

The four of them walked out of the room and the girls greeted another little girl playing on the landing with a doll made from a wooden peg. Behind a closed door, a woman shouted at someone else, and a baby wailed from a room on the floor above.

Outside, an arctic breeze tunnelled up the lane from the river. They passed a young man carrying a bucket of water and he nodded to Trixie. 'Morning, Trixie.'

'Morning, Jacob.'

'Who's this then?' He smiled from a pleasant face.

'I've a lodger, Caroline.' Trixie told him. 'Caroline, this is one of our neighbours across the landing. Jacob Adams. He lives with his sister, Sarah, she's the midwife of the lanes.'

Caroline murmured good morning and kept her head bent so he couldn't see her swelling and bruises.

They walked on just as the contents of a chamber pot splashed the cobbles ahead. Caroline stared up at the tenement houses to check for any other open windows.

Reaching Castlegate at the top, Caroline paused and looked back down the lane. The stench from human and animal waste clogged her nose. Despite the early hour, ragged children were playing on the cobbles, one little boy waddled bowed-legged, a legacy from having Rickets. Trixie lived in the Water Lanes, one of the worst slums in York. Caroline exhaled heavily. Was this awful place to be her home forever too?

Turning left, they continued on to Nessgate. The city was fully awake now and horse-drawn vehicles vied for space on the streets while hurrying people dodged the steaming deposits the horses left. The low sky held a mixture of grey and white clouds hiding a weak sun. A cold breeze blew off the river, channelling along the streets and whipping their skirts against their legs.

Crossing the river, Caroline watched as the girls pointed out different boats and the cranes working to lift cargo from them. Horns and whistles added to the noise of the rumbles of carriages and wagons crossing the bridge. On the other side, vendors sold their goods from hand carts, the smell of nuts roasting and seeing people wrapped up warmly against the chill, reminded Caroline of the winter markets in the village back home. She and Hugh would walk along the main street, buying treats to take home and eat before the fire.

The closer they got to Greenleigh House, the more nervous Caroline became. She couldn't lose her position. She'd beg the housekeeper, Mrs Claymore, beg them all if she had to, to keep her job.

'We'll wait here.' Trixie paused before a small bookshop a hundred yards down from the house. 'We can look at the lovely books in the window, can't we girls?'

'If I'm allowed to stay, I'll come out and tell you so you can go back home.'

'Good luck.'

Caroline summoned all her courage and strode up the hill. Her legs were trembling as she let herself into the back of the house through the scullery door. The warmth hit her from the open kitchen doorway and then the delicious smell of frying bacon.

'Look what the cat's dragged in,' Pammie spoke from behind Caroline, making her jump.

The cook, Mrs Townsend, glanced up from the small desk in the corner of the kitchen where she wrote her notes. 'Caroline.'

'Look at the state of her,' Pammie laughed. 'You been wrestling bears or something?'

Mrs Townsend slowly stood and crossed the kitchen. 'This is a surprise. I didn't expect to see you back after being away for two days. Mrs Claymore and I thought you'd finished with us.'

'I would have been here if I could.' Caroline wrung her hands. 'I was... I had an accident.'

'So, I see by your face. I sent Pammie to Mrs Overton's Lodging House yesterday to see where you were.' Mrs Townsend raised her eyebrows. 'Mrs Overton said you had left her premises and she didn't know where you'd gone, but she told Pammie that you had been associating with a nefarious gentleman.'

Caroline gasped in shock as did the rest of the kitchen maids, though some giggled, too. 'That's not true!'

'Nevertheless, I had to act on the information I received, and you were nowhere to be found.' Mrs Townsend tapped her fingers together. 'How was I to know if you were ever to return? I cannot run my kitchen that way, can I? I have a duty to the Greenleighs to manage this kitchen to the best of my ability and to not hire someone who had a doubtful reputation. We took a chance on you, especially as you didn't have a reference and I see now that was my folly.'

'I'm a good person. I'm here now,' she pleaded. 'I'll work hard as I did in the past. You didn't find fault with me before, did you? I am decent and honest...' She faltered. Was she decent now? She'd been beaten and held captive in a brothel. If that ever got out, she'd be shunned by all who thought themselves to better than her.

'I'm afraid it's too late. You have been replaced.' Mrs Townsend consulted her fob watch that hung on a silver chain from her apron pocket. 'Now I must ask you to leave so we can get on with our work.'

Crushed, Caroline turned away but then sprung back taking Mrs Townsend by surprise. 'May I have a reference, please?' She knew how difficult it was to get one.

'I think not. You are not reliable, why would I ever put my good name to a reference for you?' The older woman hesitated, and Caroline thought she'd changed her mind. 'However, you have wages owed and I am nothing but a fair person. Wait here.'

Humiliated, conscious of the whispers and stares, Caroline stood in the middle of the kitchen by the table.

'How did you come by that beating?' Pammie sniggered. 'A lover turned rough?'

The kitchen maids giggled and chatted loudly.

'Enough of that noise!' Mrs Townsend entered the kitchen and glared at the maids who immediately turned back to their tasks. 'Here you are.'

Caroline took the brown envelope from her. Manners made her say thank you, but a reference would have helped so much more. She'd be happy to never see the likes of Pammie again, but losing her position weighed heavily on her bowed shoulders.

Once outside on the street, she saw Trixie standing in front of a low walled garden of another grand house the street boasted. The girls were hopping up and down the gutter, singing a playful tune.

'Are they keeping you on?' Trixie asked, coming to meet her.

'No.' She refused to cry. She needed to be strong like Trixie. She needed to plan. 'I asked for a reference to help me get another position, but Mrs Townsend refused, and there's no point asking Mrs Claymore the housekeeper.'

'Is Townsend the wife?'

'No, just the cook.'

Trixie gaped at her as they walked back to the girls. 'Cook? One of us?'

'Hardly one of us. She is a valued member of the household staff, coming under only the housekeeper and butler.'

'Arses the lot of them.'

Caroline jerked at her foul language. Respectable people didn't swear, especially in public.

Trixie glowered. 'Think they're better than us, but the only difference is they've got money and we don't.'

'They don't have money, Trixie.' Caroline sighed. 'They have authority, and that power is mighty even if it's only within a kitchen.'

'What will you do?' Trixie asked, taking one hand of each sister.

'I've no idea.' The enormity of the situation throbbed in her head like a monkey clashing cymbals she'd once seen at a country fair.

'You can stay with us if you want?' Trixie flashed her a tentative smile. 'We ain't got much but we're happy to share it with you for as long as you like.'

'Are you sure? I've no job.'

'We'll find you one, don't worry.'

Caroline didn't have her confidence. She opened the envelope and counted nine shillings and ten pence. 'That's all I've got to my name, but it's yours.'

Trixie shook her head. 'Keep it. We need coal and food. I've got the rent money for this week and if you can buy the other things, then we'll be doing just fine, won't we?'

Was it that simple? A bit of food and coal, a squalid room in a filthy slum. Was that her life now? She couldn't accept it, not yet. She'd get out of this mess, and she'd take Trixie and her sisters with her. She just had to work out how to do it.

Chapter Eight

'We don't go to church,' Trixie declared stubbornly the next morning.

Caroline glanced up from putting on her boots. She'd accidentally woken Trixie up early when she climbed over her to use the chamber pot. She knew Trixie hadn't returned home until long after midnight. What Trixie did each night for her work, Caroline didn't know, and she didn't want to guess. 'But it's Sunday.'

'Just another day for us.' Trixie boiled some eggs that Caroline had bought with her wage.

'I see.' She didn't see at all. She assumed everyone went to church on Sunday morning.

'What have I got to thank God for?' Trixie pouted. 'For living in this paradise?' she mocked. 'For losing Father and Mam?'

'I don't think it works like that,' Caroline replied, smoothing down her skirt and looking for her bonnet, one she'd bought for a few pennies off the market yesterday, which in her past life she'd have not given a second glance. But she couldn't walk around with no bonnet, even as bad as the out of shape and stained one she'd bought was, it was still better than nothing.

'And what have *you* got to thank God for?' Trixie shook her head. 'I ain't going.'

'Can we go?' Elsie asked, sitting in bed.

'No.' Trixie stabbed the coals with the poker.

Caroline looked at Trixie. 'I don't mind taking them.'

'And be scorned for turning up dressed as they are? One look at them and everyone there will know we aren't good enough.'

'Who will judge us?' Caroline shook out Elsie's only dress. The grey serge without the white pinafore was passable, for the pinafore needed a good soak and a wash, something which Caroline hadn't seen anyone do in this lane.

'They *all* will!' Trixie put the eggs on a plate, her movements jerky, angry.

'It's a church, Trixie. God's house and He doesn't judge.'

'Maybe not you, but the parishioners will look at my sisters and see they aren't wearing polished boots or have ribbons in their hair. I won't have them being scorned.'

'I will protect them from any harsh words.'

'You aren't their family. You've been here only a few days, why would you protect my sisters?'

Caroline strove for patience. Trixie looked tired and worn out with shadows under her large eyes and she was so terribly thin. 'You saved me. You've allowed me to live with you. I'd like to think of you as my friend now. I thought you might feel the same.'

Silence stretched between them.

'Eat your egg,' Trixie spoke to Elsie, not replying to Caroline. 'Our Bertha has finished hers and if you're going to church, you need your hair combed and tied back, no arguments. I ain't having people say my sisters look like they sleep in the gutter. Wash your face, too.'

'Are you sure you won't join us?' Caroline asked, when ten frantic minutes later the girls were washed and dressed and wiping tears away from the pain of having their hair combed and tugged tightly into plaits.

'I've plenty to do here. I need some sleep and then I'll fetch more water and have a good wash meself.' Trixie shooed them out the door.

'I'll take them for a walk afterwards then,' Caroline suggested from the landing. 'To give you some peace for a bit.'

'If you like.' Trixie closed the door on her.

Caroline sighed. Trixie was a mixture of moods. One minute she was kind and thoughtful, or funny and talkative, then the next minute she was prickly and sour, snappy or sullen. Caroline didn't know how to take her and wondered if living there was the right thing to do. But what option did she have? The workhouse? She shuddered and dismissing it from her mind, at least for the next few hours, she took the girls' hands and went downstairs.

The closest church was St Mary's Church on Castlegate at the end of Middle Water Lane. Caroline steered the girls into the back pews, ignoring some of the stares sent their way. Elise and Bertha were wide-eyed at the novelty of being in a church. The tall narrow arched windows let in the morning light as the service began to a packed congregation.

Singing the first hymn, Caroline encouraged Elsie and Bertha to join in but they didn't know the hymn, and she realised they couldn't read.

By the end of the service, Bertha was fidgeting, and Caroline ushered them to the door to shake the hand of the vicar, Reverend Houghton, who smiled warmly at them.

'New faces. How delightful,' he said, his round glasses perched at the end of his nose. 'You are new to the area?' His gaze flicked to the girls and back to Caroline.

'I am, yes. Caroline Lawson, and these are my friend's sisters, Elsie and Bertha Wilkes.'

'You are very welcome, indeed.' Reverend Houghton bent and shook the girls' hands and they stood silent and in awe. 'Perhaps next week you can attend Sunday School before service?' He looked at Caroline. 'There is a hot breakfast served, too, for the children.'

'I'll have to ask their sister.'

He bowed. 'Of course. I hope she agrees and that I will meet you again next Sunday. We start at eight o'clock.' He turned to the next people in the line.

'A school?' Elsie said, hopping from one foot to another as they walked down Castlegate. 'Mary and Sarah who live in the rooms above us, they go to Sunday School, but our Trixie said we couldn't because she likes to sleep on Sunday mornings.'

'Well, maybe now I'm living with you I can take you? We'll ask Trixie when we go back.'

'You said we could go for a walk after church,' Elsie reminded her.

'Very well.' Caroline didn't need any persuading. She was loathed to return the tiny repulsive room, especially when the sun was finally shining after weeks of miserable weather. Although chilly, and the start of winter was only next week, she felt the need to be out in the fresh air and walk. The girls ran ahead, stopping to looking in shop windows, pointing to things they wanted, sweets and toys. None of which they'd ever had nor were likely to have.

Caroline wished she could buy them a pennyworth bag of sweets, but every penny had to be used wisely. The money Mrs Townsend gave her had bought the ugly bonnet, four eggs, half a pound of tea, four potatoes and half-priced broken pork pie and a bag of coal. She had a few coins left to buy some food this week. She'd also hunt the streets again looking for work.

Heading down to the river, they strolled across the bridge and along the docks on the other side on Queens Staith, passing warehouses and cranes, moored boats until the dockyard ended and they went up onto the street.

'We've never been over here before,' Elsie said, looking around. 'Our Trixie doesn't let us leave the Water Lanes or our side of the river.'

'This is new to me too,' Caroline told her, making a mental note to come back here tomorrow to search for work. Although there were many mills, timber and stone yards, shipyards and breweries, all who employed only men, there were some nice houses in the surrounding streets.

'Where did you live before coming to us?' Elsie asked.

Caroline smiled at her questions. She never stopped talking that one whereas Bertha spoke little. 'I lived in a lodging house when I first came to York.'

'And where did you live before that?'

'In the country, miles from here, on a farm with my husband Hugh.' Her heart twisted at the thought of Hugh.

'A farm?' Elsie's eyes grew wide. 'With lots of animals like you see at the market, hens and pigs?'

'Yes, and we had two cows and a horse as well.' She thought wistfully of her animals that she'd tended and cared for so lovingly.

'Cows...' Bertha murmured as if not fully grasping what they were.

'We saw cows once, remember?' Elsie nudged her sister before looking up at Caroline. 'There were some on a boat and they came down a ramp and were kept in a pen at the bottom of our lane. Trixie said they'd be going to the butchers' market.'

'Cows also give milk. I milked my two cows every morning.'

'Milk? It comes from cows?' Elsie asked in wonder. 'I've tasted milk once before. Our Trixie got some cheap because it was ready to turn. We drank it in a cup of tea.'

A pang of compassion for these two girls filled Caroline's heart. She'd taken for granted the fresh food and produce she grew or reared at the farm. Whereas these girls and so many like them had never tasted newly churned butter or known the thrill of digging up pale potatoes or collecting eggs still warm from the nest or picking fat blackberries from the hedgerows.

Homesickness clamped her chest like a vice. She ached for the farm, even for the freezing cold mornings when the water barrels were frozen over, and when the winds howled across the fields, or the snow drifted against the cottage and Hugh would have to dig them out.

She wondered how Leo and Lisette were coping. Did Lisette tend to Buttercup and Clover as well as she had? Did Leo know the barn door would stick in wet weather and one of the hinges needed fixing or that the roof on the hen house needed recovering for winter?

'I'm hungry,' Bertha whispered to Elsie.

Caroline heard her. 'Let us find something to eat.'

'Nothing's open on Sunday,' Elsie said. 'We'll have to go home.'

The long walk back to Middle Water Lane wasn't as cheerful as it was on the way out. Bertha's feet dragged and Elsie complained of a blister from the boots she had grown out of. Caroline was just as hungry as the girls and hoped they had enough food to tide them over until tomorrow.

Trixie wasn't in the room when they entered. The fire was low, and the water bucket gone. Shaking the kettle, Caroline was relieved it was full of water and swung it over the heat. 'A cup of tea will put a smile on our faces,' she told the girls, trying to cheer them up.

They laid on the bed looking tired and miserable.

Checking the tin box, Caroline took out the loaf of bread and cut two slices to spread them with the last of the jam. She gave them to the girls and made the tea. 'We need a teapot,' she muttered.

'We need a lot of things,' Trixie said coming into the room with a bucket of wet washing. 'How was church?'

'Lovely.' Elsie smiled, brighter now she had sat down and was eating. 'The vicar asked if we wanted to go to Sunday School next week.'

'Sunday School?' Trixie frowned, hanging the wet pinafores on the line strung across the room.

'They can have breakfast there, too,' Caroline added.

'You said yes?' Trixie slapped a cloth over the line. 'Without asking me?'

'No. I told Reverend Houghton that we needed to ask you first.'

'They aren't going.' Trixie slung a petticoat over the line.

'Why?' Caroline didn't understand. 'Elsie and Bertha will learn to read and write.'

'Hardly. It'll be all scriptures and stuff about God and being thankful and such nonsense.'

'They'll have religious teaching, yes, but the main thing is the girls will learn to read and write. Why would you not want them to do that?'

'What good would it do?' Trixie flared. 'They'll still be living in these lanes, still be poor, still have no food to eat.'

'But they can better themselves. A little education will put them in good stead for getting a respectable position some-where.'

'Huh! You're a fool to think that, or maybe it's because you've only been here five minutes and you don't know the real world of these lanes. No one gets good positions who live here. The men, when they do find work, are labourers in mills and timber yards, tanneries and brick fields. Hard, filthy work no one else will do. And the women have even less chance of finding something de-cent.'

'None of that should be a reason to not let Elsie and Bertha learn to read and write.'

Trixie gave Caroline a snort of contempt. 'Listen to yourself! You can read and write, can't you?'

'Yes.'

'And look where that's got you. *Here!*' Trixie picked up the bucket and flounced out of the room.

⁓

Staring up at the sign above the pub's door, Caroline steeled herself to walk inside the Malt Shovel. Even though she'd been inside several times before, it still wasn't natural to enter a public house. Women didn't enter taprooms unless it was a coaching inn, and this pub was simply for working men, but the landlord, Mr Warburton, was kind and accommodating and waved her on to the snug. He remembered her from her previous visits with Mussy.

Striding quickly inside and heading straight for the snug, which was tucked down a small corridor, Caroline opened the door to find it empty. Disappointment filled her.

'So, you've returned?' Mr Warburton, a lanky man of over fifty, came out of a doorway leading to the back of the pub near the snug.

'I was unable to come last week,' Caroline explained.

'Mussy was worried,' he said, tying a clean apron around his waist. 'I expect he'll be here shortly though. He said last week, he would come and hope you'd turn up. Take a seat in there and I'll get you some drinks. Do you fancy soup or stew?'

'Neither, thank you. I've no money.' She blushed with embarrassment.

'Right you are.' He nodded and left her alone.

Sitting down on the timber bench with its red cushion seat, Caroline exhaled heavily as the appealing smell of roasting meat wafted in from the pub's kitchen. She'd been constantly hungry all week. Each day she'd walked for hours along the better streets of the city, knocking on house doors, asking for a maid's position. With no reference it was difficult to even get anyone to speak to her for more than a minute and even if she did get a moment to speak, as soon as they heard she had no experience at any type of trade, the door was shut in her face. Soon, she'd have to try the less than pleasant and dangerous places, such as the factories and mills on the outskirts of the city. She was loathed to enter the filthy yards of the factories, to work twelve hours a day in gloomy dirty buildings. She had no skills of working machines in a mill and knew that because she lacked experience her position and wage would be low.

Should she consider returning to the farm? To live with Howard and his new wife wasn't ideal but would be better than the workhouse. She might find some work in the village or on another farm. She was useful in the dairy and at farmwork. The idea grew as she sat waiting. Howard wouldn't turn her away, even if his new wife wasn't as accommodating and at least she'd be in the fresh air, away from the stink of the city and the horrors it held.

Only, a tiny thought appeared in the back of her mind about leaving Trixie and the girls behind. They'd still be living in that damp room without proper food and comfort. Could she leave them? She'd grown close to the girls, telling them stories each night in bed of the farm and the animals, and although Trixie could be abrupt at times, Caroline was warming to her ways. Underneath Trixie's difficult moods was a young woman carrying a great weight. Was it any wonder she could be sharp-tongued occasionally? And what did Trixie do each night when she went out to work? Caroline had begun to guess Trixie's line of work and the thought saddened her terribly.

Returning to the farm would be humiliating, she had no doubt about that. She'd arrive with nothing and be a burden on Howard. She'd also have to deal with Leo and Lisette. Certainly, Lisette would crow over her inability to survive in York and enjoy the fact that Caroline had returned home destitute and begging for a bed. Was Howard's new wife nice? Would she want a stranger in her house?

All these thoughts jumbled around in her head, making it throb. What was she to do? There seemed no easy answer.

Beyond the snug, the noise grew of men laughing and talking. Caroline, hungry and tired sat waiting, hoping Elsie and Bertha were all right as she'd left them alone as Trixie had gone to work. She knew she shouldn't worry about the girls because Trixie had always left them at night and they were used to it, but still, Caroline didn't like it and would tell Mussy she couldn't stay long.

The snug door opened, and Mr Warburton brought in a glass of cordial and placed it on the table. 'Mussy's late,' he said.

'What time is it?'

'Just after seven o'clock.' Mr Warburton gave the table a wipe, even though it was clean. 'I hope he's here soon. I need to speak to him about something.'

'And I don't want to stay out too long.' She sipped the blackberry cordial. 'This is nice. Thank you.' Mussy always paid for her cordial, and if he didn't turn up, she didn't know what she'd do as she had no money left to pay for the drink.

'Are you out of work?' the landlord asked.

'Yes.'

'Can you clean, properly like, no cutting corners.'

'Yes, yes, I can. I'm a hard worker and take pride in anything I do,' she gushed.

He screwed up his face in thought. 'My old mother is getting on and she's had a fall recently and is laid up in bed. She has a flat on Little Stonegate, above the milliners. Would you be willing to go there each day and clean the rooms and see to her? You know, make sure she has a meal and is washed, that sort of thing?'

'Oh, well, yes...'

'I had a young lass there doing it for her, but she's got more hours at her other job and Mother won't have me help her to wash.' Mr Warburton shrugged his shoulders in a bemused way. 'I'll pay you three shillings a week.'

'Four shillings a week,' Caroline blurted out, surprising herself.

'Agreed.' He held out his hand and she shook it happily.

The door opened and Mussy strode in, his face brightening on seeing Caroline. 'You're here!' Then he scowled, seeing the faded bruises on her face. 'What happened to you? I had a right to be worried last Friday when you didn't arrive.'

Mr Warburton stepped to the door. 'Stew, Mussy?'

'Wonderful. Two bowls and bread and cheese, thank you, Bob. Oh, and a glass of wine if you please?' Mussy took off his coat. He wore a striped navy suit with a bright purple cravat and a blue silk waistcoat.

'A new suit?' Caroline asked with a dash of envy. She couldn't afford a pint of milk yet Mussy was always dressed resplendently. His wage as a gas inspector must be remarkable. She'd never seen any man dressed as impressively as Mussy.

She took the coins feeling guilty. 'I'll pay you back.'

'No, you won't. Unfortunately, that's all the coins I have on me and some to pay Bob for our meal. I don't carry much money with me these days, too worried about being done over on my walk home.'

'Maybe that's what I should do, turn to a life of crime,' she tried to joke but it fell flat.

Mussy's expression changed. He wouldn't meet her eyes and he played with his food. 'Stay as wonderful as you are. Don't ever change.'

'Change happens to us all. Sometimes I do wonder what my life would have become if I'd stayed with my father-in-law.' She often regretted her hasty decision to come to York. Living with Howard and his new wife might not have been as bad as she believed, and she'd have been warm and fed and living a life she loved.

Mr Warburton came into the snug and cleared away their bowls and glasses. He looked at Caroline. 'So, you'll see to my mother?'

'Yes. I can start tomorrow morning, if that suits you?'

'What is this?' Mussy perked up.

'Mr Warburton has asked me to care for his mother and I've agreed.' She smiled at Mr Warburton. He had no notion of how much this meant to her. 'I'll go first thing in the morning and stay with her all day, cook and clean and anything else she needs.'

The relief flowed off Bob Warburton, relaxing his shoulders. 'It'll put my mind at ease knowing she's not left alone all day. Me or my wife usually pop in and see her each afternoon before the evening rush, but my Mary, my wife, she's just had our seventh and the birth was difficult. She's not up to leaving her bed yet.'

'I'll take good care of your mother, Mr Warburton. What's her name?'

'Just call her Mrs Warburton until she says different.' He fished in the pocket of his trousers and brought out a key and gave it to Caroline. 'The door leads off the road. Next to the milliners. Just give a shout and go straight upstairs. If she wants you to do any shopping, just put it all on credit to The Malt Shovel. I'll settle the bills.'

'Now you have a job.' Mussy grinned at her. 'That's worth celebrating, isn't it?'

'I'll bring you in another drink,' Mr Warburton said and went out again.

Caroline sagged back on the bench, lightened. She had a position. She would have some money to give Trixie. Not a lot, granted, but enough to buy a bit of food, some coal. Maybe her luck was turning.

Chapter Nine

Standing outside of McCarthy Milliner's shop on Little Stonegate, Caroline noticed the black door to the side of the large window. Unlocking the thick timber door with the key Mr Warburton had given her, Caroline let herself in and closed the door. A steep narrow staircase went up before her with a door at the top that was closed.

'Morning, Mrs Warburton,' she called loudly, feeling a bit silly to be shouting up a staircase to a closed door.

No reply came so Caroline went up and peeked in. 'Good morning, Mrs Warburton,' she said in a normal voice, going further into the large sitting room. 'Mrs Warburton?'

'Who's there?' A bark came from behind another door to the left.

Caroline opened the door and found an old woman lying in a wide bed piled high with pillows and blankets. 'Good morning.'

'Who in God's name are you?' the old woman crackled.

'I'm Caroline Lawson. I've come to take care of you. Your son, Bob, sent me.'

'Did he just? Without my say? The cheek of it.' A small bird like woman, Mrs Warburton seemed dwarfed by the amount of blanket and pillows. Her thin white hair was mostly hidden in a lacey cap that matched the layers of lace on her nightgown.

'Open the curtains and come closer so I can see you, girl,' the woman demanded.

Doing as she was bid, Caroline flung back the thick dark green curtains to let in light and stepped nearer to the bed, smiling warmly.

'Hmm... You look decent enough.' Mrs Warburton scrutinised her. 'You've clear skin and a slight colour to your face... Did you spend the summer working outside?'

'Yes, on my farm.'

'A farm girl? They know hard work.' Mrs Warburton nodded approvingly.

Under inspection, Caroline hoped she'd passed the test. Her skirt needed a proper scrub, which was impossible in the tiny room she now called home, and her hair, which was usually a tawny colour, was dark from lack of washing, but she'd pulled it into a tight bun at the back of her head, so it didn't show. Her boots needed a polish, and her cheap bonnet was terrible. 'What would you like me to do for you first?'

'You can help me use the pot, that's what.' Mrs Warburton threw back the blankets. She was spindly and small-boned with no fat under her skin. Age spots marked her hands and fine wrinkles lined her face, but her grey eyes were clear and bright and held a look of suspicion.

Caroline pulled the pot from under the bed and aided the old woman to squat over it. The smell of urine hit Caroline's nose and she turned her head away until the woman was done.

'I need to be dressed and fed.' Mrs Warburton peered closely at Caroline. 'Can you cook, girl?'

'I can, yes.' She kept smiling, knowing she needed this position and hopefully it would be better than a place in a dirty factory or making matchstick boxes at home or some awful occupation as working in a laundry, lifting heavy wet clothes for twelve hours.

'Good.' Mrs Warburton pointed to her cane resting at the end of the bed. Caroline passed it to her and then became aware that the cane would be an extension of the old woman's arm as she began pointing the cane to the wardrobe, the jug and wash basin, her shoes, her hairbrush, all the while snapping out orders to Caroline like a Sergeant-Major.

Twenty minutes later, Caroline was puffing. The act of washing and dressing Mrs Warburton took more energy than she expected. She'd washed her in cold water, something the old woman insisted upon as she said it invigorated her for the day. Next, Caroline dressed Mrs Warburton in bloomers, the intimate act made her blush and look away, before she hastily applied the layers, a chemise, a corset, a shift and then a tiered linen petticoat and finally a skirt and bodice in a burnt orange colour with black braiding. Caroline finished brushing the woman's thin white hair and pinned a small lace cap over it.

'Help me into the sitting room.'

'Your son said you were bedridden from a fall.'

'My son is an idiot! I am not in my coffin just yet. Bedridden indeed! Help me, girl. I eat at the table by the window.' Mrs Warburton leaned on her stick and Caroline's arm as they walked from the bedroom to the little table with two chairs in the bay window.

Mrs Warburton sat down and peered through the lace curtains to the narrow street below. 'I see Mrs McCarthy hasn't swept outside her shop yet. She's a lazy piece and no mistake. I don't know how she makes any money, for her hats aren't that well-made and not of the latest fashion.'

Caroline made no comment, though thought it surprising that a woman of Mrs Warburton's advanced age wore the latest style and colour and littered around the room were several fashion and lady's magazines.

She hovered by the table. 'What can I do for you first?'

'Get that fire going, girl.' The cane was pointed to the embers smouldering in the grate. 'In the future, you light that fire and the kitchen range before you come and wake me at eight o'clock each morning, six days a week. I do not care to see you on Sundays, my son will see me to church.'

'Yes, Mrs Warburton.' Moving the fireguard away, Caroline knelt and attended to the fire which thankfully spluttered into flames from the kindling she found in the box beside the chimney. Resting back on her heels, she smiled at the old woman. 'What would you like for breakfast?'

'What supplies did my son bring me last night? Go and look.' Mrs Warburton waved her cane toward the other door next to the bedroom door, which when Caroline opened it revealed a small room used as a kitchen. A tall dresser stood against the far wall and a square table in the middle of the room.

On either side of the black range and the chimney were two wall cupboards and in there Caroline found food staples. She sorted through the supplies. Ham and cheese on a marble slab and covered with a damp towel, tins of oats, peas and tea. A fresh loaf of bread was placed beside jars of jams and chutneys. A wooden caddy held sugar and Caroline sighed at the sight of it for she'd not had anything with sugar in it since she left the lodging house weeks ago. Under the window overlooking a back yard, was another cupboard which held a bag of potatoes, a turnip, a bunch of carrots and a string of onions. A straw-lined basket held a dozen eggs.

Caroline's first thought was that there was so much food for one little woman, when at home Elsie and Bertha were eating stale bread until Caroline or Trixie could buy a few bits. Last night, she'd given Trixie the money Mussy gave her and that would pay the rent and for a couple of buckets of coal.

'Well, girl?' The shout came from the sitting room. 'Am I to starve?'

Caroline stood in the doorway and listed the supplies she'd found. 'What would you prefer?'

'Ham and fried eggs, two. Tea. There's a silver teapot, don't use that, use the earthenware one instead. The silver teapot is for guests. Milk is down in the cellar.'

'There's a cellar?'

'Of course, there's a cellar, girl. Go down the back stairs from the kitchen and there's a door next to the lavatory. My milk and coal are in the cellar on the right. Mrs McCarthy's are on the left. Do *not* mix it up and use hers or I'll never hear the end of it. Mrs McCarthy can be a right harridan. Well, what are you doing standing there? My breakfast won't cook itself, will it?'

Caroline hurried to the kitchen and through trial-and-error cooking in a strange kitchen with a range that was a struggle to get going, and a trip downstairs to the dank dark cellar, she finally managed to create a decent breakfast.

'An hour?' Mrs Warburton commented when Caroline set the table. 'An hour to cook a bit of ham and eggs?'

'Yes, I'm sorry. The fire kept going out.'

'I don't want to hear your excuses.' Mrs McCarthy eyed the food as if she was a judge at a food tasting fair. 'Go and fetch me a newspaper from the boy on the corner, he'll be gone in ten minutes. There are pennies in that copper tin on the mantle. Be quick about it.'

Dashing down the staircase, she heard Mrs Warburton shout because she'd left the door open but ignoring her, she lifted her skirts and hurried to the newspaper boy and bought a copy of *The Times* from him and hurried back.

'Were you born in a barn, girl? Close the door behind you when you go out,' Mrs Warburton snapped. 'Add more coal to the fire and bring me my glasses.' Mrs Warburton waved the cane to the sideboard opposite.

All morning, Caroline went from one task to other. She was ordered to dust and clean the whole flat, black-lead the range, bring up more coal, make more tea and change the sheets on the bed. When the little gold carriage clock on the mantle chimed one o'clock, Caroline was already exhausted.

'What have you made for the midday meal?' Mrs Warburton asked, sitting on the green velvet sofa, reading the newspaper.

Stopping mid-way through sweeping the kitchen floor, Caroline stared at her through the open doorway. 'I... I hadn't thought.'

'Then I guess you'd better start thinking, hadn't you?' Mrs Warburton flicked the pages of the newspaper with emphasis. 'But I do fancy a pork chop with potatoes and fried onions. You can have one yourself so buy two. Off you go.'

Caroline grinned as she finished sweeping. The cranky old woman wasn't nearly as bad as she liked to think she was. Grabbing her coat and bonnet, Caroline made for the door.

'On credit to The Malt Shovel.'

'Yes, Mr Warburton told me. He'll pay any of your bills.'

'Did he now? Thinks he's lord and master, he does. He forgets I'm still his mother and used to wipe his backside.' She sniffed and raised the newspaper to block out Caroline. 'Don't dawdle, girl.'

Walking swiftly, Caroline headed for the Shambles and the butchers there, specifically Bent's Butchers. The smell of raw meat and blood filled the cobbled laneway of the Shambles. Women shopping, some with children at their feet, crowded the open shop windows, haggling for the best cuts and the best prices. Caroline slid into Bent's Butchers and went to the counter. Charles Bent turned from weighing a slab of meat and glancing at her, smiled warmly. 'Now there's a pretty face I've not seen in a while.'

'Good day, Mr Bent.'

'Ach, call me Charles, everyone else does. I'll just serve this lass and I'll be with you.' He cut the slab of meat in half and wrapped it deftly in paper. He swapped it for a handful of coins and the customer left the shop. 'Now then, lass, how have you been?'

'Not too bad. You know how it is,' she commented. How could she really answer that question without revealing all the awful details of the last month?

'Aye, I do, lass. Life can be a struggle at times. So, what can I get you?'

'I'd like two pork chops, please, on credit to The Malt Shovel.'

'The Malt Shovel? Is that where you work now, for Bob Warburton?'

'No, I look after his mother.'

'Ah.' Charles wrapped two pork chops in paper. 'Anything else, lass?'

How she wished she could order meat to take home and cook for Trixie and the girls, but she didn't have the money for chops or chicken, or any of the other tempting meats on display under the counter or hanging in the shop window. 'No, nothing else. Thank you.'

Charles tilted his head. 'I do think that the Warburtons buy their meat from Beecham's down the lane. Did you know that?'

'No, I didn't, but I thought to come here because you were so kind to me on my first day in the city.'

'You'll always have a friend in me, lass.'

She smiled and waved goodbye and went back to Little Stonegate to wrestle with the temperamental range again.

It was past eight o'clock when Caroline wearily climbed the stairs to the little room in Middle Water Lane. She'd dashed home as fast as she could along the dark and damp streets, scared of the shadows, of any man strolling by, in case Victor Dolan was about. It seemed she didn't breathe until she had turned into Middle Water Lane and saw the neighbours she was beginning to recognise.

Trixie and the girls were sitting on the bed and Trixie was braiding Elsie's long hair. 'That was a long day.' She gave Caroline a small smile. 'I bet you're dead on your feet.'

'I am.' Caroline sat on the edge of the bed and sighed. Her feet throbbed. 'I brought this back.' From under her coat, she took out a paper parcel. Unwrapping it, she revealed a handful of fried potato skins. 'When I was cooking Mrs Warburton's meal, I thought to fry the skins and bring them home.' She handed them to the girls who devoured them in less than a minute.

'That was kind.' Trixie gazed fondly at her sisters as they ate. 'What's she like, the old woman?'

'Fine. Cranky at times. Demanding. She orders me about with a wave of her cane.' Caroline waved her arm about to demonstrate, making the girls giggle. 'But I think she's a kind person underneath the highhandedness. She allowed me to sit with her and eat the same meal as her, a chop, potatoes and onions with a cup of tea. She didn't have to do that.'

'Is she gentry?'

'No, I think she's the same as us, but she's had a wealthy husband.'

'Hardly the same as us then,' Trixie scoffed, continuing to plait Elsie's hair.

'I mean she is working class, or once was maybe. She doesn't speak like the gentry and she's not in a nice house on The Mount. She's in a flat above a milliner's shop, but her husband did well for himself from what I can gather.'

'Did she ask where you live?'

'No. She didn't talk much unless she was giving orders. She asked had I been working out in the sun during summer, and I told her I was on a farm, that satisfied her enough.'

'Didn't she ask why you left there?'

'No. She didn't seem interested in me at all.' Caroline chuckled. 'I'm sure over the next few days she'll ask more questions.'

'It's Sunday tomorrow, does the old lady want you every day?'

'No, not Sundays, thankfully. Mrs Warburton said she'd see me on Monday. I'll take the girls to Sunday School and church afterwards if that's all right with you?'

'Aye, I don't mind. There's tea if you want some. I bought some oats today that are soaking for breakfast in the morning.' Trixie finished the braid and stood to comb her riot of curls. 'Into bed, girls.'

'You're going out tonight?'

'You know I go out every night and Saturdays are the nights I earn the most.' Trixie stared into the little square mirror and pinched her cheeks.

'It's freezing outside,' Caroline murmured, coming to stand beside her. 'Be careful.'

Trixie looked at Caroline and a moment passed between them. Caroline wanted to beg her to stay home but knew she had no right to and besides they needed the money. She just wished Trixie had another way of earning it, not that Trixie had admitted her line of work and Caroline was too embarrassed to speak of it.

'Right, I'm off.' Trixie shrugged on her thin brown coat that had a button missing. 'Straight to sleep, girls.'

When she'd gone, Caroline heated some water to wash with.

'Are we really going to Sunday School tomorrow?' Elsie whispered from the bed.

'We are, and you'll start to learn to read and write. Won't that be lovely?'

Elsie's smile transformed her little face. 'I'm so happy you came to live with us. Don't ever leave.'

Caroline's heart melted. 'I'll try not to.'

The next morning, she got the girls dressed and out the door without disturbing Trixie who slept soundly. Caroline had her heard come in during the night and only when Trixie's icy cold feet had touched her back, did Caroline manage to fall into a deep sleep.

'I thought we were having oats for breakfast?' Bertha mumbled as they trod over slippery cobbles towards the church.

'No, we'll leave that for Trixie, or have it when we get home. At Sunday School, they give you breakfast.' Caroline smiled down at Bertha.

'You will stay with us?' Bertha asked, slipping her hand into Caroline's.

'If I'm allowed, yes.'

At the entrance to the Sunday School, held in a large room in the building beside the church, Reverend Houghton greeted them with a friendly face. He ushered the girls to a table, and they sat amongst other children and ate a bowl of porridge and then were given an apple each afterwards.

'An apple!' Elsie held it up like a prize. 'A whole apple for me?'

'Just for you,' Reverend Houghton said, carrying the large basket of apples down the row of tables.

Caroline helped to clear away the empty bowls and spoons, and she volunteered to wash them in tubs of hot water with a couple of other women while the children sat and recited the alphabet from a chart on the wall.

'Our dear vicar is very enthusiastic to teach the children of this parish,' one woman said, scrubbing the porridge pans. 'My Jane has done so well in learning to read. She wants to be a teacher herself one day, though I'll be happy for her to get a position as a maid with a reputable family.'

The other woman wiping down the tables, tutted. 'I know my George will follow his father into the railways whether he can read or not.'

'But at least having some education, they'll have the choice?' Caroline said to them.

'That's what I said to my husband,' Jane's mother said with a nod. 'In another five years, she'll be ten and have all this schooling. Eventually, she could become a lady's maid or something just as grand. My Jane won't be going into a mill or a factory if I can help it.'

'There's nowt wrong with a good job in a factory or a mill, Mrs Lumley.' The other woman dunked her cloth in the water bucket and wiped another table.

'I'm not saying there is, Mrs Renton! In Leeds, my mother worked in a mill, and so did I until I married my Bill, and he got a job as a warder in the prison here in York,' Mrs Lumley argued. 'But my brother was a chimney sweep's boy until he fell and broke both ankles. I ain't having my young uns getting disfigured or made lame from working in dangerous places. The things I saw when at the mill would make your hair stand on end. Little kiddies killed and maimed under the looms. I once saw a girl get scalped when her hair was caught in the machine. Stuff of nightmares it was.'

'Hey, did you hear about Nessie Elton's boy who lost all his fingers last week?' Mrs Renton said sadly. 'Got his hand caught in one of the saws at Vigger's Timber Yard. He nearly died from the loss of blood. Awful. That place has a bad reputation for treating young lads poorly.'

Caroline winced at the horrible image.

'You have two girls, don't you, Mrs... er...' Mrs Renton frowned, realising she'd not asked Caroline her name.

'Mrs Caroline Lawson,' she supplied for them both. 'Elsie and Bertha are my friend's sisters and I hope they can find suitable positions that aren't treacherous.'

'Hear, hear,' Mrs Lumley chanted. 'When I was a girl, we were working in the mill as soon as we could walk and talk. Not like now, with children under nine not allowed to work.'

Mrs Renton huffed. 'Huh, families get around that by saying their child is small for their age and employers turn a blind eye to it. Families need their children in work. How can they afford to live with children doing nothing all day?'

'Well, my Jane and her brother Tommy won't be working until they're nine,' Mrs Lumley argued. 'My Bill said he's not having his children working and breaking any law. I'm looking at getting my Tommy apprenticed to a clock maker in Coney Street in the summer when he turns nine. My Jane helps me in the house. She's becoming very good at cooking.'

'You don't sound like you're from around 'ere,' Mrs Renton suddenly said to Caroline. 'We've not seen you here before either.'

'I'm from the country, north of here.'

'What made you come to York then?' Mrs Lumley asked. 'Did your husband get a job here?'

'No. My husband died. I came to find work.'

'Ah, sorry to hear about your husband.' Mrs Lumley frowned.

Reverend Houghton came over to them and said they were finished with the lesson and the church service would start shortly. The women put away the chairs and tables and then joining the children, they went outside to enter the church with the other parishioners.

Rain fell during the service and Caroline's promise of a walk to Elsie and Bertha had to be postponed as they left the church and hurried along the slippery streets.

Back in the room, Trixie was sitting before the fire, feeding it little pieces of coal. 'How was it?' she asked the girls.

'It was good!' Elsie couldn't hide her enthusiasm. 'We learned the alphabet. Reverend Houghton said I was picking it up quickly.' She beamed.

'The alphabet?' Trixie's eyebrows rose as she looked at Caroline. 'What's that then?'

'Letters. A. B. C and so on. You need to know the letters that make up words.'

'C. A. T. Spells cat!' Elsie shouted excitedly. 'I learned that this morning.'

Trixie looked at her sister in awe. 'Does it really?'

'If we had something to write with, I could continue the lesson,' Caroline mused. 'The nuns taught me to read and write in the convent where I grew up.'

'You grew up in a convent?' Trixie scoffed. 'No wonder you love God.'

'I don't love God so devoutly as you think, not like the nuns. I never wanted to be a nun.' She remembered the harsh rules of the convent, the sternness of the strict nuns, the quietness of the cold building, the loneliness of being all alone in the world after her parents died, and the feeling of guilt for wanting more than the stale life she lived as a girl. On the rare occasions the nuns took her and the other orphaned girls out on walks, Caroline was filled with wonder at what existed beyond the convent's high walls.

'Can you teach us?' Elsie asked, hopping from foot to foot.

'We'll need something to write with, chalk or something.'

'I'm not wasting money on chalk,' Trixie said with a tut.

Caroline had a thought and reached for a piece of coal. 'We can use this.' She sat beside Trixie and wrote on the stone heath. 'I'll write the alphabet. Then the girls can copy it underneath.'

The afternoon sped by as Caroline taught the girls their letters and small words chosen from the letters. Trixie looked on as the rain ran down the window. When it was time for Trixie to cook some potatoes for their meal, she shooed them out of her way and Caroline sat with Elsie and Bertha on the bed and had them recite numbers one to twenty.

At bedtime, the girls fell asleep quickly, exhausted from all their learning.

'They'll not leave you alone now,' Trixie said to Caroline as she made weak cups of tea for them both. 'They'll be at you morning, noon and night wanting to learn letters and numbers.'

'I don't mind.' Caroline yawned and sat on the rug before the fire. 'I enjoy it.'

'You've lived such a different life to us. In a convent, then married to a farmer. We've always lived in these lanes and never had anything but each other.'

'I had no love of a family,' Caroline told her. 'My great uncle took me into his home as a help for his ailing wife. I often wondered why he didn't take me earlier but when I asked him, he said his wife was too ill to care for a child. Yet I cared for him and her from the age of sixteen until they died six years later. He was a man of the church with connections to the convent, but he didn't wish to care for me when I was little. I never felt loved until I met Hugh.' Her heart softened at the thought of him, of their quick courtship, the hasty marriage, but she regretted none of it. Hugh showed her love, made her feel special, wanted, cared for.

'You must miss the life you had?' Trixie said softly, staring into the flames.

'More than I can say.'

'I don't want our Elsie and Bertha to end up like me.' Trixie stared at her. 'And you know what that is, don't you?'

'I think so, yes.'

'I never wanted to be a prostitute. I only started because Mam was sick and couldn't work and we'd lost our father and the rent was due. Margie, in the next lane, she's an old hand at it and said she'd get me a couple of fellas who would pay well because I was young and fresh...'

Caroline watched the torment flitter across Trixie's elfin face, her large eyes sad.

'I was so scared, that first time. It was down by the river in a warehouse. He was a well-to-do young man, eager and I think not very experienced himself. He fumbled about a bit, and I felt a flash of pain and then it was over. Embarrassed, he threw a money purse at me and when I opened it had eight half-crowns in it. I was rich. I'd made that money in less than five minutes. An hour later another man come to the warehouse, and he didn't want to touch me, but have me touch him. Of course, I didn't know what to do, but he showed me. He was patient and gentle and I learned a lot about how to please a man. He said I had a gift, and my hands would be my talent. Half an hour later he left, and I had another five shillings in my purse. I was able to pay the rent we were behind on, buy food and pay for a doctor to see to Mam.'

'You did what you had to do for your family,' Caroline murmured.

Trixie glanced at the girls sleeping in the bed and back to Caroline. A steely glint entered her hazel eyes. 'I'm not ashamed of what I've become. I'm very good at it, actually. I'm not saying it's all been wonderful, it hasn't. Margie took me under her wing and taught me things, gave me lessons on how to stay alive and not get with child. So far, I've survived, and I've raised the girls, but I want more for them. A decent life, married to good men, have proper homes. I want them to have a better life than this.'

'I'll help you achieve that.'

'How?' Trixie sighed. 'I try to earn as much money as I can and still it's never enough. I can pay the rent and put a bit of food in their bellies, but not much else. They need better clothes and boots.' She glanced around the room and her shoulders sagged. 'I see all the nice houses in other parts of the city, and we live here in this rat-infested cesspit. I want more for my sisters.'

'Then we'll plan to leave here.'

'You make it sound so easy and we both know it won't be.'

'True, but we can try, can't we? We can put a penny away a week or something. I'm earning now. You've not had someone living here earning as well. Two wages can stretch twice as far as one.'

Trixie gave her a small smile. 'You'd do that for us?'

'We're friends, aren't we?'

Trixie nodded. 'Friends for life.'

Chapter Ten

Changing the sheets on Mrs Warburton's bed, Caroline kept an ear out for the old woman, who was in the sitting room replying to some letters.

Snow fell heavily outside, white-washing the city. December had roared in with wild blizzards and storms and freezing temperatures.

'There's someone at the door, girl!' Mrs Warburton called.

Hurrying out of the bedroom, Caroline went to answer the door. A young man stood there holding a basket of fresh laundry. In his hand was the bill. She took the basket and the bill from him and thanked him.

'That's good timing seeing I was just about to start on sorting the linen cupboard,' Caroline said to Mrs Warburton. 'I'll unpack this and then make you a cup of tea.'

'Whatever you do, do it quietly, girl.' Mrs Warburton instructed with a grim expression.

After eight weeks of working for the old woman, Caroline had grown used to her barbed tone, her snappish comments and her demanding ways. She refused to let the other woman bring her spirits down even though she never called Caroline by her name and only *girl*. Still, Caroline remained upbeat as she went about her tasks. Mr Warburton had upped her wages by another shilling which thrilled Caroline and despite her cantankerous ways, Mrs Warburton often gave her little tips when she ran errands or allowed her to take left over food for the girls.

Over the last few weeks, Mrs Warburton had asked a few more questions of Caroline, mainly inquiring about her current life. The old woman had been astonished when Caroline told her she lived in Middle Water Lane. Mrs Warburton had threatened to dismiss her, for she didn't want a maid who lived in the slums, but the old woman came to her senses when she realised how useful Caroline was, and that Caroline had none of the slovenly ways that marked the people of the slums.

Putting the folded linen in the cupboard in the bedroom, Caroline finished making the bed and then went into the kitchen to put the kettle on to heat.

'What are you cooking for our midday meal?' Mrs Warburton asked.

'There's stew from yesterday,' Caroline replied, making up a tea tray.

'I ain't having stew again. Do I look like a pauper to you, girl? I will not eat food from the day before. Take it home with you.'

'Thank you, Mrs Warburton,' Caroline said from the kitchen doorway.

'So, once you've made me a cup of tea, go out to the butchers. That Mr Bent of yours sells adequate steak. That's what I want.' Mrs Warburton sealed an envelope. 'And you can post this on your way, too.'

Caroline glanced out of the window at the falling snow. Her left boot had a hole in the toe, and she'd have a wet stocking for the rest of the day. She believed Mrs Warburton got a strange kind of glee out of sending Caroline into bad weather. She always sent her on errands when it was either raining, blowing a gale or snowing. Never once did she send Caroline out when it was a calm day.

Mashing the tea in the pot and adding a cup and saucer to the tray, plus a small jug of milk and a little bowl of sugar, Caroline also placed a plate of oat biscuits she'd made the day before. Mrs Warburton was pleasantly surprised when Caroline started baking little treats for her. But the old woman didn't know that Caroline also snuck some of the treats into her coat pocket and took them home with her, too.

Caroline carried the tray into the sitting room and placed it on the table. 'Do you want me to pour or to leave now?'

'I'll pour.' Mrs Warburton waved her away. 'Get my money purse from the sideboard. Buy two steaks, and also get a pork pie, I'll have that this evening once you've left for the day. Don't forget to post these letters. And don't get them wet!'

Caroline donned her bonnet and coat. 'I'll be as quick as I can.'

'It's hardly the day for strolling, is it?' the old lady snapped.

Outside, the blast of snow hit Caroline in the face. The chill of it made her shiver as she trod carefully along the narrow street which the street sweepers had cleared that morning, but the heavy snowfall had covered again within the hour. Snow was drifting up the sides of the buildings, sitting on the shop windowsills and thickly coating the rooftops.

She hoped Elsie and Bertha had kept the fire going well to keep them and the room warm. Trixie had bought a sack of coal yesterday and with the two wages coming in, the room was warmer than ever before. Caroline now brought home the old newspapers Mrs Warburton didn't want for Elsie to practice her reading with Bertha so the girls could stay in the room warm and content.

Caroline held onto a wall as she navigated an open drain, slippery with waste.

'Careful as you go, miss,' a young man said, wheeling a barrow towards the marketplace.

The snow swirled in the air, clinging to her coat and eyelashes. Caroline took her time, not wanting to slip and injure herself. She posted the letters first, noticing the address of one was for a solicitor. With the snow falling heavier, she headed for the Shambles and Bent's Butchers. Charles greeted her warmly as she entered the shop, his wife was serving another customer and so Charles came to her.

'How do, lass?'

'I'm well, Mr Bent. How are you?'

'I'm fine and dandy, lass. How's it going with Mrs Warburton today?'

'Same as ever.' Caroline smiled. She saw Charles almost every day for Mrs Warburton had been converted to eating meat only from Bent Butchers after Caroline first shopped there.

'She's sent you out on a right nasty day.'

'I think Mrs Warburton enjoys sending me out in such weather. We had stew she could have eaten but no, she wants steak, two, and a pork pie, please.'

'My, she eats well, your Mrs Warburton.' He went back around the counter and selected a small pork pie.

'I don't know where she puts it, Mr Bent, I really don't. She's as thin as a bird's leg.' Caroline grinned.

'Is that any way to speak about your employer?' Mrs Bent snarked from further down the counter. 'Be more respectful.'

Charles rolled his eyes, but Caroline dipped her head and apologised. She didn't want word getting back to Mrs Warburton that she'd been rude about her. She'd hate to lose her job.

'Have you plans for Christmas, lass?' Charles asked, rolling up two steaks in some paper.

'No. Mrs Warburton is going to her son's house for Christmas Day and the day after and doesn't need me. So, I have two days off.'

'She's spending two days at the pub?' Mr Bent chuckled. 'Bob will have his hands full with all his kids and his mother.'

'No, Mrs Warburton has another son, Gordon.' It had surprised Caroline when a few weeks ago Mrs Warburton mentioned her son, Gordon, who lived in Selby.

'Ah, yes, I do remember Gordon. I never liked him as much as Bob. He and Bob don't get on either, that's why he's never here. He owns a public house in Selby.'

'Mrs Warburton is hoping the snow stops so next week he can come and collect her and take her back to Selby.' Caroline paid him the money and stored the paper parcel in the net bag she carried.

'Well, I hope it does for your sake, so you can have a couple of days off and put your feet up. I know I'm looking forward to having a day or two of the shop being closed.'

'One day closed!' Mrs Bent barked from where she was cutting up meat behind the counter. 'Not two, Charles, just one day. The Lord's day and then we'll be open for business as usual.'

'Yes, dear.' He replied not looking at his wife but giving Caroline a wide smile and she wished him good day and headed back out into the snow.

Slipping and sliding, she made her way back along the streets, the snow crunching under her feet. She was chilled when she got back to the flat, and as predicted, her stocking was soaked on her left foot.

'You took your time, girl. What are you cooking with the steak?' Mrs Warburton asked the moment she got through the door.

'I've not decided.'

'Then be quick about it, girl. It's gone one o'clock already.'

'It won't take me long.' Caroline quickly set the pans on the range. She was searching through the vegetables, tossing up the idea to boil some turnips and cabbage or mash a cauliflower with a cheese sauce. She was still deciding when she heard voices from the sitting room. Thinking it was Bob, Caroline went to the kitchen door to greet him, but instead a well-dressed stranger stood there.

'Ah, girl, this is my eldest son, Gordon.'

The man, large with a barrel chest, greying hair and bushy whiskers turned and stared at Caroline. 'You have a new maid, Mother?'

'Yes. Bob found her for me.' Mrs Warburton waved her cane at Caroline. 'My son will have the other steak. You will eat something else, the stew.'

'Yes, Mrs Warburton.' She went back to the range, a little envious that the son would be having her steak for the midday meal. She'd only ever had steak with Mrs Warburton once before and thoroughly enjoyed it. At least she could still have her main meal here and it was less food for her to buy and eat at home. She and Trixie were determined to save as much money as they could for the plan to move away from the Water Lanes. To that end, Caroline ate what she could while at work, so the food at home stretched further.

'What is your name?'

Caroline jumped at the sound of the voice right behind her. She turned to find Gordon Warburton standing only a few feet away. 'Caroline, sir.'

'Caroline. What a delightful name.' His gaze hungrily roamed her body like a dog gazing at a sausage. He even licked his lips.

She tensed, withering at the scrutiny. 'Can-can I get you something, sir?'

He moved close enough to stroke her arm. 'My mother wants a fresh pot of tea, and we need another cup and saucer.'

His touch made her cringe, her chest tighten. 'Of course. I'll do it straight away.' She back further away from him, reaching for the kettle. All the hairs stood up on the back of her neck. She didn't want him touching her or being anywhere near her. Gordon Warburton seemed the type of man who took what he wanted and the way he stared at her, she knew that wasn't good for her.

'Oh, and I want my steak juicy.' He grinned. 'Fried in butter not lard.'

'Yes, sir.'

'Are you married, Caroline?' he asked, leaning against the dresser, arms folded, his eyes narrowed on her like a hawk.

'I'm recently widowed, sir.' She worked with jerky movements, uncomfortable by his presence, his closeness.

'Indeed? You must find that lonely?' He took another step nearer, his breath smelling of tobacco fanned her face.

'No, sir. I have friends to keep me company.' She shied away as his hand came up to her face.

'You know, I'm always in need of a... female friend when I'm in the city,' he whispered. 'I would pay you well to be that *friend*.'

Her breath caught in her throat, and she turned her head away. 'I don't think I'm suited to that role, sir.' Every part of her recoiled from his presence, and his revolting offer.

'Have a think about it. To be a man's mistress can give you a certain amount of freedom. You'd not have to work for one thing.' He took her hand and kissed it.

She yanked her hand from his, repulsed.

'I can rent some rooms, nice ones that are solely yours with an allowance to buy pretty things. How can you refuse such an offer?'

'Quite easily, sir.'

'Think it over. I can be generous and attentive when I wish to be. It's better than working as a maid for a pittance.' He straightened as his mother called from the other room. 'I'm pleased you've come to work for my mother. You brighten the place up. I shall look forward to making more visits here now.'

Caroline let out a breath when he left. She couldn't believe his boldness. A mistress? *His mistress?* She'd rather die. How did Trixie cope with such men? How could Trixie bear for them to touch her, to treat her with such dishonour?

She concentrated on cooking the steaks with boiled potatoes, but for the rest of the day she was on edge, waiting for him to reappear in the kitchen and touch her. Why did some men feel it was their right to do as they pleased? She didn't ask for his attention, nor did she want it. Yet, he was blind to everything but his own wishes and needs. Like Victor Dolan he would take whatever he wanted without thought to the person he damaged.

Caroline kept to the kitchen, cooking and cleaning. Mrs Warburton napped after her steak and her son went for a drink at The Punch Bowl pub around the corner. But he returned in less than an hour and stood at the kitchen door watching Caroline as she worked, which made her nervous. She purposely made a lot of noise to wake up Mrs Warburton and was thankful when the old woman did. He and his mother talked of relatives and local gossip and Caroline kept out of their way.

Later, she made them a supper of pork pie and pickles followed by stewed apples with cream. Caroline ate the apples and cream, sat alone at the kitchen table, one eye on the door the entire time. Gordon stayed until it was late evening, even falling asleep in front of the fire for a while. Caroline longed to be finished for the day and at home with Trixie and the girls.

When it was time for her to prepare Mrs Warburton for bed, Caroline worked fast, knowing he had to leave as soon as his mother retired for the night.

'I'll see you again next week, Caroline, when I come to collect Mother,' Mr Warburton said as she went from the kitchen to the bedroom to check on the small fire in there.

'Very good, sir.' Caroline kept her eyes downcast, relieved he was finally leaving.

She lingered for as long as she could in the bedroom fiddling with the fire, adding pieces of coal and turning the blankets down and placing Mrs Warburton's nightgown over the fire rail to warm. She could hear Mrs Warburton and her son still talking.

With nothing else left to do, she crept out of the bedroom hoping to get back to the kitchen without being noticed for Mr Warburton still hadn't left. Why didn't he just go!

'Well, I'd best be off.' Mr Warburton moved the curtains aside. 'The snow has stopped. Thankfully, I'm staying at The Punch Bowl pub just around the corner. I'll take me only a minute to walk there.'

'Go steady on your journey home tomorrow,' his mother said. 'The roads will be treacherous. Girl, clear this table.'

Caroline collected a tray from the kitchen and went back into the sitting room to place the used cups and saucers, bowls and cutlery on the tray, aware of him watching her every move.

'My coat, Caroline,' he said to her.

She left the tray and took his coat and hat from the stand near the door.

Mr Warburton's fingers touched hers as he took them from her and he grinned before turning back to his mother. 'I need to leave early in the morning. It'll take me all day in this weather to reach home.'

'Let us hope we have no more snow for the next week, or you'll not make it back to collect me for Christmas.' Mrs Warburton pouted. 'I'm looking forward to spending a few days with you and meeting your new fiancée.'

Caroline glared at him. He was getting married and still behaved as he did towards her? The cad. She sent up a quick prayer that they'd have blizzards for a week, and he'd not manage the roads into the city.

'I'll make it back, Mother, don't you worry about that. Nothing will prevent me.' He glanced at Caroline. 'Goodnight, Mother.' Mr Warburton kissed his mother's cheek. 'Goodnight, Caroline.' He smiled at her.

'Goodnight, Mr Warburton,' she replied woodenly from where she stood by the fireplace ready to bank it down for the night.

'You are very welcome to accompany Mother and spend Christmas at my home, Caroline,' Gordon Warburton said from the doorway. 'Do you not need her to see to you, Mother?'

The blood drained from Caroline's face. That's the last thing she wanted.

'No. I'll be fine with the girl you have who looks after your rooms.' Mrs Warburton raised a wry eyebrow as she looked between the two. 'I promised Caroline she could have a few days off. See you next week, son.'

When the door closed behind him, Caroline finally relaxed her tight shoulders.

'You seem quiet,' Mrs Warburton said, heaving herself up from the sofa with the use of her cane. Standing, she stared directly into Caroline's eyes. 'Anything the matter?'

'No, Mrs Warburton,' Caroline lied, placing the fireguard on the hearth.

'Did you want to accompany me to my son's home for Christmas?'

Caroline paled. 'No, madam, if that's all right with you? I'd like to spend it with Trixie and the girls.'

'And I said you could.' Mrs Warburton eyed Caroline for a moment and then shuffled towards the bedroom.

'Do you wish for hot chocolate this evening?' Caroline asked.

'No, not tonight. The pork pie and that delicious apple and cream dessert for supper was enough. Gordon enjoyed it, too. Who'd have thought he'd stay so late? It is unlike him. Usually when he is in town, I see him for an hour and then he is gone.'

Caroline didn't answer and focused on getting the old women undressed, washed and then in her nightgown. 'I've put two stone hot water bottles in the bed at your feet.'

'That is good.' Mrs Warburton declared climbing into bed with a satisfying sigh, and it was the closest Caroline would get to a thank you.

'I'll see you in the morning, Mrs Warburton.'

'Don't be late.' Was the reply.

As quickly as she could, Caroline cleaned the kitchen and made everything tidy. She donned her coat and bonnet, eager to be off. Holding the basket of leftover food, she then went down the staircase and out into the biting cold. She locked the street door, edgy at being out so late. Normally, Mrs Warburton went to bed early, allowing Caroline to head off home by seven o'clock, but tonight it was gone nine and the icy streets were eerily deserted.

The snow had stopped falling, but it had been heavy enough all day to cause it to pile in drifts against the buildings. The night sky shone with stars and the frigid air caught at her throat. Taking care with every crunching footstep, Caroline headed home along the empty streets. Ice coated the buildings' eaves and windows, shimmering in the streetlights. Golden glows spilled from pub windows, several such places on every street, the noise muffled from within them as she passed.

A lone horn sounded on the river and a dog barked in return. Caroline turned a corner and walked behind a woman carrying a heavy basket. Being with another woman felt safer than walking on her own. The darkened city streets at night frightened Caroline and trudging through the snow slowed her down. She couldn't wait for the lighter days of summer to arrive.

Rounding another corner, she bumped into a man who stood talking to another man. 'Forgive me,' she said immediately.

The man held her arm and peered into her face. A wave of beer fumes wafted over her.

Caroline blinked at the man's ragged red scars etched into his cheeks. Scars she'd made with her nails. *Victor Dolan.* She froze.

He squinted in the dim light. 'Do I know you?' he slurred.

She pulled her shawl up higher, covering the lower part of her face. 'No.' She held the basket between them like a shield, before darting around him. Her heart in her throat, with legs that trembled, she clung to her basket and hurried away as fast as she could on the icy cobbles. She slipped twice, a moan escaping, but kept going. Fear prevented her from glancing over her shoulder. She expected Victor's hand on her at any moment.

She sobbed with relief as she entered the top of Middle Water Lane where the snow wasn't so thick and had been trampled into mucky slush.

'Evening, Caroline,' Jacob Adams stopped and gave her a smile, but it fell away as he saw her stricken state. 'Nay, lass, what's wrong?'

Shaking, she shook her head, unable to speak. Her teeth clattered in her head, and she felt sick.

'Here, let me see you home.'

She sagged against him, and he cradled her against his side and took her to Trixie.

Trixie was listening to Elsie sound out words from a newspaper when they walked in. One look at Caroline and then at Jacob and she sprung up and took Caroline from him. 'Thanks, Jacob.'

'Do you need owt?' he asked Trixie.

'No, I'll see to her.'

'Just shout if you do.'

'You're a good man. Thanks again.' Trixie closed the door and led Caroline to the bed. 'What happened?'

'Victor...' she whispered.

Trixie blanched. 'What did he do?'

'He grabbed my arm, asked if he knew me...' She bit her bottom lip to stop from crying.

'And did he recognise you?'

'I'm not sure. He was drunk, I think.'

'Thank Christ for that,' Trixie whispered. 'Girls, hurry up and get washed now or the water will be cold.' She turned back to Caroline. 'We'll talk later.'

'Do you have some food, Caroline?' Elsie said, washing her face in the bowl.

She nodded and passed the basket to Trixie. For once the room was warm. Trixie kept a good fire going now they had two wages. She said coal was cheaper than a doctor if the girls got sick.

While Trixie and the girls ate the leftover stew that Mrs Warburton rejected, Caroline laid on the bed and stared into the flames. After Victor Dolan's assault, she had kept an eye on the people she passed in the streets, looking for his face in the crowds. However, as the weeks went by and she didn't see him, she'd begun to let down her guard. How foolish she was to not watch out for him, especially at night.

'Are you sick?' Elsie asked, coming over to Caroline.

'No, darling. Just tired.' And she was. She was so very tired of being frightened of Victor, of how weak Gordon had made her feel, of not being in control of anything. On the farm, she and Hugh had worked as a team. He hadn't been a demanding man, but loving and sweet. She'd run the farmhouse as she saw fit and answered to no one. But here in the city, she'd been told what to do by so many people. She was at the bottom of the class system, less than nothing and people treated her differently because of it, which was difficult to adjust to.

When the girls were asleep, Trixie made Caroline a cup of tea and they sat before the fire in silent companionship for a few minutes.

'Each night, on your way home, go a different way,' Trixie said quietly. 'Where was Victor when he saw you?'

'Outside of the Grey Hound Inn on Spurriergate.'

'Always go through Parliament Street, it's busier than any other street. I'll start to meet you there every evening.'

'But I finish at different times,' Caroline said. 'It depends on when Mrs Warburton lets me go. You can't wait around in the snow.'

'I can and I will. Each evening I'll head to Parliament Street, and we'll walk home together, except for Fridays when you go and meet Mussy.'

Caroline nodded, knowing she needed Trixie with her. The dark streets scared her witless, every shadow could be hiding Victor. 'His face, Trixie. I've scarred him for life.' Again, she pictured his appalling red scarred face.

'That's his fault, not yours. If he'd left you alone, he wouldn't be wearing repulsive scars, would he?' Trixie took Caroline's hand. 'You've done so well to get over what he did to you. Don't let this set you back. You won't be alone at night anymore.'

'I don't know how much longer I can stay in this city.' This place wasn't home, and it never would be.

'We don't have the money to leave, not yet,' Trixie reasoned, looking anxious. 'Victor can't be everywhere all the time. We just have to be more careful.'

Caroline stared at her. 'He's seen me, Trixie. If he hadn't been drunk, he'd have recognised me! He could have dragged me off the street and I'd be his prisoner again.'

Trixie poked the fire, her back to her. 'You don't know that.'

'I don't want to find out either!'

'Listen, we just have to wait. If we can make it another six months or so, saving our money and then we can go.'

'Months of wondering where Victor is? That sounds like fun,' Caroline scoffed, hating the feeling of being defenceless.

'I doubt he even remembers you,' Trixie soothed, again not meeting Caroline's gaze. 'It's a shame you couldn't live-in at Mrs Warburton's. Then you'd be on the other side of town, away from where Victor tends to be.'

'Then I wouldn't be with you and the girls.' Caroline frowned. Something wasn't right. 'Do you know something?'

'No.'

'You're lying.'

'I only want you to be safe.'

'How would living in Little Stonegate help? You said yourself, Victor has eyes everywhere, the police in his pocket. He's got dreadful scars on his face which would remind him daily of what I did to him. He'll want his revenge. So, how safe am I really?' Her voice had risen in her panic.

'Calm down,' Trixie shushed her, glancing at the sleeping girls.

'Calm down? You weren't beaten and held against your will! You don't have this hanging over your head.'

'What do you think I do each night? Hey? Do you think I enjoy what strange men do to me several times a night with their rough and filthy hands? I risk my life every night, not knowing if one stranger might be the one to really hurt me.'

'Then stop doing it!'

'Oh, yes, it's that easy and simple, isn't it? What work is out there for someone like me, hey?' Trixie glared at her, her eyes huge and dark with emotion. 'Speaking of which, I'd better get back out there and earn, shouldn't I? After all, I'm just a piece of flesh for them to manhandle. *Unlike you, I don't have feelings, do I?*' She grabbed her shawl and flounced out of the room, slamming the door behind her.

Chapter Eleven

Despite, Caroline's prayers for blizzards, the snow didn't come back during the week. It rained on and off for days, turning the snow into dirty sludge. The streets were frozen overnight, causing many people to slip over on the icy cobbles as they went about their shopping or to work. Tempers frayed and the sound of coughing and sneezing became as familiar as the clip clop of horses' hooves.

Two days before Christmas, Caroline packed Mrs Warburton's trunk being careful not to crease her clothes. Mrs Warburton sat on the chair at the dressing table, reading from a list all that she would need. Caroline went back and forth from the trunk to the wardrobe and drawers without becoming annoyed every time the old woman changed her mind about some item she'd already packed. After today, she would have three days of doing nothing but being with Trixie and the girls.

'My jewel box needs to be placed in the small leather case I'm taking in the carriage.' Mrs Warburton waved her cane at the smaller portmanteau at the end of the bed. 'I don't want it out of my sight. I don't have many jewels, but I treasure those that my husband bought me over the years.'

Caroline nodded and took the small velvet box and placed it in the case. She had learned that Mrs Warburton's husband once owned two malthouses in York that supplied breweries, hence why both her sons had public houses, though Gordon's was more of a staging inn in the country unlike Bob's pub in the centre of the city. Mrs Warburton didn't divulge much to Caroline, but she'd told her enough for Caroline to know that the old woman had been married a long time, lost a son two years ago, and her husband had meant everything to her. That last piece of information was the only thing she and her employer had in common, the love of a late husband.

'Is that everything?' Caroline closed the lid to the small trunk.

Mrs Warburton nodded. 'Gordon will be arriving shortly. Thank the Lord the snow stayed away, and the roads should be clear.'

Silently, Caroline hoped his carriage was bogged in the mud and he'd given up coming.

'Find my fur muff, the black one.' The cane waved again in the direction of the huge wardrobe. 'And the matching gloves. I'll not freeze to death on the journey just because you can't find what I need.'

It took most of the morning to satisfy Mrs Warburton that all she required for the three days away was packed and placed by the door. There was enough luggage for a grand duchess, but Caroline kept quiet and followed instructions.

When the door opened, bringing in a blast of cold air, Caroline spun and faced Gordon Warburton as he came in. She shivered not just from the cold but the way his gaze travelled her body before resting on her face. Desire narrowed his eyes.

'We meet again, dear Caroline.' He stepped around the luggage to her side.

'Good morning, Mr Warburton.' She fled to the bedroom. 'Your son has arrived, madam.'

'Ah, about time.' Mrs Warburton clasped her cane and hobbled out into the sitting room to receive her son's kiss on the cheek.

'I have the carriage waiting in Stonegate, Mother, for it won't fit in this narrow street. I've two stableboys with me to carry your luggage.' He looked at the pile. 'Is this all of it?'

'It is.' Mrs Warburton glanced around the room, making sure. 'See that it is securely tied, Gordon.'

While her son summoned the boys waiting at the bottom of the staircase and oversaw the removal of the trunks, Mrs Warburton went to the sideboard and opened a drawer. She took out a small money purse and opened it. 'Come here, girl.'

Caroline left the luggage. 'Yes, madam?'

'For you.' Mrs Warburton gave the small leather purse to Caroline. 'There's ten Florins in there. Give the girls a nice Christmas.'

Stunned, Caroline stared at the old woman. Every time Caroline mentioned Trixie or the girls, Mrs Warburton would snap a sharp retort that she wasn't here for idle chat, or she would change the subject, or brutally say she didn't care if Elsie was picking up reading or Bertha could count to twenty.

'Don't stand there gawping, girl! I want the fires banked down and the guards up and that kitchen best be spotless before you leave today. And I want you back here early on the twenty-seventh and have this place warm and welcoming for my return.'

'Yes, Mrs Warburton.' Caroline's heart sang. The money she held would make such a difference to her little bank of savings hidden under the bed.

'Now help me with my coat. Oh, and take any food home that will likely turn before I am home again. I don't want to come through the door and the place smells worse than a tannery, or a plague of rats running through my things.'

'Yes, Mrs Warburton.' Caroline fussed around the old woman, making sure she was well wrapped up against the cold.

Gordon Warburton came up the stairs and frowned at seeing his mother with her coat and hat on. 'Are we not to have a cup of tea, Mother?' His gaze slid to Caroline.

'No, son. Let us get on our way. Another cup of tea will inconvenience me on the journey. I shan't be going behind a tree on the side of the road, thank you very much.'

His face fell and a stubborn expression set the angle of his jaw. 'I've been on the road for an hour, Mother.'

'Well, another hour won't make much difference, will it? Let's go.' Mrs Warburton held out her arm for him to take.

He hesitated a fraction of a second before taking it, but his eyes were on Caroline. 'Enjoy your time off, Caroline. I will see you when we return.' His tone sounded like a threat.

She hated him and her cold stare relayed that message.

'Lock up, girl!' the old woman shouted behind her as they went down the staircase.

Within a short time, Caroline had tidied the flat and secured the guards around the fires. The range fire she scraped out clean and tipped the bucket of warm ashes in the yard. Mrs McCarthy came out of her back door at the same time.

'Good day to you, Caroline.' The milliner smiled, her glasses on the tip of her nose. She wore all black except for a ruffle of white lace going down the front of her bodice.

'And to you, Mrs McCarthy.' Caroline often saw the neighbour a few times each week and would wave or say good morning or afternoon.

'I saw Mrs Warburton go past my front window just now with her son, Gordon. She does enjoy spending Christmas with him. I'm surprised she didn't take you with her?'

Caroline stood at the bottom of the steps leading up to the flat. 'She gave me a few days off to spend with friends.'

'I'm floored she would be so generous,' the other woman snorted. 'Agatha Warburton isn't known for her generosity.'

'She's been a good employer to me,' Caroline replied honestly. In truth, as much as the old woman was tetchy and severe at times, she didn't treat Caroline badly and happily gave her food to take home to the girls. There were worst jobs and people she could work for. She also enjoyed not having to work with other maids like at Greenleigh House.

'I've known Mrs Warburton for fifteen years and she's been through about that many maids in that time. You must be doing something right for her. When I called in yesterday to see her while you were out shopping, she said she was satisfied by you. That's a rare compliment indeed.'

'That's very pleasing to hear.' Feeling the cold seep through her clothes and eager to be on her way home, Caroline climbed a few steps. 'I'd best go and lock up the flat. Have a lovely Christmas, Mrs McCarthy.'

'It'll be a quiet one for me. With no family to speak of but a cousin in Bootham, I'll enjoy a few days of peace from the shop being closed.'

Caroline hurried up to check the flat was all as it should be and happily locked the door on it. In her basket she had some bacon slices, a hunk of ham and a few eggs.

Strolling the streets, she spent some time peering through shop windows, the money purse in her coat pocket. In Swinegate, she stopped at a cobbler's shop and asked if he'd resole her boots. She was tired of putting layers of newspaper inside her boot each day to stop the water getting in, which it soon did.

While she waited, she bought new laces for Trixie's boots, having noticed her laces were broken and tied together with knots. She also bought second-hand repaired boots for Elsie and Bertha in sizes that would fit them and asked the cobbler to put them in a sack so the girls couldn't see the surprise.

Leaving the cobblers, she headed for the Shambles and Bent's Butchers.

'Ah, I wondered if I'd see you, lass.' Mr Bent grinned from the other side of the counter. 'What's the old lady want today?'

'Nothing, Mr Bent. She's gone to her son Gordon's inn for Christmas.'

'Ah yes, you did tell me.'

'I'm after something for me this time, and Trixie and the girls.'

'Indeed, you are!' He clapped. 'What a fine treat. I've just the thing.' He disappeared for a moment into the back of the shop and returned with a paper parcel. 'For you.'

'What is it? I can't spend too much.'

'It's on me, and for what's inside? Well, that's for me to know and you to find out.' He tapped the side of his nose and winked.

Caroline's chest swelled at his kindness. 'You are too good, Mr Bent.'

'You brought the old woman's business my way, I see this as a thank you.'

She wished him well and headed off to the market where she stopped at the leather stall and spoke to Walt Miller for a bit to see how he was coping with his back. He gave her a leather toggle with a fringe to tie to her house key and while they chatted, he carved a C into the toggle for her. Caroline also asked him to make one for Mussy with a carved M.

Further along the market, she bought Trixie a shawl in midnight blue from the second-hand stall, but the shawl looked in such good condition she couldn't believe it was second-hand. From the same stall, she also bought Elsie a dress in brown serge, a pinafore with only the smallest stain on it at the bottom. For Bertha she bought a pinafore, a dress in grey and she bought them both a pair of stockings each. At the next stall, she bought a handkerchief for Trixie that had a yellow daisy embroidered on it in the corner.

She wandered past the shops, standing with children to peer into the window displays, seeing lit candles, springs of holly, big bows wrapped around gifts enticing the shopper to step inside and spend their money. Being brought up in a convent, Caroline only celebrated Christmas in religious sermons with the nuns, and her uncle and aunt did the same, attending church and visiting the poor in the village. No presents were ever exchanged. Yet, here in the city, with the influence of Queen Victoria and Prince Albert, shops were embracing the joy of not only the religious element, but family togetherness. Newspaper drawings of the Queen and her family gathered around a candle-lit tree were hung in the shop windows, inspiring other families to celebrate in the same way.

Buying presents gave Caroline such joy and it hadn't been something she'd done since last Christmas with Hugh. Her thoughts drifted to that special time when Hugh had decorated the small parlour with boughs of holly. To make the cottage cheerier, she'd lit more candles than usual and had the fire roaring with the smell of plum pudding in the air and the goose roasting.

This Christmas would be so different. No Hugh. No comfy cottage. Instead, she'd be huddled around the smoking fire in the squalid damp room, and she'd try to cook whatever was in the parcel Mr Bent gave her in the one pot they had. Hugh's kisses wouldn't wake her on Christmas morning, nor would he cover her legs with a thick blanket as they drove in the cart to church.

The thrill she felt only moments ago when buying gifts for Trixie and the girls dissipated like water on hot coals. She left the market, worried she'd spent too much money when they were saving to leave. A part of her was horrified she'd spent money on boots and clothes, but another part of her argued that what did it matter? Trixie said they would need to stay another six months in the Water Lanes to save enough to move away. Another six months. Anything could happen in that time and even after that would they have saved enough money to leave? Caroline didn't think she could spend much longer living in the slums.

The basket and sack grew heavy as she walked. Head down, she trudged along the wet cobbles, stepping over horse manure, dodging people busy on their own errands. The smell of the river grew stronger as she neared the Water Lanes, as did the noise.

A large gathering stood at the end of the First Water Lane, all looking down the lane, their voices rising in anger. Thin, dirty-faced children ran about yelling, throwing missiles down the lane while men, young and old, talked and jeered, fists raised, an angry mob dressed in rough clothes.

Worried, Caroline edged around the group, then spotted Jacob Adams. 'What's happening?'

He shook his head sadly. 'The city authorities have made good their threat to start clearing the Water Lanes. They've started down by the river on this first lane and are knocking the buildings down behind The King's Arms pub.'

'Oh no!' Caroline stared around at the families displaced. Small children sat on top of carts piled high with belongings not worth a penny, but which were invaluable to those who had nothing. Distraught women, shawls over the heads, cried pitilessly at their homes being destroyed. Homes that although were slums, they were still the only place they belonged to and put a roof over their families' heads.

'It's not going well.' Jacob rubbed a weary hand over his face. 'There's been fights all day. A few arrests. The tenants against the builders. There's police down by the river protecting the men hired to bring it all down. People are angry.'

'I had read in the newspaper a couple of weeks ago that the city would be clearing this area. But I thought it would take years to happen.'

'The thing is, there's nowhere for these people to go, except to other overcrowded parts of the city, Bedern and Walmgate.' Jacob shrugged his shoulders, dejected. 'Do you think those people living there will want all of us moving in with them? There's not enough for them already living there without all of us from the Lanes going there, as well.'

'Us?' Caroline gasped.

'We'll be next, you know. Once this lane is brought down, they'll move onto ours. They say all three Water Lanes will be brought down, eventually.' His tense expression matched his tone. 'By next winter we could be out on our arses with nowhere to go.'

The idea of being thrown out of their room, as awful as the room was, terrified Caroline. What if they'd not save enough money by the time the men began tearing down their building?

Deep in thought she pushed her way through the growing crowd as rumours spread of the evictions. Once in Middle Lane, she saw Elsie and Bertha playing with some other children, their little faces red with cold, their hands freezing.

They saw her and ran up, their mouths gaping at the basket and sack.

'What have you got?' Elsie asked.

'Some food.'

'All that is food?' Elsie tilted her head, not believing her.

'What I have is my own business and you should mind yours, missy. Now go and play.' Caroline went up the staircase, wary to not tread on the second step which was rotten and to not hold the banister which wobbled dangerously.

'Heavens, what have you got there?' Trixie asked, tipping water from the bucket into the kettle.

'Food and presents.'

'Presents?' Trixie scowled. 'What do you mean presents?'

'I bought a few things for you and the girls.' She placed it all on the bed.

'Why did you do that?'

'Because it's Christmas Eve tomorrow, the day to gift family presents.'

'We can't afford to be buying presents,' Trixie snapped. 'Have you seen what's going on out there.' She flung her hand towards the window. 'They've started the clearance.'

'I know. I was just talking to Jacob Adams about it. There's a large angry crowd gathered.'

'Yes, they're angry because it's mid-winter and they've been booted out of their homes.' Trixie looked shaken.

'I understand that. Jacob said they'll probably start on this lane after the first one flattened. But I'm hoping by then, we'll be out of here, anyway.' Caroline pushed the sack under the bed so the girls wouldn't see what was in it.

'We won't be if you spend good money on stuff we don't need!'

'Will you give it a rest?' Caroline yelled, tired of Trixie always finding fault. 'Mrs Warburton gave me money as a gift to get something for the girls. That's what I did. I've bought things they are in desperate need of.'

'They can make do,' Trixie glared at her.

'Make do?' Caroline mocked. 'Bertha has no stockings. Elsie's boots are so tight her toes curl. Their dresses are so worn and ragged they'll soon be naked!'

'Are you saying I don't look after my sisters?' Trixie roared.

'You know I'm not saying that. You love those girls, but they need more than love, Trixie.'

'Food and shelter is all we need. It was your idea for us to leave here. I've been saving every farthing I can to put towards us starting again somewhere else, otherwise *I* could have found them some old dresses or boots.'

Caroline took a deep breath to calm down. 'Does it matter who buys them a dress or boots? We are in this together, aren't we?'

Trixie poked at the coals in the grate. 'We'll never have enough money to leave here, you know that don't you? It's all a dream to think we can find somewhere better. We'll be thrown out of here and have to find some filthy stinking cellar in Bedern to live.'

'No.' Caroline was adamant. 'That is not what we are going to do.'

'What's your answer then, huh?' Trixie mocked. 'We'll all go into the country and find some lovely cottage and feed hens and pigs for the rest of our lives?'

'We'll find something, yes.'

'How?' Trixie flung her hands in the air. 'Without a man to work the land, how are we to rent a farm? You're a fool to think we can, Caroline. You're living in the past, wanting the old life you had. It's not going to happen. We are stuck in this pit until we're thrown out. No amount of money saved will get us a home. It's all in your head.' Trixie grabbed her shawl and stormed out of the room.

Collapsing onto the bed, Caroline hung her head in despair. Trixie's moods were becoming harder to deal with. One moment she was laughing, tickling the girls, joking with Caroline, then the next she would be hostile or gloomy. Most of the time, Caroline ignored the bad moods and waited for Trixie to smile and chat again, but the threat of being evicted now hung over them. It was another worry they didn't need.

Sighing, she rose and poured water into the basin and then placed another bowl on the water to keep the bowl cold. Unwrapping the paper parcel Mr Bent gave her, she smiled in surprise at the amount he'd put in, no wonder it weighed so much. In her hands she held slices of tripe, several kidneys, three pork chops and four pig's trotters. She placed the meat in the bowl sitting in the water and then soaked a cloth and placed it over the meat, again to keep it cold.

From the storage tins, filled with all food she'd brought home from Mrs Warburton's kitchen over the week, she grabbed carrots and onions and chopped them up to put in the pot, along with the pigs' trotters. She'd make a stew for the girls' meal this evening. Tomorrow, Christmas Eve, they'd have Mrs Warburton's bacon for breakfast, and at midday, the chops. They could open her presents and if Trixie was in a good mood, perhaps have a singalong or she'd read to them from the bible Reverend Houghton had given the girls last week at Sunday School. On Christmas Day, after church, they could have the tripe and kidneys, if the meat was still good and not turned bad.

Despite Trixie's flare up, Caroline wanted to give the girls a better Christmas than last year when their mam had died. Then it hit her. Trixie was upset because it was the first anniversary of her mam dying.

Feeling terrible for arguing, Caroline spent her energy making a tasty stew and thanking Mrs Warburton for her leftovers which could flavour it. She lit two candles and added more coal to the fire. She pulled out the sack from under the bed and emptying the contents she made neatly folded piles and then carefully put them back in the sack and shoved it under the bed again.

The blackened kettle was filled, ready to have a cup of tea, and again with Mrs Warburton's generosity, over the weeks, Caroline had been able to replace the two broken cups with four teacups in a blue and white pattern that Mrs Warburton had buried at the back of a cupboard, ones she didn't use for the old woman preferred her green and gold dinner set.

The girls came in as night fell, their little bodies pink with cold. Caroline heated water for them to wash away the grime of the lane and, with their nightgowns on, they huddled in bed to get warm.

'It smells nice,' Elsie said, looking over at the stew simmering in the pot.

'It'll warm you on the *inside*, too,' Caroline joked.

The door opened and Trixie walked in, her expression sombre. Her gaze went from Caroline to the girls and back again. 'I didn't mean to shout.'

'I didn't either.' Caroline smiled. 'I've made a stew. Come and sit by the fire and get warm.'

'I will in a minute.' Trixie went to the girls and kissed each one on the top of the head before sitting down next to them. 'Do you remember what today is?'

Elsie frowned. 'The day before Christmas Eve.'

Bertha stuck her fingers in her mouth and shook her head.

Tears gathered in Trixie's eyes. 'On this day last year, our mam died.'

'Is that why you're sad?' Bertha whispered.

Elsie sat straighter. 'You were crying today, and you never cry.'

'Yes, I'm upset because I miss our mam.' Trixie looked at Caroline. 'I should have mentioned it was today, the anniversary of her dying...'

'I guessed only a short time ago.'

Trixie wiped away a tear and embraced the girls to her. 'We must never forget our mam, understand? She wanted the best for us, and we have to work hard to make sure we honour her.'

'We will,' Elsie murmured in a little voice.

Bertha seemed stricken all of a sudden. 'I don't remember her.'

Caroline's heart twisted in sadness at the three of them.

'Well,' said Trixie, wiping her eyes. 'We can't have you forgetting our mam, can we?' She smiled at Bertha. 'How about I tell you some stories about her and Father?'

The girls nodded and snuggled into the blankets and while Trixie told them tales of their parents, Caroline stirred the stew, adding lumps of ham into it for more flavour. She thought of her own parents long dead, of her uncle and his wife, and of her darling Hugh. She had lost them all.

'Mam would have liked Caroline,' Elsie unexpectedly said, making Caroline look up from her cooking.

Trixie smiled at Elsie. 'Yes, she would have, and you know why, because Caro helps me to look after you two and she loves you both just as much as I do. Don't you, Caro?'

Caroline grinned and rushed up onto the bed to hug all three of them in a rush of emotion. 'You're my family.'

Later, with bellies full of stew, the girls fell asleep, one at each end of the bed. Trixie and Caroline sat on the rug in front of the fire, drinking tea, watching the flames dance in the fire, the coals glowing red.

'I'm sorry about before,' Trixie said with a sigh. 'I'm the very devil at times.'

'No, you're not. You've had a hard life living in the awful place, you're allowed to be out of sorts at times.'

'I take it out on you, and I shouldn't. You've only ever been kind and caring towards me, but I treat you sometimes as though you're my enemy.'

'You've had all the strain of raising the girls, of surviving without help. It's bound to make you want to lash out sometimes and I'm the one who's here.'

'It's no excuse to take it out on you though when all you're doing is trying to help me and my sisters.'

'As I said earlier, you're my family now, if you'll let me. I've no one else.'

'Me and the girls think of you as part of our family, too. Our lives would be bleak without you in it.'

A wave of love enveloped Caroline. She had a family again. 'We must stick together, Trixie, the four of us. We've only got each other, and we will survive.'

'And get away from these streets...' Trixie murmured staring into the flames.

Chapter Twelve

Caroline and Trixie made a pact to make Christmas Eve special for the girls. Trixie said last year, losing their mam, had been hell and she'd spent days not leaving the room. Caroline didn't want to think of last Christmas when she'd been happy and in love with her husband, it brought tears to her eyes thinking of him.

To banish the sadness, Trixie made an effort to smile and be cheerful. She folded newspaper and then cut out a string of joined bells to hang above the fireplace. The girls tidied the room while Caroline made a breakfast of bacon and toast. Neighbours in the building knocked on the door throughout the morning, one asking to borrow some tea, others to gossip about the First Water Lane clearance and a few remembered Trixie's mam and came to give their condolences.

After Trixie finished chatting to their neighbour, Sarah Adams, Jacob's sister, who had come to help Trixie as her mam lay taking her last breaths, she leant against the closed door and gave the girls a smile. 'Shall we open our presents?'

THE WINTER WIDOW

'Presents?' Elsie gaped. 'We have presents?' she said in awe, eyes wide in her little face.

'A present?' Bertha frowned as though not sure what presents meant.

Caroline hugged her, her heart constricting. These poor little girls had gone so long without any joy in their lives. 'I promise to buy you both a present for every birthday and at Christmas for as long as I live.'

'That's a tall promise,' Trixie warned her.

'A present can be anything,' Caroline reminded her. 'A flower picked from a hedgerow or an apple from the market. It doesn't have to be all about spending lots of money.'

'That's good, because we don't have lots of money,' Trixie jested.

They huddled around the fire as Caroline brought out the sack. She made a performance giving out the presents.

Elsie squealed with delight over her new dress, pinafore and boots. 'My feet won't hurt anymore.' She hugged the boots to her chest and then happily tried them on.

Bertha was just as happy to receive hers. 'Can I wear my dress now?'

Trixie helped her sisters change into their dresses which made them appear a little older now they wore clothes that fitted them properly and with their shiny boots, they looked respectable.

'And this is yours,' Caroline told Trixie, passing the shawl over and the handkerchief.

'That's lovely.' Trixie took off her green tattered shawl and wrapped the midnight blue one around her shoulders. 'It's thick and look, no holes.' Trixie lifted the handkerchief and stroked the embroidered flower. 'A yellow daisy. It's so pretty, the prettiest thing I've ever owned. Thank you, Caro.'

Caroline beamed, feeling pleasure at bringing the three of them happiness. The girls twirled about, holding hands and jumping in excitement.

'Now my presents.' Trixie brought out from under the bed a few brown paper-wrapped parcels and gave them out. Elsie's gift was two yellow ribbons. Bertha received two blue ribbons and Caroline a new pair of stockings.

'Just what I need,' Caroline held up the stockings. They were new not second-hand, and she knew Trixie had spent money she'd rather have put in the savings tin.

'Now, can we promise to not spend any more money on things and put everything we have spare into the tin?' Trixie muttered to Caroline. 'We need to get away from here as soon as we can.'

Caroline stared at her in confusion. 'You said it would take us another six months or more to save.'

'We don't have that much time,' Trixie whispered back before going to tie the ribbons in the girls' dark hair.

Frowning, Caroline pulled on her new stockings. What did Trixie mean they didn't have time? Was it the concern of the lanes being cleared? All the rumours going about their lane was that it would take a while before the builders reached them. Did Trixie know something different?

Caroline had added the remaining money from Mrs Warburton to the tin last night and counted their savings. She'd been surprised to find they had fourteen shillings and eight pence in the tin. Trixie had been adding more money to their savings than Caroline realised.

'I was thinking...' Trixie said, tying a ribbon on Bertha's curly hair. 'I might come to church with you this evening.'

Smiling, Caroline watched Elsie and Bertha embrace Trixie.

'Yes, please come with us!' Elsie did a little hop.

Trixie looked over their heads at Caroline, her smile tentative and the light in her large hazel eyes unreadable.

A shiver ran down Caroline's back and she didn't know why. They'd spent a lovely day together, but Trixie, despite her best efforts, had turned edgy and it worried Caroline.

They walked up the lane to the church, joining other families. The sun was low on the horizon sending long shadows across the cobbles. Ice was forming as the temperature dropped. Inside the church, they found a pew and settled down, nodding to those they knew.

Caroline kept glancing at Trixie throughout the service, but she didn't make eye contact until she saw Caroline place a penny on the donation plate as it was passed around. A look of annoyance crossed Trixie's features, but it went as soon as it came.

They filed out at the end of the last hymn and Reverend Houghton shook all their hands at the door.

Elsie skipped with happiness. 'Can I read the bible when we get inside?'

'I can't read,' Bertha moaned.

'Soon you'll be reading just as well as Elsie,' Trixie said. 'Caro will help you.'

At the top of the lane, Trixie stopped. 'I'm going to work.'

'Work?' Caroline asked in surprise. 'I thought we agreed you'd stay home tonight? It's Christmas Eve.'

'And it the best night for me to earn good money.' Trixie dropped Bertha's hand and wrapped her shawl around her more closely. 'It'll be busy. I can do well.'

'But—'

'No, buts, Caro. I need to earn as much as I can.' Trixie bent and kissed the girls.

'Why the sudden urgency?' Caroline whispered. 'A couple of weeks ago you said it would take many months to save. What's changed?'

'*Everything!*' Trixie snapped and then shook her head and sucked in a deep breath. 'Sorry.' She gave a ghost of a smile and walked away.

Caroline watched Trixie disappear around the corner and shivered with cold. 'Let's get inside. It's freezing.'

As dawn broke, weak grey light crept into the room banishing the darkness. Caroline stirred, the cold and something else had woken her. She opened her eyes and stared at the back of Bertha's head on the pillow. Lifting her head, rubbing the sleep from her eyes, Caroline peered down the bed, but only Elsie slept there.

Alarmed, she sat up, disturbing Bertha who rolled over. Carefully, Caroline climbed out of bed, pulled on her coat and boots and went out onto the landing. There was no sign of Trixie downstairs, or out in the lane fetching water. For once the lane was deserted. Not many people were going to work today or chatting to neighbours at this early hour on Christmas morning.

Shivering in the chill, she gave one more glance up and down the lane before turning and going back up to the room.

While the girls slept, having had a late-night reading, Caroline built up the fire from the coals. She'd stayed awake after the girls fell asleep, waiting for Trixie to return home, but she must have dozed off.

Cradling a cup of tea, Caroline stood by the window, watching for any movement in the lane below, willing Trixie to appear. She'd never stayed out this long, and Caroline fought the gnawing grip of fear that something had happened to her. Perhaps she'd fallen asleep somewhere? Or she'd found somewhere out of the cold and lost track of time?

The girls woke and Caroline kept them occupied with boiled eggs for breakfast and then tasked Elsie to fetch more water from the pump. With warm water and a cloth, she made the girls wash and put on their dresses ready for the Christmas Day church service.

'Where's our Trixie?' Bertha asked. 'I don't want to go to church today. Can I stay with Trixie?'

'She's at work,' Elsie told her. 'And you have to go to church. It's Jesus's birthday.'

Caroline stood by the window again, ignoring the girls squabbling. People were in the lane now, fetching water or emptying rubbish into the drain. A couple of men leant against the opposite wall and smoked clay pipes with children playing in the doorway. A normal morning, yet not normal for Caroline at all. Trixie should be home now.

Once more donning her coat and boots, she tied on her bonnet. 'Listen to me, both of you. I need to go out for a little while. You're to stay inside.'

'But what about the service?' Elsie asked, worriedly.

'If we miss the morning service, there's another one tonight and we'll go to that one. Just behave and don't fight while I'm gone, please.'

'I'll read to you, our Bertha. Sit down,' Elsie said with authority.

'No, I don't want to listen to you,' Bertha groaned mutinously.

Caroline closed the door and met Sarah Adams on the landing. 'Morning.' She hurried past her.

'Morning, Caroline. Is anything wrong?'

Pausing at the bottom of the stairs, Caroline looked back up at her. 'Trixie didn't come home last night.'

'Oh.' Sarah grimaced. 'She could have found somewhere to sleep...'

'That's what I thought, but she would have woken as soon as it was light and come home.'

'And it's gone ten now.'

'I don't know where to go to search for her.'

'The streets around the Assembly Rooms or near the Theatre Royal. Trixie tries to select gentlemen clients if she can.'

'Really?' This was news to Caroline. She never asked detailed questions about Trixie's line of work, preferring not to know so she couldn't imagine the awfulness of what Trixie did with strangers. However, now she wished she had asked more questions and learned where Trixie went at night.

'I'll keep an eye on the girls.' Sarah opened her own door. 'Good luck.'

Caroline dashed along the lane, causing the men smoking to stare after her but she didn't care. Instinct told her something was wrong. Trixie had been acting odd for days and to not come home during the night wasn't like her.

The streets were mostly quiet as she searched the main thoroughfares. With no markets and the shops closed, there were no horse-drawn vehicles clogging the roads.

She had a stitch in her side by the time she reached the elegant streets around the Assembly Rooms. She searched a hundred yards in each direction before circling around beyond the Theatre Royal, a grand sandstone building four stories high with pointed arches and little turrets above. No one but a street sweeper cleaning the gutters of rubbish was around. The fancy row of white terraced houses along St Leonard's Place were a stark difference to the rotten buildings of the Water Lanes.

The great bells of the Minster chimed to call the parishioners to service. Smaller churches also rang their bells and the air throbbed with the sound of clanging bells. Doors opened and where there were quiet and clear streets, abruptly throngs of people clattered over the cobbles to their chosen places of worship for the eleven o'clock Christmas service.

Although unfamiliar with these streets, Caroline searched alongside alleys and snickets between rows of houses, calling Trixie's name. She wandered down Museum Street, thinking perhaps Trixie was in the Museum Gardens, but the garden gates were locked, and all was quiet inside.

Snow began to fall from low slate grey clouds as she turned into Lendal and passed the Methodist's Chapel. Opposite was the half-circle drive of the Judge's House and beside it a narrow path between the drive and the buildings next to it. Caroline ventured down the path, not entirely sure if she was on private property, but she guessed the path led to the back of the Assembly Rooms. She really didn't know where else to look and maybe it was time to start for home and be with the girls, but she didn't want to give up just yet.

As predicted, the path opened up behind the Judge's House yard and into a garden of sorts. Beyond that was the back of The Stamp Office building and to the left the Assembly Rooms. Becoming colder, the snow falling heavier, Caroline searched the area and found nothing.

She headed back the way she'd come, knowing it was silly to stay out as the weather turned bad. Snow swirled on the breeze which was getting stronger. From a window in the top storey of the Judge's House, Caroline saw a curtain move. Fearful of being somewhere she shouldn't be, she hurried back along the path. A dog barked on the other side of the wooden fence making her jump. Dashing into the yard next door, she spotted a square of white material. Her breath caught in her throat when she saw the little yellow embroidered daisy.

Picking up the handkerchief, Caroline stared at it then glanced around. Gasping in horror, she saw stocking-clad legs poking out of a woodshed. Whimpering, Caroline ran over to the open woodshed door and nearly fainted.

Trixie lay naked and exposed on the floor. Her face so beaten and bloodied, Caroline only recognised her because of the shawl she'd given her and her black curls which were matted with blood.

A sob escaped Caroline as she knelt by her friend's head, her hands hovering over her not knowing where to touch her, or if Trixie was alive or dead.

'Trixie,' she whispered, shaking her bare shoulders gently. 'Trix...' Caroline stared at Trixie's breasts begging her chest to rise and fall. There, she saw it move, just the faintest rise. Galvanized into action, Caroline tore off her coat and covered Trixie with it. She ran to the nearest door and banged on it hard and repeatedly until it was opened by a young boy wearing an apron.

'What yer banging like that for? Yer'll have me master hollering in a minute.' He glared at her. 'Well?'

'I need help. Please come with me.'

A look of concern changed his features. 'I can't help yer.' He promptly shut the door in her face.

Angered, Caroline banged hard again. 'Help! Please!'

The door was yanked open again and the boy was replaced by a tall, thickset woman who towered over Caroline. 'What is the meaning of this?'

'I need help. My friend, she's been beaten.' Caroline grabbed the woman's arm, which was as thick as her own thigh, and tugged her out of the house.

'Now hang on a minute. I've got work to do,' the woman protested.

'Just help me please, I beg you.' Caroline pulled her to the woodshed and knelt down beside Trixie. 'She's going to die.'

'Dear God in Heaven. What's she doing in our woodshed?'

'I don't know. I've been searching for her. Please help me.'

The woman knelt down on one knee with a grunt. 'She's in a bad way. Are you sure she's not dead?'

'No, she's breathing, but only just.' Caroline wasn't completely sure for Trixie was as white as the snow falling, except where the blood coated her.

'We'll need the doctor or get her to the hospital.'

'Yes, yes,' Caroline urged.

The woman heaved herself up. 'The master won't like this disturbance on Christmas morning, but what else can we do?' She strode back to the house.

Caroline stroked Trixie's hair. 'Hold on. You'll be fine now.'

Trixie's eyes fluttered open, and she groaned.

'Trixie!' Caroline squeezed her hand. 'Lie still.'

'Caro...'

'Yes, dearest. You're safe now.'

'Safe...' Trixie grimaced. 'No... not safe...' she whispered through bloodied lips. 'Must hide...'

'We'll get you to the hospital.'

'No!' Trixie reared up and then swayed with a long moan of agony.

'Stay still.'

Trixie stared at Caroline through eyes rapidly closing from swelling. 'Get me home.'

'What? No. You need a hospital.'

'Get me home. Sarah can see to me.' Trixie sucked in a breath and then cried out in pain. 'I can't breathe...'

'Please let me get you to the hospital,' Caroline pleaded.

'*No!*' Trixie gripped Caroline's hands. 'Get me home. Victor...' Her eyes rolled in her head, and she passed out.

Shaken at the mention of Victor, Caroline knelt on the floor, her mind whirling, her heart racing. Victor. Had Victor beaten Trixie? Why?

The woman from the house returned with a couple of thick blankets. 'I've sent our lad to find a hansom.' She turned as a maid came into the woodshed with a stone hot water bottle. 'Let's get her warm.'

They wrapped Trixie who was barely conscious in the warm blankets, tucking the stone water bottle under her feet. The boy ran to them saying a hansom was on the street and the woman, the size of a large man, bent and scooped up Trixie as if she weighed less than a pillow.

'Thank you so much for your help.' Caroline climbed into the cab to receive Trixie from the woman. 'I'll return the blankets and bottle.'

'Keep them, lass. You'll be needing them more than us. Good luck to you.' The big woman waved them away.

Once the cab reached the top of Water Lanes, the driver told Caroline he wasn't driving any further. Caroline told him to wait, and she ran, slipping and sliding in her haste, down the lane to find Jacob Adams. Luckily, he and another two men were sitting on the staircase playing cards.

She gabbled at them, gesturing to the top of the lane as she burst past them and into the room to find her money purse. They followed her back to the cab and while she paid the driver, Jacob carefully carried Trixie home.

'I'll fetch our Sarah,' Jacob said, laying Trixie down on the bed and hurrying out again.

'What's happened?' Elsie started crying, staring at her older sister. Bertha grabbed Elsie around the waist and buried her head into Elsie's shoulder.

'Trixie's had an accident,' Caroline said calmly, though inside she was shaking and distraught. She piled the blankets on Trixie and tucked the hot water bottle beneath her feet. 'Now I want you both to go out onto the landing while I get Trixie comfortable. Do that now, girls.' She shooed them away.

Taking a deep breath, Caroline summoned all her strength to deal with the state Trixie was in. Knowing the pain of a beating herself, though nothing as severe as what had happened to Trixie, she understood that laudanum or something just as strong was needed to ease her suffering. Caroline would use every penny she had to help Trixie. Wiping a tear away, for she had no time for crying, Caroline heated water and tore up cloths.

Sarah came in and gasped at the sight of Trixie's face. 'Dear God.'

'Can you help her?' Caroline willed Sarah to say yes. The other woman was only a bit older than Caroline but had an age of knowledge passed down from her own mother who used to be the midwife of the lanes.

Gently lifting the blankets to reveal Trixie's battered and bleeding body, Sarah gaped. 'She's been stabbed, I think, or cut... Trixie needs a doctor and the hospital. I only deliver babies and lay out the dead.' Sarah shook her head, helplessly. 'Can you afford the doctor? It's Doctor Clement, he's good, not a drunk like most of the others.'

'I can afford him.' She'd use every penny they had to pay him if need be.

'I'll send our Jacob for him. But we can start to get her warm and clean and pray it's not too late.' Sarah, a look of determination on her face, tied an apron around her waist and got to work.

Caroline glanced down at her darling friend and knew nothing would ever be the same again, whether Trixie lived or died.

Chapter Thirteen

Snow fell outside the window, brightening the darkness of the night by covering everything in white and transforming the dirty lane into something pristine and virginal. It wouldn't last of course, for as soon as dawn broke and the men and women of the lane rose to trudge to work, their footprints would turn the white snow to murky slush, reveal the open sewer drain, the slime-covered cobbles, the piles of waste that the rats would scatter over and the drabness of the ancient buildings.

Caroline leaned her hip against the windowsill and stared at the falling snowflakes. Although tired, she kept vigil over Trixie who lay sleeping, drugged by the laudanum Doctor Clement administered before he stitched the cut in Trixie's side. He also put a few stitches in the cut above her left eye. He announced Trixie had broken ribs, and a broken nose, as well as all the bruising. Doctor Clement couldn't rule out a possible head injury. He declared she'd taken a terrible beating and would be lucky to survive after spending the night in freezing temperatures. To move her to the county hospital could cause more harm than good and told Caroline to keep a good fire and, when Trixie woke, to feed her broth. He charged Caroline a fee of five shillings, money they sorely needed, and said he'd be back tomorrow.

A mangy dog ran down the lane and Caroline stared at the paw prints he left behind in the snow. Her mind flittered from one thought to another, not settling on anything. She couldn't contemplate Trixie dying, she couldn't deal with that idea at all. The image of Victor Dolan rose, and she shuddered. His red-scarred face blurred in the window, grainy and shadowy, as it had been on the night he assaulted her. Now he'd done it again, this time to Trixie, and so much more. He'd left her for dead, badly beaten, exposed and dumped in a woodshed.

In comparison, Caroline had got off lightly.

Trixie awoke an hour before midnight and moaned in pain.

Caroline, sitting on the floor resting against the bed, jumped up to see to her. 'Steady now,' she soothed, relieved that Trixie had woken and not slipped away as she feared. 'Lie still. You've stitches in your side.'

For several minutes, Trixie stared up at the ceiling through the slits in her puffy and bruised eyes and took shallow breaths. Then she slowly turned her head to look at Caroline. 'We have to get out of here.'

'I know, and we will, as soon as you're better.'

'No, now.' Trixie raised her head, a look of panic in her damaged eyes. '*Where's my sisters?*'

'Staying with Sarah Adams.'

'Get them! They're not safe here.'

'Of course, they're safe. Sarah and Jacob won't let anything happen to them.' Caroline wondered if Trixie wasn't thinking straight. Had she been dealt a bad knock to the head that addled her wits?

Trixie gripped Carolines hand. 'We have to leave *now*.'

'What? You're not going anywhere. You're too weak and need rest. Trixie, you're lucky to be alive.'

'*We* won't be if we stay here.' Trixie moaned deeply as she moved to sit up.

'What are you doing? Lie down!' Caroline urged, pushing Trixie's shoulders down.

'Listen to me,' Trixie panted, the pain etched on her face. 'Victor knows I helped you escape him.'

Caroline felt the warmth drain from her face. 'How does he?'

'The day I first spoke to you through the attic door, another girl was with me. Gina. A week ago, she told Victor what happened that day. I found out a few days ago and I've been trying to lie low and stay away from the areas he goes to.' Trixie closed her eyes, her chin trembling. 'Last night he and his men found me. He said I had to pay for what he lost, meaning you. He wanted you to be one of his *special women*. The ones he can charge a higher fee for to gentlemen.' Her eyes filled with tears. 'I cost him money and his men took their revenge.'

Caroline stroked her arm, crying too at the agony her friend must have suffered at their hands.

'The Water Lanes won't save us, Caro,' Trixie whispered.

'What do you mean? You said we were safe here.'

'Victor comes from these lanes, too, like me. The law of the Water Lanes is we don't fight with or steal from each other. Victor is one of the men in charge of the lanes' law, only he and a few others give out any punishments.' She paused for breath, wincing every time she breathed in too deeply.

Caroline frowned. 'I don't understand, you said we'd be safe here, but Victor is in control? How has he not heard about me living here before now?'

'He did, but I told him you'd gone away. That you were a live-in maid for a wealthy gentleman and that you threatened to go to the police, or tell your employer... I lied through my teeth to protect you.'

'Why didn't you tell me this before?'

'I thought I had handled it...' Trixie closed her eyes for a moment. 'For a while it worked. Victor doesn't live in the lanes anymore. He has rooms at that lodging house he held you in. But with the slum clearances starting, Victor knows his time is limited of being the big man around here. He's looking to get into other businesses, get away from the Water Lanes. I thought the danger was over, then he recognised you the other night. He's had you watched since.'

'Watched?' Caroline couldn't believe any of this.

Trixie pushed herself up further, groaning low at the pain. 'Then Gina told him it was me who helped you escape. Last night he was waiting for me near Blake Street. I tried talking him around...' She raised her damaged face to Caroline. 'I thought since he's my father's cousin, he'd go easy on me.'

'He's your father's cousin?' Shocked, Caroline stared at her. 'Why didn't you tell me that?'

'You didn't need to know.' Slowly, Trixie shoved the blankets off her. 'I betrayed Victor. I should be dead, but you found me and I'm alive.' Grimacing at the pain of every movement, Trixie eased herself up off the bed and swayed. 'When Victor knows I survived, he'll be furious. He threatened to take Elsie and Bertha. He'd sell them to the brothels who take little girls and hide them in cellars for their special clients.' With a dull look in her eyes, Trixie stared at Caroline. 'And what he'll do to you for injuring his face, I hate to imagine.'

Caroline backed away, terrified.

'So we go, understand?' Trixie hobbled a step, holding a hand to her stitches. She was panting with the effort. 'Help me get dressed.'

'Where will we go?' Caroline's teeth chattered as she hurriedly dressed Trixie in every piece of clothing she owned.

'Anywhere but here,' Trixie muttered, grey-faced from hurting.

Caroline pulled a sack out from under the bed and started packing.

'Leave it,' Trixie panted. 'We can't carry it. You'll need to help me walk.'

Throwing the sack onto the bed, Caroline rubbed her forehead in fear. 'This won't work. You're too ill. It's freezing out there. You're not in a fit state to leave your bed, never mind tramp through snow!'

'Just get me to the far side of the city. We'll wake up an inn to let us in or sleep in some stables until morning.'

'We need a few bits and the money tin.' Caroline packed some things in the sack.

'Go and wake my sisters.' Trixie leaned against the wall, holding her ribs.

Caroline dragged on her coat and felt the key and toggle in her pocket. 'Mrs Warburton's!' She spun to Trixie. 'We'll go to Mrs Warburton's flat.'

Swaying on her feet, Trixie nodded. She looked so exhausted, Caroline didn't believe she'd make it out of the room, never mind across town.

Jacob Adams opened his door to Caroline's tapping. He was still fully dressed and didn't appear as if she'd woken him. 'Do you need our Sarah?'

'No, the girls.'

'Why?' He frowned. 'They're asleep.'

'We need to leave. Now.'

Jacob gave her a long look. 'Victor?'

She blinked. 'How much do you know?'

'A bit.' He ran his fingers through his brown hair. 'I've been keeping an eye out for you and Trixie as much as I could without drawing attention to myself.' He turned and gently shook Elsie and Bertha's shoulders where they slept on a thin mattress on the floor by the fire.

Sleepily, protesting a little, the girls changed out of their nightgowns and into their dresses. Caroline wrapped shawls around them tightly and led them out onto the landing.

Jacob joined them. 'Trixie's not fit to go anywhere.'

'We have no choice.' Caroline found Trixie sitting on the bed, her breathing shallow, her face as pale as death.

'Let me carry her.' Jacob said.

'No.' Trixie put her hand up to stop him. 'The less you know the better.'

'Victor won't get nothing from me, you know that. He could beat me to a pulp, and I'd still tell him nothing.' A look of love was written all over Jacob's face as he stared at Trixie. 'Let me help you.'

Trixie reached out a hand to him. 'Only halfway.'

In the eerie quiet streets, Caroline held the girls' hands while Jacob carried Trixie who he'd covered completely with a blanket. The snow fell lightly, drifting about their heads. They walked without speaking, the girls half asleep and not inclined to chatter as usual. Caroline's gaze searched every shadow, her nerves on edge. She jumped when a cat dashed across in front of them. At any moment she expected Victor and his henchmen to spring out at them.

Along Finkle Street, Trixie raised her head. 'Put me down, Jacob.'

He slowed his steps but didn't stop. 'Not yet.'

'Jacob, please. I don't want you to know where we are. Enough damage has been done. I can't bear to think of you getting involved as well.'

Carefully, Jacob placed Trixie on her feet and held her until Caroline could take his place. 'Will I see you again, Trix?'

'I don't think so.' Trixie gave him a wounded smile. 'I'll not forget you, Jacob Adams.'

He leant forward and softly kissed her cheek. 'Take care.' He thrust his hands into his coat pockets. 'I'll wait here until you're out of sight.'

The flat was deathly cold. Caroline helped Trixie into Mrs Warburton's bed, making her comfortable before settling the girls on the sofa with a blanket. Next, she built fires in the range, the sitting room and the bedroom to heat the freezing flat.

Checking on Trixie, she grabbed another blanket from the top of the wardrobe and spread it over the bed.

'I'll rest for a bit,' Trixie said quietly. 'Then we'll decide what to do.'

Caroline nodded. Her head ached from fatigue and worry. What would they do?

Loud knocking on the door woke Caroline a few hours later. She scrambled off the sofa where she slept with the girls and hurried to the street door at the bottom of the staircase.

Mrs McCarthy stood there, arms folded, but relaxed on seeing Caroline. 'Oh, it's you. I thought someone had broken in. I saw smoke coming out of the chimney when I was in the yard just now and knew Agatha wasn't expected home until tomorrow.'

'Good morning, Mrs McCarthy. Yes, it's just me. I thought to come and light the fires and keep the place warm ready for when Mrs Warburton returns,' Caroline lied effortlessly. 'You know how Mrs Warburton hates a cold room.'

'That is very true.'

'I thought I could get some cleaning done, too, while she's away,' Caroline added.

'You are an excellent maid, Caroline.' Mrs McCarthy nodded, stepping back to her shop door. 'Agatha is fortunate to have you.'

Upstairs, Caroline went into the bedroom. Trixie was awake. 'How do you feel?'

'As if I've been run over by six horses pulling a wagon.' Trixie winced as she moved. More swelling and bruising had come out on her face, misshaping her nose and eyes further. Dried blood caked her split lip and her hair.

'Let me see if your stitches are bleeding.' Caroline took off the dressing, relieved to see the wound wasn't weeping. She replaced the bandage with a clean one from the supply kept in the kitchen because Mrs Warburton, as most old people did, bleed easily with any knock to her body.

Making Trixie comfortable again, Caroline straightened the blankets. 'Could you manage some porridge? I soaked some oats last night.'

'Yes. I need to build my strength up, don't I?' Trixie sighed. 'We need to be gone by nightfall.'

'I've been thinking.' Caroline sat on the edge of the bed. 'I'll find Mussy. He'll be able to help us.'

'How?'

'I'm not sure yet, but I'll ask to borrow some money. We'll get the train south.'

'The train...'

'We'll be away from York by this evening.' Caroline stood. 'I'll make breakfast and get the girls up. Go back to sleep.'

By mid-morning, Caroline was entering Bob Warburton's pub by the back yard and going in through the scullery. She'd wrapped her shawl around her face, leaving only her eyes showing beneath her bonnet. At first, Bob didn't recognise her.

'Who the hell are you?' Bob demanded, carrying a tray of dirty glasses and tankards.

'It's me, Caroline Lawson.' She pulled down the shawl.

'Ah.' Bob put the tray on a bench by the wall. 'I'm glad you've called. I'd hope you'd turn up.'

'Oh?'

'Come with me.' He went out of the kitchen.

'I've only come to ask if you know where Mussy's accommodation is? He told me he has rooms near St Williams College, but he's never said exactly where, and I didn't think to ask,' she babbled, stepping quickly to follow Bob up the hallway.

Near the snug, Bob stopped. 'He's not lodging near St Williams College anymore.' He flung open the snug door. 'He's camped in my snug!'

The smell of stale wine and body odour hit Caroline. She gaped at Mussy laying sprawled across the bench seat, his luggage trunks open with clothes spilling out. Empty wine bottles were scattered across the table and on the floor.

'He's been here for two days.' Bob walked in and started collecting the empty bottles. 'He was thrown out of his lodgings.' Bob glanced at Caroline. 'I don't know how much you know about Mussy, or understand... Anyway, his *friend,* the tailor on Blake Street, he wants nothing more to do with him either.' Bob came back to the doorway, arms loaded. 'Mussy has been drinking for two days straight, perhaps longer for he was drunk when he turned up here the day before Christmas Eve.'

Caroline's shoulders slumped. She needed Mussy's help, but he also needed help. 'Has he still got his job?' she asked Bob when he came back from the kitchen.

'Job?' Bob looked uncomfortable. 'He's never had a job.'

'He's a gas works inspector.' She still stood by the door, hoping Mussy would wake soon.

Bob scratched his chin. 'Mussy isn't who you think he is, Caroline.'

'I don't understand.'

'He's a gentleman's son from Manchester.'

'I gathered he wasn't working class, not with his accent and clothes.'

'He doesn't work for a living either. He has an allowance from his grandmother.'

'Why would he say he's a gas inspector then?'

'It's his cover... he didn't want anyone to know he was a gentleman's son, yet he dressed so extravagantly he brought attention to himself, anyway.' Bob shrugged. 'He did study chemistry at university though.'

'How do you know all this?'

'Mussy knew my brother.'

'Gordon?'

'No. Douglas. They met at university. Douglas was the cleverest of us three brothers. Our father saw his potential and sent him to St Andrews in Scotland. Our father was Scottish, you see.'

'Mrs Warburton told me she'd lost a son two years ago.'

'Yes. Mother has never got over it. She rarely speaks of Douglas. He was her favourite.' Bob began to clean up the snug and Caroline helped him even though she was keen to return to Trixie.

'So, Douglas and Mussy were friends?'

Bob closed a trunk and fastened the straps. He straightened and gave Caroline a long look. 'They were more than friends, do you understand?'

She didn't. What did more than friends mean?

'They were lovers.'

It took several moments for her to process his meaning and even then, she didn't fully comprehend how that was possible. Men didn't love men. She'd never heard of such a thing. At the convent it was drilled into her to not give into the temptation of the flesh, but to only honour thy husband once married for the procreation of children. However, she had desired Hugh and cherished him and sharing a bed with him had been one of the highlights of being married. Their intimacy meant everything to her. Now she was learning that those same feelings could be between the same sex. It was mindboggling.

'Don't hate Mussy for it,' Bob said sadly. 'I know it's hard for us to figure out and it's against the law for men to be together, of course it is, but it happens.'

Abruptly, Bob slumped to the other bench seat and stared at the sleeping Mussy. 'I adored my brother. I thought there was no other man greater than him. Douglas was clever, funny, kind and generous. But he had an affliction which tormented him. He wasn't interested in girls, women. Mother refused to accept it, and Gordon was totally disgusted by it, but Father knew and tried to tolerate Douglas's tendencies. We all did because we loved him. Mussy loved him too. He's never been the same since Douglas died.'

'That's why you've allowed him to come here.' Caroline abruptly felt older, wiser. Love was love. Poor Mussy.

'I have.' Bob pushed himself to his feet. 'But I'm worried Mussy is going down a path he can't return from, as Douglas did...'

'What do you mean?'

Bob collected a few more bottles. 'Douglas killed himself.' He walked out of the snug.

Caroline blinked in shock. She gazed at Mussy. Was that his future, too? Rubbing her hands over her face, Caroline didn't know what to do.

'So that's my story,' said Mussy, unexpectedly. He still had his eyes closed but had obviously listened to their conversation about him.

'So, it is.'

He opened blood-shot eyes and sat up with a groan, holding his head. 'Do you hate me?'

'No.' That was the truth. He was her friend.

'I'm pleased. I have very few friends. Actually, two. You and Bob, and I think I'm trying Bob's patience.'

'You'll always have a friend in me.'

He smiled a melancholy smile. 'I doubt I deserve you.'

'It's not for you to decide. I wish you had told me.'

Mussy glanced away guiltily. 'I wanted to, I nearly did one night...'

Caroline heard the clock in the hallway chime. She counted them. Eleven o'clock. She had to get going.

'What's wrong?' Mussy stood and tucked his shirt into his trousers and buttoning his purple waistcoat.

'Trixie has been beaten by the fellow who attacked me. He nearly killed her.'

'Bastard.'

'We need to leave York today. We're in danger.'

Mussy's expression fell. 'Dear Lord, no.'

'I came to find you to see if you could help us, but...' She waved her hands at the mess of the snug. 'You're in no position to help.'

'Nonsense. I'll do whatever you need.' He screwed up his face and wiped his eyes with a hand that held a slight tremor.

'You're worse for wear. Still drunk probably. Don't worry about it.' She went and kissed his whiskery cheek. 'I'll be in touch. I'll send a letter here to Bob when we're settled.'

'Caro, you can't do this on your own. Where will you go? Do you have any money?'

Tears filled her eyes. 'We'll get by.' She swallowed, forcing herself to not give into weakness. She had to be strong for Trixie and the girls.

'What are your plans?'

'To get a train to somewhere. Leeds maybe. Anywhere, it doesn't matter. We just have to leave York, today. Mrs Warburton will be back tomorrow, and she can't find us in her home.'

'Her home? That's where you're staying?' Mussy's eyes widened.

'We had nowhere else to go and she's away.' Caroline glanced at the door and hoped Bob hadn't heard her. He wouldn't be pleased to know she was lodging at his mother's place. 'I have to go. I've been gone too long as it is.'

Mussy dragged on his long grey coat and found his top hat under the table. 'I'm coming with you.'

'Coming with me?' She jerked in surprise.

'There's nothing for me in York. I stayed because I felt closer to Douglas here. This was his home. He's buried here.' Mussy went to his trunks. 'But people know of me, know who and what I am. I won't take another beating or make another run for my life... No, it's time I started again somewhere else.' He stopped searching through a leather case. 'That's if you want me to accompany you?'

She couldn't think. What would Trixie say? Oh, what did it matter? As long as they escaped the city, that was all she cared about. 'Yes, come and join us.'

It took another twenty minutes for Mussy to sort himself out and have his luggage sent to the train station. They said farewell to Bob and hurried along the streets. Being Sunday, church bells rang and some people were about, but the cold and snow kept most indoors.

Caroline led Mussy up the stairs to the flat. She opened the door and skidded to a halt. There, sitting at the table was Mrs Warburton and pacing the room, was Gordon.

Her insides turning to water, Caroline looked for the girls and found them standing in the bedroom doorway wearing frightened expressions.

Chapter Fourteen

'Well, isn't this a situation?' Mrs Warburton said, glaring at Caroline. 'You can imagine my surprise to walk into my home and find two small girls sitting on my sofa and a beaten woman in my very own bed? I go away for a couple of days and find my home taken over by strangers!'

'I'm very sorry.' Caroline wrung her hands. 'I didn't expect you back until tomorrow and we'd have been gone by then.'

'Gone?' Mrs Warburton's grey eyebrows rose. 'You were *abandoning* me as well?'

'I shall call the police, Mother.' Gordon rocked on his heels. 'No doubt they would have robbed you blind.'

'That's a lie!' Caroline stepped forward, angry at being accused. 'I respect your mother and would never steal from her.'

'You've brought strangers into her home without her permission! How is that respectful?' Gordan spat.

'Enough!' Mrs Warburton waved her cane at them. 'There will be no police. My business will not be fodder for the gossips. Go home, Gordan. I shall deal with this.'

'I'll not leave you alone, Mother,' he protested, with a sneering glance at Mussy. 'Not with the likes of him here.'

As though it was painful for her to look at him, Mrs Warburton finally addressed Mussy. 'Mr Casey. I didn't realise you were an acquaintance of my maid.'

'I am, Mrs Warburton.' Unshaven and still affected by days of drinking, Mussy was not at his best.

Caroline was eager to see to Trixie but dared not move.

Using her cane, Mrs Warburton left the table. 'Gordon, I have all this in hand. Return home before the snow begins again. I shall write to you tomorrow.'

'Mother, I can't leave you alone with this lot.' He gestured towards Caroline and Mussy.

'I will send for Bob should I have the need. Now kiss me and go.'

Stiffly, Gordon bent and kissed his mother's cheek. He was fuming as he collected his hat and stomped down the stairs.

'Now,' Mrs Warburton said. 'I need a cup of tea. Then we are going to discuss what has been going on here.'

Caroline went to the kitchen to boil the kettle, her head aching with tension, her hands unsteady.

Elsie sidled up to her, tears slipping over her lashes. 'You left my bible behind.'

'Oh.' Caroline sagged. 'I'm sorry, sweetie.'

'Can we go back and get it?'

'No. But perhaps I can buy you another one soon.' Caroline set out the tea tray. 'How's Trixie?'

'She was asleep until that lady and man came in. They frightened us and we ran to Trixie.'

Caroline kissed the top of her head. 'Go back into the bedroom and wait in there with Bertha. I'll be in shortly.'

Taking the tray into the sitting room, Caroline noticed Mussy standing near the fireplace and Mrs Warburton sitting back at the table staring out the window.

'I never expected such deceit from you, girl,' Mrs Warburton stated.

'And it was never my intention to deceive you, but we had nowhere else to go.' Caroline poured out a cup of tea.

'Fetch two more cups, girl. Mr Casey looks ready to drop and I suspect you need something as well.' The old lady turned to Mussy. 'Come sit down, Mr Casey. It has been a long while since we last met.'

'Two years ago, Mrs Warburton.' A shadow crossed Mussy's features as he joined her at the table.

'And yet it feels like only yesterday,' she murmured. 'Don't you think?'

'Absolutely.'

Caroline stepped away to get the two extra cups and saucers. Her employer's grief matched Mussy's. They'd both loved Douglas.

'Why do you need to leave?' Mrs Warburton asked as the three of them sat at the table.

Caroline told her the truth, explaining everything that had happened since she arrived in York.

'What a grave experience you've had, girl.' Mrs Warburton lifted the teapot and poured more tea into each cup.

'Trixie isn't safe here, nor am I.'

'Indeed. And where do you wish to go?'

'Home. To the country,' Caroline blurted without hesitation.

'The countryside is harsh, especially in winter. Without a place to stay, you'll die on the road.' Mrs Warburton sipped her tea thoughtfully.

'My father-in-law will put us up.' At least Caroline hoped Howard would welcome them.

'And what of you, Mr Casey?' Mrs Warburton asked.

'I shall go with them. My time in York has come to an end.'

'Chasing ghosts isn't a life,' the old lady murmured. 'Douglas is gone.'

'Yes...' Mussy played with his teaspoon.

'You and my son chose a difficult path, one which I doubt will bring you any great joy. The hiding, the secrecy. You need to find something else to do, to throw your passion towards. Do you understand?'

'It's easier said than done, Mrs Warburton.'

'But what other choice do you have? Do you want to end up like my Douglas?'

Mussy stood and walked back to the fireplace, his back to them.

Caroline's heart broke for him. To not be free to love someone must be the hardest of burdens.

Abruptly, Mussy took his coat and hat from the stand. 'I'll be back in an hour.'

'Mussy!' Caroline jerked up from the chair. 'We need to plan!'

'I'll be just an hour. Whatever you decide I'll go along with.' He looked pained and wouldn't meet her gaze.

'He's a troubled soul,' Mrs Warburton said when they heard the door slam. 'You're going to need a carriage. I will hire one for you and pay the fare to take you to your father-in-law's farm.'

Impulsively, Caroline clasped Mrs Warburton's arthritic hand. 'Thank you. That is generous and kind.'

Mrs Warburton pulled her hand away. 'Settle yourself, girl. There's much to do.'

With a note from Mrs Warburton, Caroline went to the nearest stables and hired a carriage and driver, a fee was discussed and paid. Next, she went to Mr Bent's and bought a meat pie for Mrs Warburton's supper that evening, which Caroline could leave warming in the oven for her.

'This is goodbye, Mr Bent,' Caroline said, paying him. 'I'm going away.'

'Well now, that saddens me enormously.' He came around the counter and took her hands in his giant ones. 'I will miss seeing your pretty face and no mistake. Where are you going?'

'Home, to the country.' She walked out to the doorstep with him.

'Then I wish you well, Mrs Lawson, indeed I do.'

Two men walking by stopped and stared at Caroline.

'Mrs Lawson?' one asked, a shady-looking character.

Caroline shrank back, her heart nearly exploding in her chest.

The two men advanced. 'Mrs Lawson? The one who lives with Trixie Wilkes? You've a debt to settle!' They both reached out for Caroline, and she screamed.

Mr Bent lunged forward and pulled her behind him. He spun fast for a big man and landed a punch on one fellow's jaw, sending him staggering back. Mr Bent turned in a flash and grabbed the other fellow by his coat and hauled him off the ground before flinging him across the cobbles to thump into a butcher's display table opposite.

The butcher stormed out. 'What's all this, Charles?'

'Scum, Kel, scum!' Mr Bent rushed on them as the fellows struggled to their feet. 'Go on! Get! We'll not have the likes of you around here!'

Shaken, Caroline clung to the doorframe.

'Nay lass, you're all right now. They've gone.' Mr Bent rubbed her back.

Her legs had gone to mush. They were Dolan's men. She had to get back to Trixie and get them in that carriage as quickly as possible.

'Where do you need to go, lass?' Mr Bent asked kindly. 'I'll walk with you.'

Grateful, she made her legs move and kept close to his side until they reached the flat.

'There now, lass. Can I be of any more help to you?' Mr Bent asked with a kind smile.

'You've been a good friend, Mr Bent and I thank you.' She clasped his hands.

'Call in for a chat anytime you're back in York, lass. Fare well and good luck.'

She didn't tell Trixie what happened at the butchers when she got back to the flat, but her pale face alerted Mrs Warburton that something was wrong.

'Do you have the carriage sorted?'

'Yes.' Caroline glanced at the clock. It had gone two o'clock. There would only be a few hours of daylight left. They needed to get going. 'Where's Mussy?' she worried.

'Just concentrate on getting your friend and these girls in that carriage,' Mrs Warburton instructed.

Caroline wrapped the girls up warm and told them to wait at the bottom of the stairs. Elsie held the sack of their few belongings.

Trixie was suffering terribly as Caroline wrapped the blanket around her. The pain from the cut, her broken ribs and other wounds caused her to cry out when she moved.

'Here.' Mrs Warburton thrust a small green bottle of laudanum at Caroline. 'Take it. She's going to need it.'

'Where is Mussy!' Caroline was annoyed he'd not returned yet.

'You'll have to leave him behind or you'll not reach your destination before nightfall,' said Mrs Warburton. 'What's the name of the farm?'

'Hopewood, near the village of Melliton, on the Stockton-Lee estate.'

'I'll send him there.'

Staggering down the stairs with Trixie groaning with each step, Caroline thrust Mussy from her mind. He'd left her when she needed him. What kind of friend did that?

She leant Trixie against the wall and turned to her employer. 'I'm sorry to leave you like this.'

'Needs must, girl. You've a weary and troubled road ahead of you and I don't envy you any of it.' She gave Caroline a weighty money purse.

'I can't take it, Mrs Warburton. You gave me money only a few days ago.'

'Don't argue with me, girl. You've three people depending on you. You need to pay your way. I'm old. I don't need much money anymore.'

'Thank you. You've been kind and forgiving. I won't forget you.' Caroline embraced her even though the old lady remained stiff and unbending.

'Get along now. You're wasting daylight,' Mrs Warburton snapped, pushing Caroline away.

Caroline gathered Trixie against her to help her walk through the sludgy snow.

Mrs Warburton stood at the door. 'Good luck to you, girl.'

Caroline didn't look back, concentrating on getting to the carriage waiting at the end of the lane. The girls climbed aboard, full of excitement. Trixie leant weakly against Caroline and, using all her strength, Caroline heaved her up onto the seat.

Caroline paused and waited a moment, looking up and down Stonegate, willing Mussy to appear, but deep down she knew he wasn't coming. Saddened and disappointed, Caroline stepped up into the carriage and held Trixie to her.

After a wretched journey through ice-rutted roads and thick snow drifts where the driver swore and complained as he repeatedly dug the carriage wheels out of the mud, they finally rolled through the gates of Hopewood Farm just after sunset.

Tired, hungry and apprehensive of her welcome, Caroline stepped down from the carriage as the front door opened.

A woman stood framed by the light behind her. Mrs Aspall from the candle stall in the village market, the woman Howard had spoken of as his soon-to-be wife.

'Good evening, Mrs Aspall... er...Lawson,' Caroline called, believing Howard had remarried.

'Who are you?'

Caroline walked closer into the light, slipping and sliding on the ice. 'It's me, Caroline Lawson.'

'Caroline?' The other woman peered forward as if to make sure. 'Goodness. I never expected to see you again.' She gripped Caroline's cold hands, her eyes friendly. 'Howard will be so pleased, so very pleased to see you. Come in.'

'I have my friends with me,' Caroline waved towards the carriage. 'Is it possible we can stay? My friend is ill.'

Taken aback, Mrs Aspall blinked rapidly. 'Ill?'

'Nothing contagious. She met with an accident.'

Mrs Aspall, a plump short woman nodded. 'Aye, I suppose so... Howard would never forgive me if I turned you away.'

'I appreciate it very much.'

'There's a spare room, you'd know, of course, but Howard is unwell, you see, and...' Her words petered out as she wrung her hands in her apron.

'Howard is unwell?' Caroline felt guilty for adding to their problems.

'Has been for months, but more on that later. We're letting out all the warmth.' Mrs Aspall took a hold of herself. 'Bring your friends inside.'

Easing Trixie down from the carriage proved difficult for she was moaning in pain and stiff from the arduous journey. The girls, tired and cold, followed Caroline as she half-carried Trixie inside the farmhouse.

'Oh, dear God in Heaven!' Mrs Aspall exclaimed on seeing Trixie's wounded face. She stared at Trixie, then at Caroline. 'What is going on?'

'It's a long story and I will tell you it all, but first I need to put Trixie to bed and the girls. Can we have some tea? Oh, and the driver. I'll need to let him sleep in the barn.'

'Right, er... yes, right...' Mrs Aspall dithered. 'I'll go out to the driver and see to him. You know your way upstairs? I sometimes sleep in the front room and Howard is in the back bedroom. There's the other spare room which has a bed...'

'We'll manage. Girls stay down here by the fire and get warm.' Caroline gathered Trixie to her and went out of the kitchen down the hall to the narrow staircase. Trixie, as small and thin as she was, grew heavy on Caroline as she guided her up the stairs. A lantern on a table on the landing lit the way to the small bedroom Caroline remembered used to be Hugh's bedroom when he was a boy. Her chest twisted at the thought of him. She was in his home again, but she had no time to ponder on memories.

She slipped Trixie into the cold bed. Trixie's teeth started chattering for the room was chilly and unused. Caroline closed the thick drapes shutting out the black night, even with the snow whitening the landscape, the night was darker than in the city. She'd forgotten the sheer blackness of the country at night, unlike the city which had lights on in windows until late and gas streetlamps.

Retrieving an extra blanket folded on a chair, Caroline placed it over Trixie to warm her up. 'I'll get you a cup of tea and a hot water bottle. Just rest.'

Trixie barely registered her.

Concerned, Caroline hurried downstairs to the kitchen. Mrs Aspall came in bringing in a waft of cool air. 'Is there a stone water bottle I could use, Mrs Aspall? I mean Mrs Lawson.'

'Under the sink. Howard has one and I use one for my bed when I stay.'

'When you stay?' Caroline bent to retrieve the stone bottle.

'Howard and I aren't married, Caroline. We've not got around to it as he's been ill since you left in September. I still live in my cottage and come up here every day to see to him. Sometimes I sleep the night when Howard has a bad turn, or the weather is freezing, like tonight. We had snow most of the day and I didn't fancy walking back to the village in it.'

Caroline poured warm water from the kettle on the range into the bottle. 'What's wrong with him?'

'His lungs aren't good, Doctor Pike says.' Mrs Aspall mashed some tea in the teapot and brought out a large blackberry pie which she cut into thick wedges and gave a slice each to the girls. 'Do you want cream?' She smiled at them and poured cream from a small jug.

Caroline took the bottle upstairs and placed it under the blankets. Trixie had fallen asleep and so she crept back down to the kitchen.

Mrs Aspall passed Caroline a cup of tea. 'Howard is asleep, and I'll not disturb him. You can see him in the morning. I thought you and the girls can share my bed? I'm happy to sleep on the sofa in the parlour. It's large enough for me and I'll light the fire in there.'

'That's kind, thank you.' Relief at being safe and home in the country drew out a long sigh from Caroline. There was still a bumpy road ahead but at least they were away from the Water Lanes, away from Victor Dolan.

'They look dead on their feet, poor little lambs.' Mrs Aspall nodded to the girls.

Having eaten the pie and drank their milky sweet tea, the girls' eyes drooped, their cheeks rosy from the warmth of the fire.

'I'll take them up.' Caroline ushered them up to the large bed that Caroline knew used to be Leo and Lisette's bedroom. Already warmed from a bottle, the girls climbed into bed wearing their shifts, yawning. Caroline laid their dresses on the chair near the small fire that glowed in the hearth and felt guilty she was putting Mrs Aspall out of her room. She kissed the girls. 'There's a pot under the bed if you need it during the night. I'll be across the landing with Trixie.'

'Is this your farm you told us about?' Elsie asked.

'No. My husband, Hugh, he grew up on this farm and when we married, we moved to Springwood Farm a few miles away.'

'Why can't we go there then?'

'Because someone else lives there now. But Hugh's father, Howard, lives here and he's a very nice man so we'll stay with him.'

'Can we see the animals tomorrow?' Bertha yawned and snuggled down further in the blankets.

'If the weather is clear.' She turned down the lantern. 'Sleep well.'

Once more in the kitchen, Caroline sat at the wide pine table, a pale cream colour from years of being scrubbed with lemon and salt.

Mrs Aspall came into the room carrying a bucket. 'I've just lit the fire in the room your friend is in. My, she's in a right state, isn't she?'

'I was going to do it, thank you, and yes, she is.'

'You look as if you could get your head down as well.' Mrs Aspall washed her hands and sliced some of the pie. She placed it in a bowl and poured over the cream. 'Here, eat this first before you go up.'

The sweet and tart flavours of the pie sent Caroline back to last autumn when she'd made a similar pie for Hugh. She glanced around the kitchen, a place that had been Lisette's domain. Not a lot had changed since Caroline's last visit, yet the room seemed cluttered, uncared for. The cooking range needed a good black-leading, the net curtains that hung at the square window above a long wooden bench could do with a wash and the stone-flagged floor would shine with a decent scrub.

'You've had a rough time of it in the city, lass?' Mrs Aspall asked with sympathy, wiping a strand of dark grey hair away from her face.

'I have.' Caroline finished her pie and sipped her tea. Warm, fed and safe, she felt a wave of tiredness come over her.

'I'm sure you've a lot to tell me, but it can wait until tomorrow.' Mrs Aspall took the empty plate and placed it in the sink in the scullery before returning to the range to bank down the fire. She straightened and smiled at Caroline. 'How long can you stay? I could do with the help.'

'Depends on Howard.'

'Of course, he'll want you to stay. He never wanted you to go. He's always thought of you as a daughter and, to be honest, I'd like the company of having you here and, as I said, the help. I know that's selfish of me, but it's demanding going between two houses and then doing the market twice a week and coming up the hill to see to Howard every day. I'm not a young woman anymore.'

'Doesn't Leo and Lisette help you?'

She laughed without humour. 'Them? Leo can see to nothing but his own needs, which includes drinking heavily, and she's not much better.'

'I'm sorry to hear it.' Caroline hated the thought of those two awful people living in her and Hugh's cottage. But that was a thought for tomorrow, first she needed to sleep and after that, get Trixie well again. Everything else she'd sort out later.

Chapter Fifteen

A tap on the shoulder woke Caroline the next morning from what seemed like a few minutes nap. She raised her head and squinted tiredly at Elsie through blurry eyes.

'Can we see the animals now?' Elsie whispered.

Rubbing the sleep from her eyes, Caroline sat up where she lay across the end of the bed so as not to disturb Trixie. She stared anxiously at Trixie, but she still slept. A cool shiver went over Caroline's skin as she slipped out from under the blanket. The fire had gone out.

'Go downstairs. I'll be down in a minute.' Caroline needed to use the pot and wash the sleep from her face before she faced another long day.

A comb and brush set on the small dressing table came in useful to tidy her hair. It had grown so long, nearly down to her bottom. A good wash and a trim was in order. Smoothing her skirt, the state of her clothes dismayed Caroline. She looked like a beggar, but then, wasn't she one?

On the landing she heard soft murmurings coming from Howard's bedroom. She waited and Mrs Aspall come out carrying a jug and towel. 'Good morning.'

'Good morning, Caroline. How did you sleep? And your friend?'

'Well enough, when I managed to nap, but I kept waking to check on Trixie.'

'I've told Howard that you're here and he's beside himself with happiness. I've not seen him smile like that for many months, not since before your Hugh died. Go on in and sit with him.'

Caroline went into the bedroom after a slight tap on the door and smiled lovingly at the man she thought of as a father. 'Howard.'

'My dear, dear lass.' He held out his hands for her to take and she rushed to the bed to envelope him in a tight embrace.

She leaned back, emotion caught in her throat. 'I've missed you,' she managed to say.

'Not half as much as I missed you, daughter.' He took her hands as she sat on the bed beside him.

'I'm back now, and you must get better,' she chastised gently. Howard appeared older, his sparse hair now pale grey and white. He'd lost weight, his cheeks sunken and had dark shadows beneath his eyes.

'You're here to stay?' He coughed into a handkerchief.

'If you'll have me?'

'Absolutely.'

'But it's not just me here. My friend, Trixie, and her two little sisters are with me as well. Trixie is... has been through a lot and needs to rest and recover. I couldn't leave her behind. They've become my family now.'

'As I said to Annie, any friend of yours is welcome in my home, you should know that.' He studied her face. 'The time away hasn't been easy on you. No longer do I see the young, sweet girl who left with a broken heart.'

'Those three and a half months in York have changed me. There's no denying it.'

'Well, you're home now, and I know this was never your farm, but it once was Hugh's home, and it is my home, and you can stay as long as you wish.'

Caroline embraced him again only to break away when they heard the sound of girlish giggles from downstairs.

'Now isn't that a magical sound? It does me good to hear it.' Howard sighed contentedly. 'This house needs laughter in it. It needs life.'

'I'd best go down and make sure they aren't running rings around Mrs Aspall.' Caroline rose from the bed.

'Annie will enjoy every minute of it. Her one regret in life is having no children, she adores them.' Howard squeezed her hands. 'Come back up soon. We've much to discuss.'

Downstairs in the kitchen, Caroline smiled at the scene. Mrs Aspall had Elsie and Bertha kneeling on chairs, their hands in flour, aprons around their skinny waists.

'We're baking bread, Caro,' Elsie said. 'Mrs Aspall is teaching us. Bread!'

'Right, girls, concentrate on what you're doing.' Mrs Aspall kneaded a round piece of dough. 'Use the heel of your hand, Bertha, dear, that's it.'

Caroline poured herself a cup of tea and ladled a large dollop of porridge into a bowl for her breakfast. 'Howard is happy for us to stay.'

'I told you he would be.' Mrs Aspall placed the dough into an earthenware bowl. 'The bread has to prove now, girls.'

After finishing her porridge, Caroline went upstairs to Trixie with a cup of tea and a bit of scrambled egg. Only, her steps faltered as she noticed the sweat beading on Trixie's forehead. Setting the tray down, Caroline felt her forehead and her stomach twisted in fear at the heat coming from it. *Fever.*

She raced downstairs and Mrs Aspall jumped as she rushed into the kitchen. 'We need a doctor, Mrs Aspall. Trixie has a fever.'

Mrs Aspall nodded. 'I'll go. Now, girls, I trust you are old enough to wash up the breakfast dishes in the sink in the scullery? And when I get back, we'll put those loaves into the oven.' She pinned on her hat and pulled on her coat. 'It's just started to rain. What awful luck. I'll be as quick as I can.'

'You'll be all right, girls?' Caroline asked them as they tidied the table.

Elsie wiped the flour off the table with a damp cloth, swiftly looking so grown up. 'I'll see to this and watch our Bertha. Our Trixie needs you.'

Impulsively, Caroline kissed the top of her head. 'You're a good girl.' She did the same to Bertha.

Upstairs, Caroline placed a damp cloth on Trixie's forehead and washed her arms with another cool cloth. Trixie's skin burned and where there was no bruising, her face and neck glowed red. 'Now listen to me, Trixie Wilkes. I don't have time for any of this nonsense, you understand? We're at the farm and we're safe and the girls are excited to see all the animals. We need you up and well.'

Trixie moaned and thrashed her arms. Her hair wet with sweat. Caroline fought the inner panic that rose up to choke her. She had caused this. Dragging Trixie out of a warm bed and into a carriage in the middle of winter had been a foolish decision. She'd put her need of wanting to be back at the farm before the need of her sick friend. What had she been thinking?

It seemed hours until Mrs Aspall returned with Doctor Pike, an elderly man with a round stomach and a thick white beard. He came into the bedroom with his black leather case and a nod of acknowledgement to Caroline. 'Mrs Lawson. We meet again.'

'Yes.' She couldn't make eye contact with him. The last time she saw him was when Hugh died. The memory was too painful.

'Now tell me everything that has happened to this poor girl.'

While he examined Trixie, Caroline told him the details of Trixie's assault and all that had happened since.

'And before the attack?' he asked, listening to Trixie's heartbeat.

'What do you mean?'

'Where did Miss Wilkes live? What was her position?'

Caroline blanched. 'She lived in the Water Lanes in York.'

'Ahh.' His bushy eyebrows rose. 'That explains her undernourished condition which will not help her fight this fever. She is very weak.'

'But she'll survive?' she whispered.

'That remains to be seen, Mrs Lawson. The beating she has received has damaged her body. It has to heal and fight the infection of the fever... That is a tall task in her current state.'

'What can I do?' She needed to do something.

'Keep her comfortable. Ideally, if we could get her to take some broth that would be beneficial.' He packed away his instruments. 'I've a bone to set and a birth to attend, then I'll return.'

'Thank you.' She walked with him downstairs and into the kitchen where Mrs Aspall was placing beef bones into a large pot.

Once the doctor had left, Caroline wasn't sure what to do next.

'I'm making some broth, lass.' Mrs Aspall said, stirring the bones. 'Howard drinks a cup of it every day and we're running low. I expect Doctor Pike says to give it to Trixie?'

'Yes.' Caroline poured fresh water into a jug. 'I shouldn't have brought her out in this weather. The journey here was too much, but I wanted us to be safe.'

'You did what you thought was best. No one can blame you for that. You said you couldn't stay in York. What other option did you have but to come home?'

Caroline could hear Elsie talking in the parlour. How would she ever face those two girls if something happened to Trixie, and it was her fault?

'Elsie is reading, bless her. I showed the girls the parlour when we took some wood in for the fire. Elsie spotted the newspaper and said she'd read it to Bertha.' Mrs Aspall grinned. 'There she is reading advertisements about soap or ironmongery to Bertha who sat and listened. I was astounded.'

Caroline smiled with love for them. 'They've been going to Sunday School, and I've been teaching them as much as I could when not working. Elsie is a keen learner, Bertha not so much.'

'This house owns no books of any interest except farming manuals, I know I've looked.' Mrs Aspall chuckled. 'I'll see what books I have at home and bring them here. There's a Sunday School held in the village as you know. I can take the girls there this Sunday before church.'

'That'll give them something to look forward too. Elsie is rather bright. She'll benefit from it.'

'And it gets them out under your feet while you nurse Trixie back to health.'

Caroline spent the next few hours bathing Trixie's hot flushed body. Mrs Aspall brought a fresh nightgown up, one of her own, and they stripped the damp sheets and changed the bed. Caroline tried to get Trixie to sip cooled boiled water but most of it dribbled down her chin.

It was late in the evening when Doctor Pike returned. He declared Trixie no worse nor no better. He said he'd be back in the morning. Caroline kept vigil by Trixie's bed, delicately wiping her damaged face and begging her to wake up, but the fever held Trixie in a tight grip.

As the sun went down, Caroline stood at the window and watched it dip below the fields on the horizon. With a start, she realised that she'd not heard the cows or sheep, or any of the animals.

She left the bedroom and knocked on Howard's door. He was sat up in bed, sipping soup.

'How is your friend, lass?' he asked, biting into a slice of bread and butter, the bread the girls had helped make.

'The same.' She stepped closer to the bed. 'Howard, I can't hear any of the animals.'

'That's because there aren't any.' He gave a small cough.

Shocked, she stared at him. 'Where are they?'

'Leo took them when I became ill.'

'Took them?'

'Well, yes. He said he didn't want to keep travelling between the two farms to see to them all. I couldn't expect Annie to care for them, she has enough on her plate with everything else.'

'But the animals are your income.' She felt it wrong to discuss money, which wasn't really any of her business, but if Hopewood Farm was to become her, Trixie and the girls' home, she needed to know they had a future here.

'I've always had some money set aside for bad times. I gave Leo money to pay the rent for this quarter. I've money for the next quarter, too.' He nodded to the set of drawers next to the window. 'There's a money tin in the bottom drawer.'

Deflated at the news of the farm being empty, Caroline couldn't keep the upset from her voice. 'I had hoped to help you with the farm, to earn my keep. There won't be many positions available in the village for me to earn money.'

'Lass, listen to me. Leo is taking care of the stock. Come spring I might be on my feet again and then you can help me get this farm back to how it used to be.'

She nodded, hoping it would be true.

Howard gave a smile. 'I had a thought that we could start the dairy side of things again. You had a decent dairy at Springwood, and my late wife had a good concern going when our lads were younger. Lisette couldn't turn her hand to the dairy shed and it's been neglected for years, but you could do it again, couldn't you?'

She nodded eagerly, hearing the positive note in his tone. 'I could. We'll need some good milking cows.'

'Well then, that's a plan for the spring.' He glanced out of the window where the rain pitted against the glass. 'I'm looking forward to the warm weather.'

'Me, too.' Caroline squeezed his hand. 'It's a new year in a few days and a new start for all of us.'

'In the morning, bring those little girls to me. I want to see them and get to know them.'

'I will.' She left him and went back to Trixie. Mrs Aspall was refilling the water bowl with fresh warm water.

'The girls are having supper.' Mrs Aspall told her. 'I'll bring you up a cup of tea shortly.'

'I'll come and get it, Mrs Aspall. You've been on your feet all day.'

'I like to be busy.' She paused by the door. 'Tomorrow, I need to go home and finish setting a few boxes of candles for the market on Thursday. I could take the girls with me, if you like? They could help me.'

'They will enjoy that.' Caroline sat on the chair beside the bed and once more began to wipe Trixie's hot face.

'The girls have been asking about their sister.'

'I have no news to tell them.' Caroline willed Trixie to turn a corner and open her eyes, beat the fever.

Throughout the night, Caroline administered water between Trixie's cracked and dry lips. Sometimes Trixie took it, nearly choking, other times it trickled down the side of her mouth. While Trixie ebbed in and out of sleep, Caroline kept the fire going, tidied the bedsheets, paced the floor or napped on the chair, before waking to bathe Trixie's face and neck once more.

She thought a lot about Mussy, still a little annoyed with him for not coming with them or telling her the truth about his past. What was he doing now? Her mind flittered to Mrs Warburton, and she hoped the old woman would soon find another maid to look after her.

By dawn, Caroline was numb with fatigue. She felt she hadn't slept for more than a few hours together since Christmas Eve. Her scalp itched from the lack of washing, her eyes were gritty with tiredness. The state of her creased clothes and the staleness of her own body scent disturbed her. She longed for a bath. Something she'd not had since leaving her own farm in September.

A tap on the door brought her head up where it rested on her folded arms on the bed. She smiled at Mrs Aspall who carried a cup of tea.

'I thought you could do with a cup before breakfast.'

'You are wonderful,' Caroline praised her, standing up to stretch her body before taking the cup.

'No change?'

'No.' Caroline gazed down at Trixie who for once lay still without moaning or moving about in the heat of the fever.

'She looks better. Not as hot.' Mrs Aspall peered closer, placing a hand on Trixie's forehead.

'That's cold!' Trixie unexpectedly mumbled.

Mrs Aspall jumped back as if scalded.

'Trix?' Alarmed, Caroline put her cup on the bedside table. 'Trixie?'

'Why are you shouting?' Trixie murmured, eyes still closed.

Tears sprang to Caroline's eyes, and she gripped her friend's hands, that were still a little too warm, but at least Trixie had woken. 'Your fever has broken.'

'Can I sleep now?' Trixie pouted. 'You're too noisy, Caro.'

Smiling through her tears, Caroline kissed Trixie's hands. 'Go to sleep, dearest.'

'You should do the same, lass,' Mrs Aspall suggested. 'I'll take the girls with me, and Howard is fine reading a farmer's journal. Go and get a few hours kip.'

With a last look at Trixie sleeping peacefully, Caroline went across the landing to the room the girls had been sleeping in and fell onto the bed fully dressed. She didn't even have the time to think of anything as exhaustion closed her eyes.

When Caroline woke, hours later, she felt disorientated and lay for a moment to gather her bearings. She'd slept heavily and a glance at the little clock on the mantlepiece showed it to be four in the afternoon. It took an effort to climb from the bed and more sleep would have been nice, but she went across the landing, needing to see Trixie.

'You're awake.' She smiled happily, see Trixie propped up with pillows. 'How do you feel?'

'Battered, weak, but alive. That's the best I can hope for at the minute.' The bruising on Trixie's face was turning darker in shades of blue and purple. The swelling was easing, but movement still caused her pain from her ribs.

'Help me use the pot.' Trixie winced sitting up, holding her ribs. 'This must be how old people feel when their bodies stop working. Everything is a struggle.'

'You'll be back to normal soon. You're young and you'll heal.'

'That's what Doctor Pike said an hour ago.'

'Oh, he's been again?' Caroline took the pot out from under the bed for Trixie to use and then helped her to slip back into bed and arranged the blankets around her waist.

'He believes time and rest will heal me.' Trixie folded her hands over the blankets. 'Mrs Aspall seems nice enough.'

'She is.'

'She brought me up a bowl of soup and bread. Apparently, our Elsie and Bertha helped bake the bread.'

'Yes, that's true.'

Trixie's eyes grew thoughtful. 'Can we stay here?'

'Yes. Howard is in full agreement of us living here.'

'Does he know about me?'

'He knows enough. No one needs to know what work you did if you don't want them to know. We'll tell them you worked as a barmaid.'

Relaxing against the pillows, Trixie sighed. 'Yes. That's all we'll say.'

'Do you remember what happened when you were attacked?'

Trixie pushed away the tray. 'I don't want to talk about it.'

'Victor left you for dead in a woodshed.'

'He didn't do the worst of it. His men did. Victor hit me once, I'm a relative after all, to teach me a lesson.'

'How kind of him!' Caroline fumed, taking the tray and placing it on the bedside table. 'His men could have killed you. You would have been dead if I hadn't found you.'

'That's probably what Victor wanted. I'd messed about in his business.' Trixie looked at Caroline. 'Victor said a beating was the least I could get for ruining his plans. He warned me that if he saw me again, he'd take the girls and sell them to a brothel.'

'He won't find us here,' Caroline said with determination.

'Maybe not. But we can never go to York again.'

'That's fine by me.'

'We'll have to go somewhere else to find work.'

Caroline jerked. 'Somewhere else? Why? We can stay here, I just told you Howard is happy for us to stay.'

'And what work will I do in a village?' Trixie scoffed tiredly.

'You'll help us on the farm.'

'Are you mad?' Trixie closed her eyes with a long sigh. 'I know nothing about animals or farm work.'

'I'll teach you and the girls.'

Trixie pulled the blankets up over her chest. 'This is all very different to what I know, Caro. What if I don't like being in the country?'

'We'll face that if it happens. Promise me you'll give it a try though, please?' Caroline begged. 'Anything has to be better than what you did before, surely?'

Trixie turned her head away. 'We'll see, won't we?'

Chapter Sixteen

The new year of eighteen fifty-three rolled in with days of wild wind and rain, which turned the ice and snow into slush and the roads into muddy bogs. Hopewood Farm became isolated where it sat in the fold of a hill two miles from the village. The stream at the bottom of the home field flowed fast and the drinking well filled with ice cold water. Elsie and Bertha found it amazing to have fresh water whenever they wanted. No queuing at the pumps in the Water Lanes as they were used to; a pump that was only turned on for a limited time each day. At the farm, all they had to do was carry the buckets down to the well.

Mrs Aspall took Elsie and Bertha to the market with her each week throughout January, where they learned to sell her candles to customers, and every Sunday, she accompanied them to Sunday School and church.

With the girls content, Caroline spent most of her time with Trixie or Howard. Both of whom were becoming stronger and leaving their beds for longer periods each day.

On the first clear sunny day in mid-February, Caroline helped Trixie and then Howard downstairs to sit in the kitchen. The back door was open to a fresh breeze that didn't have an icy bite to it. The touch of spring was coming. Snowdrops bloomed white in the two garden beds on either side of the door along with the yellow buds of early daffodils. Birds chirped on the roofs of the house and barns and in the small orchard, tiny buds swelled in anticipation of warmer weather to come.

'We'll all catch our deaths with that door open,' Mrs Aspall said to Caroline. 'It's not spring yet.'

'No, but it's the best day we've had since we arrived, and I want to start airing out the cottage.' Caroline said, scrubbing the floor.

'It's too early for spring cleaning.' Mrs Aspall tutted where she stood at the table cutting round scones. As usual, Bertha stood on a stool beside her, helping, for cooking had become Bertha's passion. Whereas Elsie was content to read and draw and venture outside at any excuse to wander the empty barns and play down by the stream.

'I can help clean,' Trixie said, sipping the tea Mrs Aspall had poured for them all.

Caroline gave her a warning look. 'None of that nonsense, thank you. You might be out of bed, but your ribs are still sore.'

'I feel useless just sitting here watching you work.'

Howard snorted and lowered the newspaper he was reading. 'I know what you mean.' He looked at Caroline. 'I need to visit Leo. It's time the animals came home.'

'You can't walk to Springwood Farm.' Caroline emptied the bucket of dirty water in the scullery sink. 'I'll go.'

'Is that wise?' Howard frowned. 'You and he never got on.'

'No one gets on with Leo,' Mrs Aspall commented, putting the tray of scones into the range oven. 'I'll send him a note on Thursday when I'm at the market, unless I see him or Lisette on the day, but they weren't at the market last week that I saw.'

Caroline swept the doorstep and noticed a rider coming along the village road and turn into the dirt track leading to the cottage. 'Someone is coming.'

'Leo?' Howard asked with relief in his voice.

Caroline squinted in the sunshine. 'No, it's not Leo, unless he's lost a lot of weight?'

'Not the last time I saw him,' Mrs Aspall tutted. 'As wide as a bull, he is.'

The rider dismounted and Caroline untied her apron and went out to meet him with Howard close behind her using a stick as a cane that Elsie had found for him on her many jaunts to the woodland.

'I don't know him,' Howard wheezed, his breathing laboured from taking only a dozen or so steps.

'He might be lost.' Caroline smiled at the stranger as he walked towards them, leaving his horse to graze beside the drive. The man was taller than average and dressed in tailored tweeds of expensive quality.

'Good morning,' the stranger said, his well-bred voice held a slight trace of the Yorkshire accent. 'Mr Howard Lawson?'

'I am.' Howard frowned. 'Do I know you, sir?'

The man held out his hand for Howard to shake. 'Maxwell Cavendish. I'm the new estate steward for Lord Stockton-Lee.'

'New? What happened to Mr Craven?' Howard seemed surprised by the news.

'He retired.' Mr Cavendish supplied, then glanced at Caroline and tipped his hat. 'Madam.'

'This is my daughter-in-law, Caroline Lawson,' Howard made the introductions.'

'Not your son, Leo's wife?' Mr Cavendish frowned in confusion.

'No, not Leo's wife. My younger son, Hugh was married to Caroline. He passed away last year.'

'Ah, yes. He tenanted Springwood Farm.' Mr Cavendish gave Caroline another look from eyes as blue as the sky above their heads.

'Will you come inside, Mr Cavendish and have some tea?' Caroline remembered her manners at last. This stranger had a way about him that disturbed her senses. Not only that, he was the new estate steward and they had to tread cautiously around him. On his say, they could either lose the farm or be given a helping hand, depending on what type of gentleman he was.

'Thank you.' Cavendish followed them into the kitchen. He nodded to the others, smiling at the girls.

Mrs Aspall already had the kettle boiling and fresh tea leaves in the teapot. Howard made the introductions to everyone and then sat heavily in the chair by the fire. 'So, Mr Cavendish, are you here to inspect the farm?'

'I am, but also to clear up some questions I have.' Maxwell Cavendish sat at the table in an easy manner, though his handsome face was unreadable, his blue eyes watchful.

Howard gripped the chair arms. 'Which are?'

'My information is that you currently have no animals stocked on the land.'

'That's true. Since my illness my son, Leo, has taken them to Springwood Farm to care for them there.'

'Part of your tenancy agreement is to have the land stocked at all times, or under cultivation.' Cavendish accepted a cup of tea from Mrs Aspall. 'Or how else are you to pay your rent?'

'I have money for my rent.' Howard bristled. 'My animals will be brought back to this farm now I'm up and about again and Caroline is here to help me.'

'Mr Lawson, I am a fair man, and new to the workings of this estate, but my uncle has given me full rein of all accounts and ledgers going back years. I have been researching—'

'You're Lord Stockton-Lee's nephew?' Howard interrupted.

'On his wife's side, yes.' Cavendish sipped his tea, his gaze direct. 'The ledger reads that you didn't pay your rent last quarter.'

Howard jolted in his chair. 'Not paid! That's a lie! I gave my son the money to pay it to Mr Craven. There has been a mistake.'

'That is what your son says, too.' Cavendish said, yet his tone belied his belief in the statement.

'You've spoken to Leo?'

'Briefly, in the village this morning. He was making his way from the stables at the Fox and Hound. A rough night sleeping in the inn's hayloft apparently...' Cavendish shrugged. 'Your son didn't seem inclined to converse with me. His language left a lot to be desired.'

'It would be if you accused him of not paying my rent.'

'Not just yours, but his as well.'

Caroline gasped. Damn Leo. Hugh had always paid their rent and she knew Howard did as well. What was her brother-in-law playing at?

Howard sat in stunned silence for a moment, frowning. 'Are you sure he did this?'

Cavendish nodded. 'Mr Craven left a note beside the rent entries in the ledger. Both this farm and Springwood Farm had the note stating rent not paid due to illness. Double rent due next quarter.'

'I shall speak to my son.' Spots of angry colour appeared on Howard's cheeks. 'I have this quarter's rent money upstairs, shall I get it for you now?'

'No, Mr Lawson.' Cavendish stood, his shoulders relaxing. 'I'll call again in a day or two and we'll discuss it more then. First, I need to speak to your son when he is not under the effects of liquor.'

'I apologise for him.' Howard pulled himself up to his feet. 'We Lawsons pay our debts, Mr Cavendish.'

'I believe *you*, Mr Lawson.' Cavendish replaced his hat on his head. 'But I would fail in my duty to not inform you that should the rent be left unpaid and that the farm isn't stocked or the land tilled, then I'll have no choice but to inform Lord Stockton-Lee and he may not be as lenient as you hope.'

'It won't come to that,' Caroline said suddenly, making Cavendish look at her. She raised her chin in challenge. 'The rent will be paid and the animals back on this farm before the month is out.'

He studied her for a long moment. 'I'll be glad to see it, Mrs Lawson.' Cavendish bowed and left the kitchen.

Caroline stood in the doorway and watched him mount. He raised his hand to her and rode away.

'Goodness,' Mrs Aspall said. 'What a lot to take in. A new steward, and a mighty good looking one at that, and now this news about Leo.'

'I need to see Leo.' Howard stepped toward the scullery where the coats and hats were kept.

'You'll never make it that far,' Caroline said. 'I'll go.'

'We need Dossy back.' Howard grumbled.

'Dossy?' Trixie asked with raised eyebrows.

'My horse. I need to have the horse and cart. We can't live out here without them.' Howard tapped his thigh in frustration and then had a bout of coughing.

'Go upstairs and rest,' Caroline soothed him. 'I'll speak to Leo.'

'I'll go with you,' Trixie said to Caroline.

'You aren't up to it.'

'I am. I can walk a few miles.' Trixie looked down at herself. 'I've put weight on with all this sitting around eating good food.'

It was true. Caroline could see the change in Trixie. As she slowly healed, the nourishing food had filled out her gaunt face a little. Her skinny body didn't look as skeletal as it had done in the Water Lanes. Trixie had also become more at ease, not as tense as she used to be. Being away from the slums and the nightly work she endured, and for once being cared for allowed her to be less prickly. The girls too had benefited from the solid food. They'd both grown an inch it seemed, and Mrs Aspall mentioned the need to let down the hems of their dresses.

'I'll be fine.' Caroline said, tying on her bonnet. She glanced at Howard. 'I'll tell Leo you wish to speak to him urgently so that he comes back with me.'

'Thanks, lass. If he's busy with lambing, then tell him to come as soon as he can.'

She set off with a determined step, cutting across the fields to take the shorter route to Springwood, a way she'd gone so many times in the past. She retraced the walk she'd done with her arm through Hugh's whenever they visited Howard. Memories came rushing back as she walked through the wet fields, her heart full of love for Hugh. Most times they took the cart, but sometimes in fine weather she liked to walk the fields with Hugh, and he'd inspect the sheep or cows as they went, pointing out to her new spring lambs or bird nests. He'd show her the traps he set to catch rabbits or the large holes the badgers made.

Soon her boots were covered in mud and also the hem of her skirt, but she didn't care. For the first time in many months, she felt she could breathe without the pain of deep grief or the fear she felt living in York. This is where she belonged.

She leapt from one steppingstone to the other across the stream, the same stones that Hugh had played on as a boy. On the other side she was on Springwood Farm, her old home, the one place she'd felt such contentment and peace. How would it feel going back to her and Hugh's cottage? Resentment, or that awful feeling of loss?

But as she walked, she noticed signs of neglect and grew concerned. The bottom field was boggy, the drainage Hugh had dug was clogged with mud and debris. A part of a dry-stone wall had collapsed, and she noticed a lone cow in the adjacent field, which bellowed at her mournfully. It wasn't Buttercup or Clover. Where was Hugh's herd, or her two milking cows? Where was Howard's herd?

Closer to the barns, the disrepair became more visible. The hen house roof had fallen in, but chickens still pecked about inside. The barn door lay lopsided, off its top hinge and several shingles were missing from the stable roof. Weeds grew between the cobbles in the yard and a thin mangy cat stalked the top of the kitchen garden wall.

Whiffs of smoke escaped the chimney, showing some sign of life, but the yard was eerily quiet. Caroline took a deep breath, readying herself to face the two people who'd she'd never liked, and knocked loudly on the back door.

A noise came from within, and the door was yanked open. Lisette's features twisted with loathing as she stared at Caroline. 'It's you. I heard you were back. I hope you're not staying long.'

'Good day, Lisette.' Caroline ignored her rudeness. 'I've come to speak with Leo.' She was shocked at Lisette's unkempt appearance. The woman might have been lazy and demanding in the past, but she always dressed well. Yet now, Lisette wore a stained bodice and a dirty skirt. Her black hair lay in a tangled mess about her shoulders.

'He's not home.'

Snoring came from the other side of the door. Caroline lifted a wry eyebrow at her sister-in-law. 'Howard needs to see him immediately.'

'I'll tell him when he wakes.' Lisette went to close the door in her face.

Caroline jammed her boot in the door. 'It's the middle of the day. Wake him. This is important.'

'You don't get to tell me what to do.' Lisette's stale breath wafted over Caroline. 'You're nothing to this family anymore.'

'Howard thinks differently.' Angered by Lisette's nastiness, Caroline pushed open the door and stepped inside the kitchen. The state of the untidy room, *her* lovely room she'd cleaned and polished hours a day, shocked her. Used plates and cups covered every surface. Newspapers lay strewn across a floor that hadn't been scrubbed in a long time, probably not since Caroline left. The window was grimy, darkening the room. The cooking range was dull from lack of black leading, and the fireplace grate heaped with ashes. Smoke puffed back down the chimney to rise like a cloud near the ceiling. The whole room was bare and without any of the nice pieces Caroline had decorated the cottage with.

'Leo!' Lisette kicked her husband's feet where he sat before the dull fire in what used to be Hugh's chair. 'Leo!'

Emotion rushed to Caroline's throat, nearly choking her. She was furious at the state of her old home, but also utterly sad that all her dear memories were being eroded by the sight of those two horrible people living in what had been her happy place.

Leo snorted, then coughed, hawking up a mouthful of spit which he directed into the fire. He glared at Lisette. 'You stupid witch. Why have you woken me?'

'Because I told her to.' Caroline came into his view. 'Howard needs you. It's urgent.'

Leo gave her a filthy stare. 'Why did you have to come back, hey? Go back to where you came from!'

'Your father needs to speak to you.' Caroline wouldn't back down, not to him. Once she would have, but months of living rough in the Water Lanes, witnessing all she had, gave her a newfound strength of character. She was sick and tired of being swept aside as though she didn't matter, that she was less than worthy.

She squared up to the large brute. '*And* as to where I came from? I came from *here!* This house! This *farm* I shared with my *husband* who was a better man than *you'll* ever hope to be. Now get up and get Dossy harnessed, or I'll take the poker to you, so help me God!'

Both Leo and Lisette stared at her as if she had two heads. They'd never seen her angry or heard her raise her voice and the shock of it rendered them mute.

'What are you waiting for?' she shouted.

Leo shook himself like a dog in the rain and blinked a few times.

Suddenly, Lisette grabbed Caroline's arm and pulled her sharply out of the door. 'Get away from here!' She slammed the door in Caroline's face.

Stunned by her own rage and Lisette shoving her out of the cottage, Caroline swore a terrible word she'd heard the men use in the lanes. She sucked in a deep breath. A fleeting idea of marching back inside came and went. Going back in there wouldn't work. Those two would do as they pleased.

A horse's snicker came from the stable. Dossy.

Lifting her skirts high, she dashed across the yard to the stable and brought Dossy out of her stall. 'There's a good girl.' She rubbed her nose and led her to the other side of the stable where a small gig stood. Caroline looked for the correct harness hanging on the wall and hurriedly selected what she needed. She kept glancing at the cottage for any sign of Leo as she worked to secure the leather straps on Dossy. She thanked the fates that Hugh had taught her how to harness a horse to a cart, for there were times when she'd gone into the village while he worked in the fields, and she'd taken the gig instead of the large farm cart.

Hurrying as fast as she could, she coerced Dossy backwards into the gig's shafts and buckled the final straps. Nervously, she gathered the reins and climbed aboard. Dossy was Howard's horse, not her sweet-natured Belle, where she might be Caroline couldn't guess. However, she had no time to think about it as she clicked her tongue and urged Dossy out of the wide barn and down the drive.

Once on the road to the village, Caroline let out a yell of triumph that frightened Dossy, who side-stepped a little. 'Steady, girl, that's it,' Caroline soothed, turning off the village road and onto the track leading up to Hopewood Farm.

She couldn't wipe the grin off her face at her small victory. Leo would be livid, but Howard had a right to use his own horse and it would give them transport into the village instead of walking.

Elsie and Bertha helped her to clear out the stable of old straw and replace it with some fresher straw piled in the barn. The girls didn't complain as Caroline issued instructions, showing them how to properly care for the horse and explaining why.

Howard slowly walked across the yard to rub Dossy's nose. He listened as Caroline told him what happened.

'I don't know my son anymore.' He sighed heavily. 'Hugh would be disappointed in his brother for neglecting your farm.' Howard's eyes saddened. 'To not pay the rent... and it seems as though he hasn't, doesn't it? All the animals are gone. Why? I can't understand it.'

'Leo's been neglecting you, too. He left your care solely to Mrs Aspall. What kind of son does that make him?' Caroline finally said the thoughts that had been plaguing her since she arrived.

'Not a good one...' Howard murmured, before turning to Elsie. 'There'll be some hay up in the loft, throw some down for Dossy.'

Elsie scrambled up the ladder, eager to please him, with Bertha content to stay on the ground and fork up the hay Elise tossed down. Howard showed the girls how to feed Dossy a bruised apple from the barrel in the cellar with an open palm while Caroline filled the water trough with fresh water.

'Thank you for bringing her back.' Howard rubbed Dossy's neck. 'She needs a good brush.'

'I'll do that tomorrow.'

'One animal on this farm... when it used to be full of livestock.'

'We'll get it back to how it was, I promise.' She patted Howard's arm. 'The farm will be thriving before you know it.'

'Someone is here.' Bertha pointed down the drive.

Through the wide, open barn doors, Caroline watched as Leo walked into the yard. He'd washed, his hair damp, and wore a clean shirt under his coat. She stood next to Howard, ready for a confrontation.

'Can we talk, Father?' Leo asked, hat in hand.

'We can.' Howard took Caroline's arm, and they walked back inside the kitchen.

Mrs Aspall was knitting in front of the fire, but stood as they came in. 'Trixie's gone up for a nap.'

Caroline gave her a brief smile. 'The girls are out in the barn.'

'I'll go and be with them.' Mrs Aspall gave Leo a sharp look and left.

Sitting at the table, the three of them waited for someone to speak first. Caroline refused to offer Leo some tea.

'This is between you and me, Father,' Leo muttered with annoyance, eyeing Caroline.

'Caroline stays. She's living here now and is family.'

Leo's lips thinned.

'Now, what's this I hear from the new estate steward that you've not paid the rent?' Howard's clipped words matched his direct gaze.

'I meant to...' Leo's head bowed.

'You know how important it is to not be in arrears!' Howard barked. 'Where's the money?'

'I've spent it.'

'On what?' Howard ground out. 'Or perhaps I should say where? Likely the Fox and Hound I'd wager.'

'On tickets.'

'Tickets?' His father scowled in confusion.

'Lisette and me are emigrating. To Canada.' Leo couldn't look at his father and kept his gaze on the table. 'The rent money bought the tickets for the voyage.'

'*Canada?*' Howard barely got the word out. 'You're leaving your home to travel to a distant country?'

'Aye.' Leo sighed. 'Lisette has several cousins over there and they're all doing well, farming or in some kind of industry in the new towns that are getting built all over the place. They're forever writing to her saying how good it is there.'

'You didn't think to tell me?'

'You weren't well enough. I... we... were waiting to see if you...'

'If I died?' Howard finished for him.

'Well, yes.'

'So, you could get whatever money I had, or even sell everything in this house?' Howard waved his arm to encompass the whole cottage. 'Just like you've sold my animals?'

'I'm your son, why wouldn't I have had it when you died?'

A spasm of pain etched Howard's features for a moment then was gone. 'Only I'm not dead, am I? Did I disappoint you?'

'Father, we were being respectful by waiting.'

'Really? I'd call it something else.' Howard shrugged. 'Nevertheless, you can go now. Go to Canada.'

Leo nodded. 'I'm glad I have your blessing.'

'You don't have my blessing, because you don't need it or care for it. However, bring what's left of my stock back before you go.'

Leo flushed and looked away.

Caroline knew the truth. 'You've sold everything, haven't you? Furniture and animals alike. Springwood is bare of anything of value. How could you do that to your father? To go behind his back, to sell his livelihood!' Caroline's estimation of Leo dropped to an even lower level.

Leo held up his hands. 'We had to! Father couldn't look after them and we didn't expect him to recover. We need as much capital as we can find for the journey and to start again in the new country.'

Rage burned in her. 'Yet *I* had to leave with *nothing!*'

'That was your choosing.'

'Because I had little other choice. You took all that away from me and for what? Six months later you're giving it all up? We could have worked both farms together if you'd been a decent person and put family first.'

'Me and Lisette need this new start.' Leo glared at Caroline. 'I'm not answerable to you. Who the hell do you think you are, anyway? You married my younger brother, but you carry on like you're a royal princess or something. You're nothing but a convent-raised brat who thinks she's better than everyone else because she's been educated! Hugh might have thought the sun shone out of your arse, but I don't!'

'Enough!' Howard banged his fist on the table. 'No more, Leo. Not another word. I can't tell you the disappointment I feel. You robbed me, left me with nothing. You're no son of mine.'

Leo grabbed his hat. 'I'm going and I'm bloody glad to be leaving this place. There's no future in this country!' At the door he paused and looked at his father. 'I'll come and say goodbye when we leave in a few days' time.' He slammed the door shut behind him.

Caroline reached for Howard's hand and held it.

He gave her a sad smile in return. 'We've got nothing, lass. They'll take the farm off us.'

Caroline's stomach twisted at the thought. 'No, I won't let that happen. We will fight for it.'

Chapter Seventeen

After the argument with Leo, Howard withdrew to his room and his appetite faded. Caroline cursed Leo several times a day as she thought of ideas to get Howard's enthusiasm back, but he wasn't interested and said the farm was lost.

She refused to believe it and sat late into the night with Trixie and Mrs Aspall discussing new plans.

'I think you should speak with the new estate steward,' Mrs Aspall said one night as they sat up drinking hot chocolate, a rare treat that Trixie and the girls had never experienced before and thought it was the best drink they'd ever tasted.

'No.' Caroline baulked at that idea. 'He has a duty to do and that's to have tenants who pay their rent and farm the land. We're doing neither at the moment, and it'll give him more reason to get rid of us.'

'Where will we get money from though?' Trixie asked, blowing to cool the hot drink.

Caroline tapped her fingers on the table. 'Howard has money upstairs for next quarter's rent.'

'That still makes us behind because last quarter wasn't paid.' Mrs Aspall added wood to the fire. 'And we have to buy animals.'

Grabbing a piece of paper and a pencil that Elsie had been using earlier, Caroline began to write. 'We need milking cows to get the dairy up and running to sell butter and cream at the market. Hens for eggs. Sheep for wool and meat. Pigs for meat and breeding to sell piglets.'

'Add geese.' Mrs Aspall pointed to the paper. 'For meat and feathers. They keep the foxes away, too.'

'Seed potatoes and other vegetable seeds.' Caroline continued. 'I'll plough the bottom field with vegetables and the top field with hay as we'll need feed for next winter.'

'Ploughing?' Trixie blinked in surprise. 'That's man's work.'

'Not on this farm it isn't, not anymore.' Caroline read the list, her heart sinking at the cost to restock the farm. It seemed an impossible task.

'That's a lot, lass,' Mrs Aspall folded her arms, her expression unreadable.

'I'll talk to Howard. We could go to the bank and ask for a loan.'

'A loan?' Mrs Aspall's eyebrows rose almost to her hairline. 'They'll not give loans for a few animals and vegetable seeds.'

'They might.' Caroline left the table and went up to Howard.

In his bed, he lay with his eyes closed, the room lit by a single lantern and the glow from the fire. 'Howard?' she whispered, not wanting to wake him if he was asleep.

'I'm awake.' He opened his eyes, but they were dull with no spark of interest in them.

'I've been thinking. We could go to one of the banks in York and ask for a loan.'

'No, lass.' Howard reached for her hand. 'I'm too old for loans. We have to face it, the farm is lost.'

She sat on the edge of the bed. 'Don't give up. We can fight for it, together.'

'I don't have the strength, daughter.'

'Find it, find the strength for me!'

He shook his head. 'Sell up everything you can in the house and ask Annie if you can all go and live with her in the village until you can find some place to work. She won't mind.'

Caroline stood and turned away. 'I can't do that, not without trying.'

'Leo has lost it all, lass. He's taken it all.'

'Once before Leo took everything I had, I'll not let him do it again.' She clenched her fists in anger. 'I haven't survived the slums of York to come home to nothing, Howard. There has to be a way. We just need money to buy the animals, the seeds to plough.'

She paced the floor, an idea germinating until she stopped and smiled. 'I have a plan.'

'Whatever it is you're wasting your time, lass.' Howard closed his eyes.

Caroline raced downstairs and into the kitchen making Mrs Aspall and Trixie turn to her. 'In the morning I'm going to York, to visit Mrs Warburton. I'll ask her for a loan.'

Trixie's face paled. 'No, Caro. Not York. We have to stay away from there. What if Victor sees you?'

'Can't you send her a letter?' Mrs Aspall asked.

'It's too important to put in a letter. Mrs Warburton would rather I asked her in person, I know she would, and I need the answer fast.'

'Would she want you to put yourself in danger?' Trixie pushed back her chair, annoyed. 'We got away. We're safe. Why would you go back there?'

'Because we have no other option.'

'If it's as dangerous as you say, then I'll come with you.' Mrs Aspall gave Caroline a direct look that meant no argument.

'Thank you, Mrs Aspall,' Trixie answered quickly. 'If Caro is determined to go, then she can't go alone.'

The next morning, Caroline woke early and harnessed Dossy to the gig. She embraced Trixie who was still uncertain the plan was a good one.

'This time it'll be different, Trixie. I'm driving with Mrs Aspall. I'll stable Dossy in Stonegate and walk straight to Mrs Warburton's home. I'll see her and then drive straight back home again. I'm not going anywhere near the Water Lanes.'

'Make sure you don't.' Trixie still bore the evidence of their time in York, with sore ribs and recently suffering nightmares that woke Caroline.

'We'll be back before dark.'

The long drive to York gave Caroline time to run through her proposition to Mrs Warburton. Her stomach did a flip at the idea of being in York again, but she had to push that from her mind. Saving the farm was too important and she couldn't give into her fear of returning.

As planned, she drove them straight into the outskirts of York, along The Mount, passing Greenleigh House, and Caroline couldn't help but sigh in relief that she didn't end up spending the rest of her life as a scullery maid.

They crossed the bridge over the River Ouse and turned left to follow the streets towards Stonegate. Driving Dossy through the crowded noisy streets took all of her concentration. Dossy threw her head whenever a wagon or carriage came too close in the narrow streets. Caroline spoke calmly to her but the disturbance of so many people and loud sounds meant the horse baulked at the slightest movement.

Eventually, they made it to Stonegate and the stables where Caroline had hired the carriage to take them to the farm. It felt like a lifetime ago and not just six weeks.

'Here we are.' Caroline walked past Mrs McCarthy's hat shop and knocked on the door leading up to the flat. She knocked again after a minute, wondering if Mrs Warburton had found a new maid, if not, it would be doubtful the old lady would even hear the knock.

'She might be out shopping?' Mrs Aspall said, looking up and down the cobbles.

'Mrs Warburton didn't go shopping. She ordered other people to do it.' Suddenly, Caroline missed the old woman, even her harsh words, the waving of her cane. For all her brusqueness, she'd been patient with Caroline and helpful when she needed her the most.

Caroline tried the door handle, but it was locked. She knocked again.

Mrs McCarthy came out of her shop, a shocked expression on her face, her glasses hanging by a ribbon around her neck. 'Caroline?'

'Mrs McCarthy. How are you?' Caroline walked over to her.

'I'm fine, busy, but fine.' She glanced at Mrs Aspall and then at the locked door.

'I need to see Mrs Warburton, but I don't think she can hear me knocking.'

'No, she can't.' McCarthy's shoulders sagged. 'We buried her last week.'

The words hit Caroline like a slap. 'She died?'

'Yes. She was fine one minute and gone the next. After you left, she had a girl come in a few hours a week, but she wasn't very good, and Agatha became low in spirit. She missed you. I tried to go in everyday to see how she was. I visited Agatha on the Monday evening, and we had a little chat as we normally do, mostly Agatha complained about the girl and how she wasn't as capable as you were. Then Tuesday morning the girl came screaming into the shop saying she'd found her dead on the floor.'

'I can't believe it.' Sadness filled Caroline. Mrs Warburton gone, dying alone with no one to give her comfort.

Mrs McCarthy raised her hand to a customer entering her shop and turned back to Caroline. 'If I'd known where you'd gone,

I'd have written to let you know so you could have come to the funeral.'

'Her sons must be devastated.'

'Aye, they are. They buried her next to her husband and her son, Douglas.'

'May she rest in peace now,' Caroline murmured.

'I shall miss her, as cranky as she was most times.' Mrs McCarthy clasped a hand over Caroline's. 'Anyway, I'd best get back inside. Call in any time for a chat.'

Caroline nodded, full of sorrow. Mrs Warburton was gone, which was awful enough but now Caroline had no one to ask for money.

'We'd best go home,' Mrs Aspall said.

'No. I need to see Bob Warburton.' Caroline strode down Little Stonegate.

'Lass!' Mrs Aspall hurried after her. 'Is that wise? Trixie said not to go anywhere else, to go straight home.'

'I shall pay my respects, and he might have word of Mussy.' She longed to know how Mussy was doing.

'Write a letter!' Mrs Aspall pleaded.

Caroline slowed and linked her arms with Mrs Aspall. 'Victor will know by now we have left the Water Lanes, he'll not be looking for me or Trixie. Besides, it's the middle of the day and we are together. Nothing will happen for Victor haunts these streets at night not in the middle of the day.'

Mrs Aspall shivered. 'Just be quick. I want to go home. I've a terrible dislike for cities.'

'Me, too.' Caroline quickened her footsteps but detoured to the Shambles first and stopped outside of Bent's Butchers. She studied the meat hanging on hooks.

'Now's not the time to buy some meat,' Mrs Aspall whispered, looking about the narrow lane as though they'd be attacked at any minute.

'Butchers buy meat as well as sell it...' Caroline murmured, an idea forming.

Mr Bent saw her through the shop's open display and grinned as he came out to her. 'Mrs Lawson. I never expected to see you again.'

'How are you, Mr Bent?'

'Well, lass, well, and you?'

'Actually, I'm in a bit of a situation which I would like to talk to you about. Do you have a few minutes spare?'

'Aye, lass, come inside and out the back to the office.'

Mrs Aspall eyed Caroline as though she'd lost her mind.

In the cramped office, Mr Bent turned to Caroline. 'We can go upstairs if you'd prefer for some tea? There are no chairs in here but my desk chair.'

'I don't need to sit down.' Caroline put him at ease, but her mind worked frantically to gather her scrambled thoughts. 'I'll get straight to it, Mr Bent. My farm needs some stock on it. I don't have the money to buy the beasts. So, I would like to put a business proposition to you, Mr Bent.'

'Oh, aye?' He seemed interested, yet also surprised.

'If you were to buy a herd of cattle and a flock of sheep, I would breed and fatten them up on my farm. You would take a percentage of the beasts for your shop and to pay off some of the initial investment and I'd take some to market and keep the rest to breed with. We'd split the profits eighty-twenty.'

He frowned in thought.

'Sixty-forty,' a woman's voice came from the doorway. Mrs Bent stood there, her face stern, arms folded.

Caroline knew who ran this business and knew who was the backbone behind the friendly and kind Mr Bent. Caroline faced the other woman. 'Seventy-thirty. I will have to feed and care for the beasts more months.'

'Done.' Mrs Bent held out her hand and Caroline shook it. 'Once the initial investment is paid back, we want first refusal of any beasts going to market and we get to pay a discounted price.'

'Agreed.'

'Write down your address and I'll have our solicitor draw up the contract.' Mrs Bent scowled. 'I want it done all proper mind. There will be consequences if you fail to fatten the beasts to a suitable standard for our butchery, understand?'

'I understand and I'll sign the contract.'

'Charles and me will go to the next cattle market and select the animals we think are worth the money. I'll hire a drover to take them to your farm.' Mrs Bent's eyes narrowed at Caroline. 'We'll come out and check the quality of your farm's fields. If we find them not fit for purpose, we'll take the beasts back and you'll repay us all the costs.'

'Agreed.' Caroline's heart was beating fast.

'Write down how many cattle and sheep you need.' Mrs Bent found a piece of paper and a pen. 'We aren't your friends, remember, this is business.'

'Purely business, Mrs Bent.' Caroline wrote down all that was required and when she straightened Charles winked at her and she smiled at him while his wife scrutinised the list.

Mrs Aspall let out a long breath as they left Bent's Butchers. 'My God, lass! You're a marvel and no mistake. What made you do that?'

'It just came to me.' Caroline grinned, feeling excited and relieved all at once. 'Who else is better to do business with than a butcher who needs meat? Mr Bent was so nice to me while I was living here. I thought it worth the gamble to ask and I honestly thought he'd probably say no, but it was worth trying.'

'And it worked. His wife though?' Mrs Aspall huffed as they walked along. 'She has a face like she's just chewed a wasp!'

Caroline laughed. It felt so good to laugh. It had been too long since she had.

At the pub, Caroline walked inside, encouraging Mrs Aspall to do the same when she hesitated at the door saying she'd never entered a public house in her life.

A young barman was throwing fresh sawdust down on the floor, but stopped on seeing Caroline. 'Can I help you?'

'I wish to see Bob Warburton, please.'

'Aye, I'll fetch him.'

Caroline stood in the dim bar which always looked different in the daylight than at night when it was lit with golden gas lighting and held a cloud of smoke hovering beneath the ceiling. There were not many men sitting on stools during the day compared to an evening when the place was heaving with workers chatting and smoking, occasionally fighting.

She thought of Mussy, of all the times she'd met him here. Where was he now?

'Mrs Lawson!' Bob Warburton came along the passage, smiling. 'I didn't expect to see you back in here.'

'It's good to see you, Mr Warburton.' She shook his hand.

'Come through to the snug. Johnny fetch two glasses of cordial for the ladies,' he called to the young barman.

In the snug, more memories flooded back of Mussy. Caroline missed him, missed his cheeky grin, his flamboyant mannerisms, his charm, his friendship.

'How have you been?' Mr Warburton asked.

'I'm well, and this is Mrs Aspall, a friend.' Caroline made the introductions. 'I've just learned from Mrs McCarthy the news about your mother. I'm so sorry to hear it.'

'Ah, yes.' He reclined back on the bench, his face thoughtful. 'It was a shock to us, of course. Even at her great age, you are still never ready to lose a parent.'

'Mrs Warburton was kind to me when I needed it.'

'My mother was a paradox of a woman, but deep down had a warm heart. And she liked you. She felt your loss for sure.' He waited while Johnny brought in the two glasses of cordial. 'You are settled in the country? Mussy told me that was where you intended to go.'

Caroline winced. 'I am, but could I ask that you tell no one, please?'

'Aye, I know how to keep a secret, Mrs Lawson, never fear. Mussy told me what went on with you, your friend and that Dolan rat.'

'He nearly killed Trixie. She's only just back on her feet. She didn't want me to come to York, felt it was too unsafe, but I wanted to see your mother, and also ask her about a business loan.'

'Oh?' Bob Warburton grew interested. 'Would it be one that I might be interested in?'

Caroline told him the general details of the proposition she made with the Bents.

'Will that be enough for you to get the farm up and running again?'

'I hope so. We must pray we don't have any diseases affect the stock and that we have a good summer, for we'll be planting late and need to harvest decent crops in the autumn. We need to make enough money to last us next winter and then do it all again.'

'Wait here a moment.' He left them and returned within a few minutes. Sitting down, he passed Caroline a small leather pouch.

'What is this?'

'It's from Mussy,' Bob said sadly. 'I just remembered he'd left it for you. He told me to give it to you if you should ever call in here.'

She opened the pouch and gazed at the coins inside, deeply touched that he thought of her even when his own life was in such disarray. How dear he was to her. 'Where *is* Mussy? He was meant to come with us to the farm. He didn't turn up when we were leaving.'

'He felt bad about that, but he felt it wasn't the right time to go with you. He knew you needed to focus on Trixie, to get her away.' Bob ran a hand over his bearded chin. 'I was so pleased he and Mother talked. They both needed to tell each other stories of Douglas, to heal. Mussy spent a few weeks after you left with Mother.'

'But where is he now? He could come out to the farm to visit.'

Bob sighed heavily. 'He's in prison.'

'Prison!' Caroline jerked back, nearly upending her glass. 'Prison?' she repeated. 'Why?'

Bob glanced at Mrs Aspall.

'Don't worry, Mrs Aspall knows everything,' Caroline murmured.

'Mussy was caught... with a man... He was arrested and jailed for three months.'

Caroline gasped.

'They say he got off lightly. I believe a member of his family intervened and spoke with the judge.' Bob shrugged. 'I sent Mussy a letter about Mother. Who knows if he received it? I don't even know which prison he's been sent to, but I'm fairly certain it's not here in York. I think Mussy's family would have got him in somewhere away from here if they could.'

'Poor Mussy. He'll feel so alone.'

Mrs Aspall touched Caroline's arm. 'I know it's difficult news, but we've got to get a move on, lass. We need to head for home before it gets any later.'

Caroline nodded and stood. 'Goodbye, Mr Warburton. If you see Mussy again, tell him he is always welcome at the farm.'

'I will, Mrs Lawson, and perhaps he will go this time. There's nothing for him in York, and he needs to realise that once and for all.'

The drive home passed in near silence. Caroline was caught up in her own thoughts. Her sadness for Mrs Warburton, her worry for Mussy and her joy at the business deal. What a day it had been. She longed for a cup of tea.

'Howard will be pleased by your efforts today, lass,' Mrs Aspall said as they neared the farm.

'It'll give him a purpose to get better. Howard will be excited to have animals on the farm again. He might now find the opportunity to marry you, Mrs Aspall.'

Mrs Aspall laughed. 'Lord above, I think our time might have come and gone for all that.'

'You'll make a beautiful bride, Mrs Aspall.'

'Now, lass, I've been meaning to mention this. I think it's only right that you call me Annie. We've been thrown together for months now and well, I consider you a friend at least and possibly family at most. What do you think?'

Caroline let go of the reins for a moment and embraced Annie to her. 'I never had a mother, but you've become the closest thing to one.'

Annie blushed. 'Now you're embarrassing me.'

They chuckled as they drove into the yard, both glad to be back until Trixie ran out of the kitchen, her face pale, her elfin eyes wide. 'Come quick, it's Howard!'

Chapter Eighteen

'What's wrong with him?' Caroline asked with dread, slowing Dossy.

'I took him up a cup of tea, but he was barely breathing.' Trixie wrung her hands anxiously. 'I couldn't go for the doctor because I don't know my way to the village, so I sent our Elsie and she's been gone two hours!' Panic filled her voice. 'What if she's got lost or something?'

'I'll go find her and Doctor Pike.' Caroline waited for Annie to climb down and turned Dossy about in the yard only to see another cart coming up the drive. Elsie sat up on the seat next to Doctor Pike.

It was all chaos as Trixie embraced Elsie while Annie and Doctor Pike hurried inside. Caroline praised Elsie as Bertha came out of the house crying because she'd thought Elsie would never come back.

Caroline calmed them down and sent them inside before unharnessing Dossy. She kept busy, feeding Dossy and getting her fresh water. She brushed her down with long smooth strokes as tears gathered in her eyes. Howard had to pull through. She couldn't think of the alternative. Today had been difficult enough without Howard collapsing. She needed him to be strong, to be by her side as her plans for the farm came together. Howard would be her tutor, her guide, the one she could ask advice from, learn from.

He was a father figure to her.

He was the last link to Hugh.

She stayed in the stall brushing Dossy until the light faded. Not daring to go into the house and face bad news. When Trixie came into the stable, Caroline knew the worst had happened. Her broken heart shattered.

Trixie came to her and held her tight, but Caroline was numb from shock. This wasn't meant to happen. She'd come home. Howard and this farm were her home.

'He didn't wake up after his collapse,' Trixie told her quietly. 'Doctor Pike doesn't believe he was in any pain.'

'No, the pain is for those left behind,' Caroline murmured and walked with her into the kitchen. Annie was still upstairs with Doctor Pike and the girls had been sent into the parlour, they could hear Elsie teaching Bertha her numbers.

Trixie poured out tea and Caroline drank it because she didn't know what else to do. All the plans she'd made were nothing but dead ashes now. On this day she had learned such bad news, first Mrs Warburton, then about Mussy being in prison and now Howard. Each event was horrible enough on their own but all three together was too much, too difficult to comprehend. She was numb, shocked and full of grief.

Unable to sit still, Caroline went back outside into the deepening dusk. Birds swooped low into the trees to settle for the night. It was all so unnaturally quiet for a farm. No bellows from the cows, or bleats from the sheep. No soothing sounds of the hens roosting or little squeals from piglets fighting for their mothers' teats. Barren fields. Barren barns. Was it even a farm when stripped of every animal and seed?

Annie came outside with Doctor Pike. 'I've washed and laid Howard out. We've dressed him in his best suit,' she said softly, her eyes red from weeping.

'And I'll call in at Springwood Farm to inform Leo of what has happened,' Doctor Pike said, placing his bag in his gig.

Caroline nodded. A sudden spurt of anger burned in her chest for Leo. He had done this. If he'd kept the animals here, kept this farm alive for Howard, then his father would have recovered sooner, she was sure of it. Leo's announcement of emigrating to Canada was the final straw for Howard. He had nothing to live for.

Doctor Pike climbed up onto the gig's seat. 'I'll call in at the undertakers, too. Ask Fred to come up and see you tomorrow.'

Annie thanked him and waved him off. Caroline turned and went inside. Grief gave way to some other emotion that was cold and hard, curling into a knot in her chest and sharpening her mind.

On the table was the money pouch from Mussy. She opened it and counted the money. Twenty-five shillings. More than she ever expected. She turned to Annie. 'How much will Doctor Pike's bill be?'

'I've paid him,' Annie stated, adding wood to the fire. 'Howard might not have been my husband by law or by God, but I loved him. I did what any wife would do. It was my right to pay for the doctor.'

Caroline nodded, knowing that was how she had felt when Hugh died. 'Then I'll pay for the funeral.'

'It's paid for. Howard had Fred Wright visit here when he first became ill. They planned Howard's funeral and he paid for it there and then.' Annie put a frying pan on the range top. 'At the time I thought it all too macabre, of course. However, Howard was determined to see it done. The Wrights have all the details, tomorrow when they come will just be a formality.'

While Annie cooked ham and eggs for their evening supper, Trixie and the girls set the table. Caroline stared at the pile of money. She could pay the arrears on the rent and have enough left over to buy a crate of hens and a rooster, perhaps even vegetable seeds. Could she keep the farm? Or should she take this money and go with Trixie and the girls somewhere new and find work? The thoughts whirled in her head.

After they'd eaten, which they did even though the three adults had no appetite because wasting food wasn't an option, Caroline tidied away while Annie went up to sit with Howard.

Trixie heated water to give the girls a wash and then put them to bed.

Alone in the kitchen, Caroline cleaned. She needed to do something. Her thoughts were jumbled, her body restless. She emptied the cupboards and wiped the shelves before restocking them again. The table received a scrub and she even wiped down each chair.

She was on her knees washing the stone flags when the back door opened. Leo and Lisette stood there. Caroline stared at Leo. They stared at each other. Then slowly, Leo closed the door behind him as Caroline got up off her knees. Silence stretched between the three of them. For once Lisette kept her sharp tongue in her head.

'I want to see my father.' Leo's hands flexed, his eyes dull.

Caroline remembered how he showed no tears when Hugh died, but his hands flexed the whole time. 'Go on up. Annie is sitting with him.'

He nodded, then hesitated as if he wanted to say something but Lisette took his arm, and they continued out of the kitchen.

Clearing away the bucket and cloths, Caroline untied her apron. The little clock on the dresser chimed seven times. She couldn't wait for this day to be over.

Annie and Trixie came into the kitchen and while Annie made tea, Trixie sat with Caroline at the table. Trixie didn't speak, she just was there, which was all Caroline needed.

'I thought they'd come in the morning,' Annie said, spooning tea leaves into the teapot. 'Now he and Lisette can go to Canada without worrying about Howard.'

'Did they worry about him?' Caroline scoffed. 'They weren't worried about him when they sold all his stock.'

'No...' Annie sighed heavily.

Leo and Lisette entered the kitchen surprising them that they'd only been upstairs a short time. 'I know father paid for his funeral,' Leo said, not looking at any of them.

'Yes. Mr Wright will be here tomorrow,' Annie said. 'Howard will be buried next to your mam.'

Lisette lifted her chin. 'We've received a letter today that our ship is sailing in a few days. We're to leave in the morning to travel to Liverpool.'

'In the morning?' Annie gasped and almost dropped the teapot.

Caroline glared at them. 'You'll not stay for the funeral?'

'We... We can't miss the ship.' Leo's hands flexed.

'You'll miss your father's funeral!'

'I would stay for it if I could, obviously, but the tickets are paid for.'

Lisette bristled. 'If we were already in Canada we wouldn't be traveling back to attend, would we?'

'But you're not *in* Canada yet.' Caroline wanted to scream.

'We *aren't* waiting.' Lisette's harsh tone matched the expression on her cold face. 'Howard would want us to go.'

'You know *nothing* about what Howard would have wanted!' Caroline jerked to her feet angrily. 'You two are selfish and only care about your own needs! Howard would never have wanted his only remaining son to be thousands of miles away. Your plans broke his heart.'

Leo flushed and stared down at his boots.

'Oh, be quiet, Caroline.' Lisette waved a dismissive hand at her. 'You think you know everything, but you don't. Howard hasn't been the same since Hugh died and then *you* left without any thought to him. You did the exact same thing as what we are doing! Hugh and then you broke his heart if you want to be so dramatic about it.'

'When I left, I thought Howard would marry Annie and be happy. I was only fifteen miles away not thousands, hardly the same.' Still, guilt niggled at her.

Lisette tossed her head. 'Think what you like. Leo and me are leaving in the morning. It's all arranged, and we aren't changing it.' She marched to the back door. 'Come on, Leo. We're done here.'

As Leo walked past Caroline, she gripped his sleeve. 'Don't go. Stay at Springwood and help me run this farm. We can do it, together, have both farms be successful like they used to be before Hugh died. We can do it, you know we can. Honour Howard and Hugh, please!' she begged.

'Leo!' Lisette barked. 'We're going.'

He glanced at Caroline and shook his head. 'I can't.'

When the door shut, Caroline fell onto a chair, crushed.

Trixie took her hand. 'Don't give up. *We'll* do it. We don't need them.'

'But you do need a man,' Annie said softly. 'It's in the tenancy agreement. A man must be the tenant. The moment Lord Stockton-Lee or Mr Cavendish hears Howard has gone, they'll want you out.'

Caroline bowed her head. Tears burned hot behind her eyes. She didn't want to cry, not for Howard, not for the farm, because if she did, she didn't think she'd ever stop.

'You can come and live with me at my cottage,' Annie told them. 'I think of you all as my family and would hate to see you go away.'

'Thank you, Annie.' Trixie smiled sadly. 'But we need to find work.'

'Well, we'll sort that out when we come to it.'

Caroline raised her head. 'I told Howard we'd fight for the farm. That's what I'm going to do.'

'How, lass?'

'I'll go and speak to Mr Cavendish in the morning,' she said with determination. 'A woman can run a farm as good as any man.' She went to the door leading to the stairs. 'I'll go up and sit with Howard for a bit. I want to tell him my plans.'

~ele~

Caroline turned Dossy into the second drive of the Stockton-Lee estate. The main drive went between large black iron gates and through an avenue of oak trees to the grand Misterton Abbey, the Stockton-Lee's country house. The second drive followed parallel to the main drive for a few hundred yards before veering off to the left, away from the abbey and its ornamental gardens and headed towards the service areas of the estate, the walled vegetable garden, the impressive stable block, and the outbuildings housing the laundry and dairy. A wing of servant quarters was attached to the main house and beneath the servant quarters were the offices used for running the estate.

Caroline knew from previously accompanying Hugh to pay the rent, that the estate steward's office was in this wing, along with storerooms, the gun room, the staff dining room and many other areas.

She steered Dossy past the gates leading to the stable block and drove into the cobbled yard near the laundry and dairy. The yard was a hive of activity. Footmen were carrying crates of food or baskets of neatly sawn logs. Two maids came out of the laundry holding baskets of wet clothes. Beyond the yard, a stretch of green lawn was crisscrossed with poles and lines where sheets hung in the sunshine.

A smartly dressed young man came down the stairs from one door of many along the wing. 'Can I help you, miss?'

'I'm Mrs Lawson.' Caroline smiled confidently as he helped her down from the gig. 'I wish to see Mr Cavendish.'

'Do you have an appointment?' he asked.

'No, but it's urgent. He'll want to see me,' Caroline said, hoping it was the truth.

'Follow me.' The young man led her into a long corridor full of tall windows looking out over the yard. Opposite each window was a door. Under each window stood a wooden bench, and he stopped and pointed to one. 'Wait here, please.'

Caroline sat down as instructed, wondering what his role was when he seemed no more than twenty, but he wore neat clothes of good quality and spoke well. She smoothed the material of her dark blue skirt, one Annie had given her to wear that was in better condition than her own clothes.

She'd woken early that morning and washed her hair before plaiting it and curling it up at the back of her head. She also wore Annie's best bonnet, black with pale yellow material roses on the side. Her cheap bonnet wasn't fit for wearing to such an important meeting. Her boots needed polishing, so she tucked her feet under her skirts to hide them.

'Mrs Lawson?' Maxwell Cavendish came out of a room further down the corridor.

Standing, Caroline watched him walk towards her, her stomach churning. So much depended on this meeting, so much. She held out her hand. 'Thank you for seeing me, Mr Cavendish.'

His smile was welcoming, and genuine as he clasped her hand. 'I am surprised to find you here. My brother said it was urgent?'

Oh, the other fellow was his brother.

Caroline walked with him back into the room which was a wood panelled office with two tall sash windows looking out to another courtyard filled with flowering bulbs of daffodils, crocus and snowdrops. One wall of the office was filled with books and the other walls showcased paintings of country scenes. Two desks dominated the room. A large walnut map desk and a green leather-topped desk which was where he worked. Piles of paper and ledgers vied for space along with farming books and stationery.

'Please, do sit.' He indicated to one of the two leather chairs facing his desk.

Suddenly nervous, Caroline took a deep breath, anxious to not make a fool of herself.

'Now, how can I help you today?' Cavendish asked, sitting behind his desk. His blue eyes had an honesty about them which eased her a little.

'My father-in-law, Howard, he died yesterday.' That was hard, but she said the sentence without her chin quivering.

'That is a terrible shame, Mrs Lawson. You have my sincere sympathy, and I know Lord Stockton-Lee will want me to pass on his condolences, too.'

'Thank you.' She summoned all her courage. 'I wish to discuss with you the farm, Hopewood Farm.'

'You wish to give it up, naturally.'

'No!' she spoke the word harshly. 'Forgive me, no. I want to run the farm myself.' Then, as he went to speak, she rushed on. 'I know the estate policy is only have male tenants, but I can make the farm successful. I learnt a lot from my late husband and my father-in-law. I had a successful dairy at Springwood, and I helped my husband in every other aspect of the farm work. I am educated, and clever. I'm a quick learner and can work hard, all day every day. I have a business deal in place to restock the farm, with Mr Bent, a butcher in York. Oh, and I have the money to pay our arrears.' She pulled her reticule off her wrist. 'I can pay next quarter's rent in advance as well.'

'Mrs Lawson!' Cavendish held up his hands to halt her flow of words.

She stared at him, chest heaving.

He smiled again, a slow steady smile. 'Mrs Lawson, shall we have some tea?' He got up to pull a bell rope beside the fireplace.

Her shoulders slumped. Tea? No, she didn't want tea! She wanted a tenancy agreement in her hands with her name on it.

Cavendish tilted his head, studying her. 'Over a cup of tea, we'll discuss your tenancy. Do you have a financial plan for the farm?'

From her reticule she took out a small square of folded paper which she opened and passed to him to read. 'That is my restock list. Obviously, we are late to plough. The fields should have been sown over winter for most of the crops, but I can plant vegetables, and maybe a couple of acres of late season hay. The bottom fields need the drainage cleaned out and dug to the stream. I'll run a flock of sheep up on the top fields and small beef herd around the woodland. I thought to start with a few milking cows to begin with and build a dairy herd over time. Naturally, I'll have hens and geese, pigs and possibly a goat.' The whole time she was looking at the list he held until she gazed up and found him staring at her.

'You sound confident that you know what you want to do,' he stated as he beckoned a maid in and requested a tea tray.

'I'll make it work, Mr Cavendish, I have to. It's my home, not just for me, but for my friends who are my family now.' She gripped her hands together. Did he believe she could do it?

'I will need to discuss this with Lord Stockton-Lee.'

She nodded, throat dry.

He wrote some notes in a small notebook, referencing her list often. 'I have found that my predecessor had some certain ways of running this estate that are different to my thoughts, to the practices I wish to implement.' He kept writing with a fluid hand. 'I feel a woman can run a farm just as a man can, if not perhaps do all the physical work, but most, and she can hirer labourers to do the heavy manual labour. I have studied cases of this happening on other estates in this country. In many cases, it is the widow who carried on the farm after her husband dies, bringing up her children to take over when she is old.'

The maid returned with the tray and set it on a small round table near the map desk.

Cavendish walked to the tray and poured out two cups of tea. He handed her a cup and saucer, again with that smile which Caroline was beginning to like a lot.

'Lord Stockton-Lee has given me full responsibility for the estate, for he spends most of his time in London and if not there, then in India, where he owns a tea plantation. He trusts me to keep this estate profitable, that can only be done with good husbandry and tenants paying their rents. My thought is that as long as a tenant is taking care of the land and paying their rent, then who actually works it, male or female, doesn't matter.' Cavendish sat down behind his desk once more. 'I am confident you can make Hopewood Farm a success, Mrs Lawson.'

Caroline couldn't drink the tea, her hands were shaking too much. 'You mean...'

'I'll have a new tenancy agreement drawn up with your name on it. I'll speak to my lord, first, of course, but I do not foresee any concerns on his part. He knows little of farming, unlike me. Lord Stockton-Lee was a soldier, and this estate is simply a place for him to pass onto his son when he dies. My role is to keep it profitable and improved for the next generation.'

Caroline stopped listening after he said *a new tenancy agreement with her name on it*. She couldn't take in what he was saying. 'Are you stating that I can-can stay? Stay at Hopewood? Me?'

His warm smile became a grin. 'Yes, Mrs Lawson, that is exactly what I am saying.'

Shocked, she gripped the teacup in fear her trembling hands would spill it all over her lap. She wanted to jump and embrace him and shout and laugh and cry. Naturally, she did none of those things, but inside she was bursting with happiness.

'You won't disappoint me, will you, Mrs Lawson?' he half-joked.

'I give you my word I will work hard every day or die trying,' she said sincerely.

'I believe you, and please, do not hesitate to come to me if you need any guidance or want to discuss anything. A good estate manager takes care of his tenants.'

'Thank you, Mr Cavendish.'

He rose with an apology on his lips. 'I must be going, Mrs Lawson. I have an appointment in the village. My duties go beyond this estate and since my lord owns the village as well, my days are very full.'

'Yes, yes.' She returned her cup to the tray untouched and faced him. She held out her hand and he took it in a strong warm grip. 'I can't thank you enough, Mr Cavendish. You have saved me.'

An emotion entered his blue eyes that was tender and soft. 'Oh, I think you're stronger than you think you are, Mrs Lawson.'

He walked with her to the gig and handed her up into the seat. His smile sent her on her way and as she drove out of the estate, she grinned and then whooped for joy, then she remembered Howard and the tears fell. 'It's a start, Howard,' she whispered. 'I won't let you down.'

Chapter Nineteen

Most of the village turned out for Howard's funeral. March sunshine shone on the mourners. Whispers ran riot about Leo and Lisette leaving the country only days before, but Caroline ignored them. She kept strong for Annie who wept for the man she loved and never got to marry and although Caroline cried, it seemed a kind of healing cry.

As the mourners began to file out of the churchyard, Caroline showed Trixie Hugh's grave and put a bunch of daffodils at the base of the headstone.

'I can't believe he's been gone over seven months.' Caroline ran her hand over the top of the grey headstone. 'Sometimes it feels like yesterday and at other times like it was years ago, a dream even.'

'I feel like that about Mam.' Trixie gazed over to where Elsie and Bertha were talking to some other girls they knew from Sunday School. 'Look at them, Caro.'

Caroline turned and smiled at Elsie laughing at something and Bertha twirling. They were happy little girls now. Annie had sewn them new dresses in light blue and new white pinafores. Both Elsie and Berth had grown since coming to the farm. Decent food, a warm and clean home and lots of loving care from Annie had changed the girls. They no longer looked like the frightened, skinny dirty urchins from the Water Lanes. Now they were rosy-cheeked with good health, their limbs strong, their hair shiny and wearing clothes that fit. They attended Sunday school in the village and were learning their letters and numbers.

Trixie wore a serious expression. 'I know nothing about farming, but I'll work hard beside you so that those two will never know another hungry day.'

'Nor will we.' Caroline said, determinedly. She slipped her arm through Trixie's, who was wearing a new skirt and bodice in dark red that Caroline bought her from the money Mussy left her. Annie had enough to do with making the girls' clothes, so Caroline and Trixie had gone to Mrs Fenby in the village and been measured for a new dress each. Trixie, the deep red and Caroline, emerald green. They wanted to look the best they could for Howard and couldn't possibly wear the same old stained clothes they had.

'Mrs Lawson.' Maxwell Cavendish came to stand beside her and Trixie and with him was his younger brother.

'Thank you for coming, Mr Cavendish.' Caroline shook his hand, liking his firm grip.

'May I formally introduce you to my brother? Thomas Cavendish.'

'We meet again, Mr Cavendish.' Caroline shook his hand and introduced them both to Trixie.

'If I may, I'd like to call by the farm one day next week?' Cavendish asked. 'I have the new tenancy agreement for you to sign.'

'You have?' Surprised, Caroline's widened. 'Yes, of course. Unless you'd prefer me to come to your office?'

'No, no. I'll call by at the farm. I'd like to have a walk around it with you. We can discuss your farming practices.'

'Absolutely,' she said eagerly. She still couldn't believe the farm would be hers. The day she held that agreement would be one of the best days of her life.

Cavendish glanced at Hugh's gravestone, his expression thoughtful. 'Thomas will be also moving into Springwood Farm for a year before he goes to university. I hope that won't be a cause for upset to you? We haven't found any suitable tenants since Leo Lawson left, and I thought it would be a perfect way for Thomas to learn how to run a farm.'

Caroline wasn't sure how she felt about Springwood. 'It crossed my mind to ask for Springwood instead of Hopewood, but then I decided against it. There are too many memories there for me,' she said sadly, looking at Hugh's name on the gravestone. Her old home wasn't the same place without Hugh. 'Hopewood is better for me, and I want to make it successful again to honour Howard and Hugh.' She smiled at Thomas. 'I hope you will enjoy your time there, Mr Cavendish.'

Thomas bowed slightly with a twinkle in his eye. 'Thank you, neighbour.'

'Your late husband and father-in-law would be proud of you,' Maxwell Cavendish said.

'Well, that remains to be seen. I've some hard work ahead of me for some years,' she said ruefully.

Thomas grinned at Caroline, his laughing eyes were a deeper blue than his brothers but just as striking. 'We'll both be starting afresh, Mrs Lawson.'

'It will do my heart good to see my old home once more full of life, Mr Cavendish.'

'I may not even go to university, but stay at Springwood instead,' Tom joked.

His brother frowned. 'You'll be going, Tom, no arguments. You need to study as I did, especially accounting. Without a good head for figures, you won't be a decent estate steward.'

'Land agent, brother. That's the name for it now.' Thomas nudged his brother's arm in jest.

Cavendish raised an eyebrow at him, then looked at Caroline. 'Until next week? Wednesday?'

'Yes, until then. Good day to you both.' Caroline walked away with Trixie to where Annie was standing with the girls, talking to some of the villagers.

'I don't think I've ever seen two men more handsome than that in my life and I've seen some men,' Trixie said in awe.

'Are they?'

Trixie tutted. 'Are you blind?'

Caroline frowned. Indeed, the two Cavendish brothers were handsome, but she'd not thought much of it. She had too much else to think about.

'Maxwell Cavendish looks at you a great deal,' Trixie mentioned.

'Does he?' Caroline blushed. 'I've no time for a man, any man. I've a farm to build and that's all I'm focusing on.'

Trixie gave her a worried look. 'I'm pleased as I'd hate to lose you, not yet anyway.'

'Put that nonsense from your mind,' she admonished. 'Come on. Let's go home.' The thrill she got from saying those words was immense.

Two days later, Caroline attended the market. They all went as Trixie's bruises were gone and Trixie no longer felt the need to hide her face. Trixie also wanted to see more of the village. Annie was keen to show her the little cottage she called home, and her candle making business, which Trixie was interested in.

Helping Annie to set up her stall in the busy market held along the main street in the village, Trixie wore her bonnet and remained shy, but as the morning wore on, she eventually started to smile at the local women who came to chat to Annie. Many remembered Caroline and gave their condolences for Howard.

In a lull between customers, Annie turned to Caroline who'd just returned from buying a crate of hens and a rooster.

'Trixie's taken the girls to Enid Webster's stall to get them a toffee twirl each,' Annie explained. 'I usually get the girls one when they come to the market with me.'

'They'll enjoy that.' Caroline eyed the other stalls. She was after some leather work gloves to wear on the farm.

'Listen, lass. While we have a moment alone,' Annie lowered her voice. 'I've been thinking.'

'Oh?' Caroline gave Annie her full attention.

'Aye, you see the weather is getting warmer and my bees need my attention. I've let my wax stocks go down and I need to make more candles. So, I think I'll move back to my cottage again, especially now Howard is gone...'

'Oh, I see. Yes, you must be eager to be in your own home again.'

'Well, I am and I ain't.' Annie frowned. 'I've adored being at the farm with you girls. We've become a little family, haven't we? And I'll miss Elsie and Bertha so much.'

'They'll be down that hill to see you every day given the chance,' Caroline told her with a smile. 'And you're welcome to come up to the farm any time you want because we'll miss you, too.' Impulsively, Caroline embraced her. 'Since we arrived at the farm you've been like a mother to me, and to Trixie, and a grandmother to the girls.'

Annie wiped a tear away. 'Well, that's how I feel, too. I've always wanted a family.'

'And now you have one,' Caroline declared.

'You know that the cottage is mine, don't you?' Annie suddenly said. 'I don't rent it from Lord Stockton-Lee like most people in the village do. My late husband bought it many years ago, an unheard-of thing to do back then, but my Wilf was left an inheritance by his grandfather who was a member of the royal household, would you believe?'

Caroline raised her eyebrows in surprise.

'My Wilf's grandfather bought several properties in London. When he died, many were sold and the money split between his twelve children. My Wilf's father died young, and his share of the money went to my Wilf and his two sisters. The cottage and four acres were bought by my beloved Wilf. Anyway, I don't know why I'm telling you such a long story.' Annie laughed. 'Suffice to say, you, Trixie and the girls will always have a home with me as I've made my will and left you all the cottage. You will never be homeless again.'

'You are a dear and special woman, Annie Aspall.' Caroline held her tight.

Trixie and the girls returned. Elsie and Bertha sucking on toffee twirls while Trixie had bought some produce from the vegetable stalls with some of the money Caroline gave her to use. 'This should last us a week.'

'It will now I won't be there,' Annie said. As she explained her decision to Trixie and the girls to live again at her cottage, Caroline went to the other end of the market to purchase some geese and look at the few sows in a pen.

'Mrs Lawson!' Thomas Cavendish hailed her. 'We seem to be of the same mind?' He gestured to the sows.

'Good day, Mr Cavendish. I am in two minds at the moment.' Caroline glanced at the old farmer who was haggling the price of another pen of sows to another farmer. 'Old Mr Meehan doesn't have a good reputation. My late husband, and his father, always said Meehan sold stock that was past their usefulness.'

'Then we should steer clear.' Thomas gave a critical eye to the beasts. 'I am not from around here so local knowledge is something I lack.'

'I'm happy to pass on anything I know.' She smiled. 'Where is it that you hail from?'

'My brother and I were born in Lincoln.' Thomas stepped to where two kid goats were tied to a stake.

'And you left there to come live with Lord Stockton-Lee?'

'Maxwell got the posting through our aunt, and he promised he wouldn't leave me behind.' Thomas grinned. 'I don't think he trusted me to stay out of Lincoln's many fine inns if left alone.' He laughed.

Caroline chuckled. 'Mr Cavendish seems a caring older brother.'

'An overbearing one sometimes,' Thomas snorted. 'But it's not his fault. He's had to care for me for years when he should have been seeing only to himself.'

Intrigued, Caroline would have liked to have known more but Farmer Meehan came to them and started extolling the virtues of his goat kids to Thomas.

'I'm also interested in them,' Caroline told him.

'Indeed, you are...' Meehan squinted in the morning light at her. 'You're Hugh Lawson's widow, aren't you?'

'I am.'

'Both he and his father were good men. Where do you live now?'

'At Hopewood. I aim to farm it.'

Meehan laughed scornfully. 'A young pretty thing like you? Farm? What *hens?*'

Caroline stiffened at his mocking. 'No, cattle, sheep, possibly a few sows, a few acres under plough, oh, and some *hens.*'

'You'll never do it by yourself, lass. You need a man.'

'No, I don't. I'm quite capable.'

'You weren't even born on a farm, aren't you from a convent or something I remember someone once telling me?' Meehan scratched his straggling grey beard.

'I've learned a lot since marrying Hugh,' she snapped.

'I'm a widower meself if you're looking to get wed again.'

Caroline blinked as if she'd misheard.

Thomas burst into laughter.

Scowling, Meehan raised his hands in protest. 'Hey, you young pup, I've a lot of years left in me yet.'

Thomas took Caroline's elbow and they walked away. 'Do you fancy becoming the next Mrs Meehan?'

'I certainly do not.' Caroline grinned.

'You would suit my brother though,' he replied cheekily.

She stopped and looked at him. 'I'll remain a widow if you don't mind.' She hadn't thought of ever remarrying and the idea of it seemed too soon to even contemplate. 'I'd best be getting back. Good day, Mr Cavendish.'

'And to you, Mrs Lawson.' Thomas bowed.

The following morning, Caroline rose early and started the fires in the kitchen for Annie, who cooked breakfast for them all. Today Annie was going back to her cottage, and they were all rather sad about it.

Taking the empty buckets, Caroline filled them at the well at the far end of the yard and returned them to the scullery. Today was washing day and she lit the copper boiler and filled the large tub with water. It took several trips to the well and back to get the required level before she grated soap into it. In another tub clothes were soaking that she'd placed in there the day before.

Trixie came into the scullery, yawning, rolling her sleeves up ready to help. They squeezed the water from the clothes soaking and plonked them into the boiler. While Trixie plunged a dolly stick in to mix the clothes through the soap, Caroline added a bluing agent to a smaller tub for the final rinse.

The washing line was soon filled with wet clothes dripping in the morning sunshine. Elsie and Bertha had jobs to do as well. Bertha fed the hens and Elsie let Dossy out into the small field behind the barn and then cleaned out her stall.

'What's that noise?' Trixie paused in transferring the last of the clothes into the large stone sink to drain.

Caroline straightened and listened. Bellowing. A lot of cows bellowing.

She raced out into the yard and stared. A herd of brown and white cows plodded up the drive. A black and white dog barked to keep them in order, darting about like a flash of lightning.

Behind the herd a drover walked, carrying a large staff. At the very end was a cart and a lone driver.

'My heavens, that's a lot of cows,' Trixie said, half afraid.

'Quickly, we have to get the gate open!' Caroline lifted her skirts and ran down the drive to open a gate leading into the field on the right. 'Stand in the drive, Trixie. We need to turn the herd into the field. Wave your arms.'

Trixie flapped like a bird and Caroline laughed, but the dog knew its duty and turned the lead cows into the field and the rest followed, eager to graze the new spring grass.

'Mr Bent!' Caroline waved to the butcher on the cart.

He pulled the cart to a stop beside her and Trixie, his friendly face a welcome sight. 'I thought to come along and see for myself the place you call home and where my investment will be growing fat.'

'Come up to the house for some tea.'

Once in the kitchen, Caroline set out cups. 'Have you had some food?'

'Aye, lass.' Mr Bent took off his hat as he came through the door. 'We had some porridge at the inn before we set off. We stayed overnight at an inn on the road here as we were late leaving York yesterday afternoon after the market.' He nodded to Annie and Trixie as Caroline introduced them.

'Right, Caroline.' Annie collected her bag by the door. 'I'll be off home. I'll see you on Thursday at the market.'

'You're going now?' Trixie asked.

'I am, while you're busy. No fuss.' Annie held up her hand. 'I'm only in the village and will see you every Thursday at the market and Sunday at church. Ta-ra!' Annie walked out with tears in her eyes.

'I didn't mean to interrupt anything,' Mr Bent said anxiously.

'No, no, you haven't.' Caroline reassured him, knowing Annie had picked this precise moment to leave to lessen the painful tug of goodbyes. Annie had thought that one day she'd be married to Howard, and she'd be living on this farm, but all those dreams had vanished when Howard died. The poor woman had to go home and re-adjust to the old life she once lived.

'So, is it good to be back in the country, lass?' Mr Bent asked, accepting a cup of tea.

'Very good.' Caroline smiled.

'It's quiet, that's for sure.' He took the slice of pound cake that Trixie cut for him. 'Different to York for certain.'

'But friendlier,' Trixie added. 'People in the village like to stop and have a chat.'

Caroline glanced at Trixie. That was the first time she'd heard her friend say such a thing. Was Trixie learning to like the countryside? 'How is Mrs Bent?'

'Quite well when I left yesterday. She would have come, but she didn't want the shop to be closed.' He pulled out a rolled document. 'This is the contract for you to sign and that other piece of paper has all the details about the cows, age, breed, and so on.'

'Lovely.' Caroline took it and read through it while Mr Bent spoke of York news to Trixie.

Mr Bent sipped his tea. 'They are getting on with knocking down First Water Lane. They'll be nowt left of it soon except the King's Arms pub down by the river. But the people are rising up against it. There's nowhere for them to live. It's making the other areas of the city overcrowded and making conditions even worse. There's a rumour that Middle Water Lane won't be knocked down for a while yet.'

'I'm glad we got out when we did,' Trixie murmured.

'Aye, times are difficult. Criminals are becoming bolder. Just last week a jewellery shop was robbed in Coney Street.'

Caroline finished reading the contract which was straight forward and went into the parlour to sign both copies. When she returned, she noticed Trixie was pale. She frowned in a silent question to her.

'Mr Bent just mentioned Victor Dolan,' she said softly. 'He's been causing trouble.'

'Oh?' Caroline's stomach churned at the mention of Dolan's name and looked at Mr Bent.

'The villain needs locking up.' Mr Bent ate more cake. 'He and his men were involved in a forgery scandal. His lodging house was raided by the police, but he wasn't arrested. Slippery as an eel that rogue is.'

'One day Dolan will get his comeuppance.' Caroline gave one copy of the contract back to Mr Bent.

'And not a day too soon.' Mr Bent stood with a smile. 'I'd best be off. We want to be back in York before nightfall.'

'Take some cake with you for the shepherd.' Trixie wrapped a piece in paper.

'Thanks, lass.'

They walked out with him into the sunshine. The shepherd was already sitting up in the cart. Elsie and Bertha were down the drive, standing on a fence railing watching the cows.

'Write to me with updates on the beasts when you can, lass.' Mr Bent tipped his hat and climbed up onto the seat. 'Good luck!'

Caroline and Trixie waved and stood together watching the cart rumble down the drive.

'Are you all right?' She asked Trixie.

'Just hearing Dolan's name gives me the shivers.' Trixie wrapped her arms about herself.

'It sounds as though he's becoming a big name in the criminal world. Forgery now on top of everything else?' Caroline wished the police had thrown him in jail.

'We can never go back to York, Caro,' Trixie whispered. 'Not even when the cows go to market.' She looked at her with frightened eyes. 'Promise me you won't go again.'

'I have to get the beasts to market, Trix. I've signed a contract with the Bents.'

'Then we hire a man to take them. You can't go, none of us can. If Victor sees us, he'll take us, or maybe even have us followed back here. He can't be trusted, and we can't let down our guard.'

Caroline put her hand on Trixie's shoulder. 'There might be a chance he's forgotten all about us by now. He took his revenge on you and left you for dead. In his mind, that may be the end of it.'

'I took something he valued, something he could have made a lot of money from. *You*. And you disfigured his face. We did him wrong. He won't forget any of that, especially if he sees you walking the streets of York. I wished you hadn't signed the deal with Mr Bent but found somewhere else away from York to sell the beasts.'

'I had to secure the rent of this farm, you know that, and the only way I could was to stock it and make the place profitable. I needed Mr Bent's help to do that. Where else would I have found an investor?'

'Let's hope this farm is worth it then.' Trixie turned and walked inside.

Caroline stayed looking out over the fields down the hill. Had she made the right decision to stay here? Or should they have moved further away? In the peacefulness of the farm, she didn't feel Dolan was a threat, not now, not here. That monster was the past. They had a whole future ahead. She had to believe that. She refused to be forever looking over her shoulder. No. This farm was their home and she'd work hard to make it a good life for them all.

Chapter Twenty

By the end of April, Caroline was making headway on getting the farm back to its former glory. The cows were fattening up and she had selected those she was keeping as breeders and those she'd send to market at the end of summer. A small flock of ewes and their lambs, bought by Mr Bent, now grazed on the highest slopes of the hill. They'd arrived a few weeks ago, the same shepherd and his dog guiding them up the hill fresh from the market.

At an auction Caroline attended with the Cavendish brothers a fortnight ago, she'd bought two milking cows and their calves, with the last of the money Mussy gave her. Maxwell Cavendish had been immensely helpful in aiding her to select the best cows and she'd enjoyed her day with the brothers, which included a roadside picnic on the way home.

Now she had milkers, she needed the dairy scrubbed clean. The task was made more difficult when working on a hot day in late April. While Caroline threw buckets of soapy water over the floor to scrub the stone flags clean, Trixie and the girls were white-washing the walls. Out in the warm sunshine, milk buckets, butter paddles, the milk churn and all the other utensils and tools Caroline would need to make butter and cream were drying after having been scoured and washed.

By midday most of the jobs were complete and Caroline and Trixie sat out on the grass to rest and wipe the sweat from their brows as Elsie and Bertha went into the kitchen to pour glasses of cordial for them all.

'Someone is coming.' Trixie nodded towards the bottom of the drive where a cart has just turned in.

Caroline blocked out the sun with her hand and squinted. She sat up straight. 'It's Mr Cavendish and Thomas.'

Both Caroline and Trixie stood and brushed off the grass from their skirts. Caroline wasn't looking her best. She was hot and sweaty and wore no bonnet while cleaning the dairy and her tawny hair had escaped its bun.

'Ladies,' Thomas called as he jumped down from the cart.

'Good day to you, Thomas.' Caroline enjoyed his company very much. She saw a great deal of him at the markets or animal auctions. He'd moved into Springwood and visited them several times in the past weeks. Thomas was always cheery, happy to joke and laugh whereas his older brother showed her a serious side, though still friendly, if in a slightly intense way. 'Good day, Mr Cavendish.'

'Mrs Lawson. Miss Wilkes.' Cavendish climbed down to greet them.

'We have brought gifts!' Thomas declared, walking around to the back of the cart.

Caroline's eyes widened at the crate of piglets and the large sow tied to the inside ring of the cart. 'Pigs?'

'A sow and her eight piglets.' Thomas opened the back of the cart.

'Why have you brought them to me? Surely you need a sow yourself?'

'I have four sows. My brother and I visited a farm this morning, another estate tenant, but the poor man is ill, and his wife wants them to move to Leeds to her family.' Thomas and Cavendish took a side of the crate each and brought it down to the ground. The piglets' squeals hurt all their ears. The sow grunted for her babies.

'Anyway,' Thomas continued. 'As you know, at Springwood, there's only room for four sows in the pigsty so I thought you would like the fifth one?'

'I can't pay you, Thomas.' Caroline felt guilty that they'd gone to all this trouble for nothing.

'No payment necessary, Mrs Lawson,' Maxwell Cavendish said. 'We got them at a good price because the wife just wanted them gone.'

'I must pay you something.' She thought of the few shillings she had left of Howard's money she'd found in his bottom drawer when they cleaned out his room so Caroline could use it as her own bedroom. That money was to buy them food and basics until she had her first stall at the market.

'Please, think nothing of it.' Cavendish smiled that thoughtful smile he wore. 'You'll be doing us a kind gesture by taking her off our hands.'

'How about you cook us a nice meal one day? Roast pork!' Thomas laughed. 'That is payment enough.'

'As long as you're sure?' Caroline still felt a bit guilty for not paying them.

'Absolutely!' Thomas told her.

Elsie and Bertha came out of the house carrying trays which they promptly gave to Trixie so they could kneel beside the crate and coo over the little piglets.

'Can we give them names?' Elsie begged.

'You know we don't give names to those animals going to market,' Caroline warned.

'Are they all going to market?' Bertha asked. She'd turned six two days ago and was keen on all aspects of the farm and Caroline had an inkling that she'd be a wonderful farmer one day. Whereas Elsie preferred to read a book or draw and only wanted to do some tasks on the farm such as feeding the hens.

'No, not all.' Caroline bent and inspected the pink piglets. 'Any boys will go to market. You can name the mother pig.'

'Let's take them to the pen and we can check what you have,' Cavendish said. He and Thomas grabbed the crate and walked across the yard to behind the stable and barn to the stone-walled pigsty.

'I've not cleaned it up yet.' Caroline frowned in concern. 'I've left it to last as I knew it'd be a few months yet before we bought a sow.'

'We can help you,' Cavendish said. He and Thomas went to wrangle the sow from the cart and herd her to the pigsty while Caroline and Trixie quickly swept the winter leaves and old straw from one of the stalls. Elsie and Bertha carried fresh straw from the barn to lay on floor and then filled up the trough with water.

'Get the bucket of food scraps we were going to give the hens and we'll give it to the sow,' Caroline told Bertha, who ran to do her bidding.

'What will the hens have then?' Elsie asked.

'They can have some grain, but they've also been pecking around the farm all day, so they can do without scraps tonight. The sow needs it more as she's feeding these little ones.' Caroline checked that the stone walls of the whole pigsty were strong and intact and the wooden gate secure.

With the sow in the stall, they opened the crate and took out the piglets. The squealing was loud and intense. Elsie covered her ears, but Bertha laughed as Trixie winced at the horrendous noise the babies made.

'You'd think we were harming them from the noise they make!' Trixie scoffed.

For a while, they all leaned on the wall and watched the farm's latest inhabitants settle. The sow grunted and slobbered over the food scraps and her piglets ran about or fell asleep in the straw.

'This is a good enclosure,' Cavendish said to Caroline, gazing around the open grassed area that the stall led into so the pigs could root around in the dirt and grass. 'Most pigsties I've seen are all stone flags and walls, nowhere for the pigs to root.'

'Pigs were a favourite of Howard. He liked to make them happy and having an open area for them to roam about in the summer he felt was ideal for them to grow big and healthy.'

'I wish I'd been able to converse with him. I think he'd have a lot of knowledge to impart.'

Caroline nodded sadly. 'I think you two would have enjoyed each other's company.'

'I'm as parched as a desert,' Thomas announced, tickling Bertha. 'Did I spy some cordial?'

'Yes. I'll fetch two more glasses.' Caroline went inside as the others went to the grassed area at the front of the house. A large pear tree grew near the edge of the drive, throwing shade. In time, Caroline wanted to buy some wrought-iron chairs and a table so in summer they could eat outside in the warm evenings, but for now they sat on a large blanket.

Elsie helped her to pour out the cordial and share some oatmeal biscuits they'd baked yesterday.

'These are delicious,' Thomas exclaimed to Elsie. 'What a clever girl you are.'

Elsie preened and blushed.

'Heavens, more visitors,' Trixie said, watching the drive.

They all stared at the slow progress of the two men who walked up the drive, one swayed a little as though drunk and the other reached out to steady him.

Cavendish stood, instantly alert. 'Do you know these men?'

'Are they drunk?' Thomas stood beside his brother.

Caroline's skin prickled. Trixie stepped closer to the girls. She glanced at Caroline, fear in her eyes.

Angry that their little piece of paradise might be ruined, or threatened, Caroline strode away from the group and down the drive, ready to have it out with whoever dare intrude on her property. Cavendish and Thomas were right behind her.

'Mrs Lawson,' Cavendish grabbed her elbow to slow her down. 'Let my brother and I handle this.'

'No, I...' Caroline frowned. There was something familiar about the taller man's walk. She held her hands up over her eyes to stare down the drive. The taller of the two wore a grey striped suit and a red cravat...

'Mussy!' Caroline screamed and picking up her skirts she ran towards her dear friend.

She nearly knocked him flying as she embraced him.

He staggered but held onto her. 'Caro. Darling, Caro.' He sobbed into her shoulder and then coughed so badly it bent him double.

Caroline held him tight, then realised she could feel all the bones of him. She leaned back to stare at him and gasped. Mussy was a skeleton. His eyes sunken, his face gaunt, his black hair cut short to his scalp. His suit hung on him as though made for a bigger man. He looked like death walking. 'Mussy?'

'I'll be fine...' He sucked in a breath, pale and haunted.

'You found me,' she whispered tearfully.

Mussy closed his dull eyes as though the feat had almost killed him, that or prison.

'Caroline,' murmured the man standing next to them.

Caroline whipped her head around and stared at Jacob Adams. He'd been beaten terribly and swayed on his feet.

'We need help, Caro,' Mussy murmured, coughing again.

'Trixie!' Caroline yelled, but thankfully Cavendish and Thomas caught Jacob as he fell in a faint.

Mayhem ensued as they brought Mussy and Jacob into the house and upstairs. Caroline helped Cavendish lay Mussy in her room and Thomas and Trixie eased Jacob onto Trixie's bed.

'What can we do?' Cavendish asked on the landing.

'We need Doctor Pike.' Caroline told him as she raced downstairs to heat some water.

'Mrs Lawson, these men...' Cavendish followed her, wanting answers, Caroline knew.

'They are our friends, Mr Cavendish. We are in no danger from them.'

'Are you sure? For it seems they were in some danger themselves, by the state of them, and they might have brought that danger to your door.'

Swallowing a moment of panic, she busied herself pouring water into the pans and kettle. 'I must help them.'

'What's happening?' Elsie asked, coming in from the parlour where both girls had been sent. 'Why is Jacob here?'

Caroline paused. 'He's been hurt and needs us to care for him, but I think it's best if you and Bertha go and stay with Annie tonight.'

'But I want to help,' Elsie pleaded.

'And you can, in a day or two, but for now it's better if you go to Annie's.' Caroline looked up at Cavendish. 'Would you take the girls into the village to Annie Aspall's house, please?'

'Certainly, and I'll call and ask Doctor Pike to come here.'

'Thank you.' She gazed into his blue eyes. 'You are a true and good friend.'

His gentle smile was his only reply and she told the girls to go and pack their nightdresses as she boiled the water and tore a large cloth into strips. Jacob needed his wounds cleaning. His face was battered just as Trixie's had been. What other injuries did he sustain? And Mussy? He looked ready for his coffin.

Thomas went with Cavendish and the girls, telling Caroline not to hesitate if she needed his help.

Carrying warm water up to Trixie's room, she kept her mind on the task ahead and tried not to let her mind whirl with questions.

'I've taken his boots off,' Trixie said, covering Jacob with a blanket. 'He's had a right beating that's for certain.'

'Like you did.' Caroline looked at her and placed the bowl on the bedside table.

Trixie paled. 'You think Victor Dolan has done this?'

'Perhaps.' She didn't know. She hoped not. 'Mr Cavendish has taken the girls to Annie's for the night.'

'Oh, good.' Trixie nodded, taking a cloth and starting to clean the blood from Jacob's poor face.

'And he's gone to fetch Doctor Pike.'

Trixie delicately wiped Jacob's forehead. 'And Mussy?'

'I'll go and check on him.' Caroline found Mussy asleep on her bed. She pulled his boots off and noticed the blisters on his feet. He wore no socks. His suit was grubby and stained. She'd never seen him look anything but dashing. Her heart melted for him, for he'd obviously been through an ordeal. She covered him with a blanket and closed the curtains. He needed the healing benefits of sleep.

Caroline and Trixie waited on the landing while Doctor Pike examined both men. Evening had fallen by the time the doctor indicated for them to go downstairs to the kitchen, where they sat at the table and Caroline poured out cups of tea.

'Well,' Doctor Pike removed his glasses and cleaned them on a square of velvet from his pocket. 'Your friends are in no immediate threat of meeting their maker. Mr Adams has suffered a terrible beating. I fear he has broken ribs.' He glanced at Trixie. 'In fact, he has very similar injuries to those you suffered. Does everyone get beaten up in York?'

'Only the unfortunate ones, Doctor,' Trixie answered quietly.

'Mr Casey is severely malnourished.' Doctor Pike replaced his glasses on his head. 'Has he been in prison? Shaved heads and malnourishment are often a sign.'

'Yes, he has.' Caroline sighed. 'He will be well again though, won't he?'

'I fail to see why he wouldn't be, in time. He needs his strength building up again. He's a tall man, he'll need plenty of nourishing food and rest. I do not like the sound of his chest. My guess he has pneumonia or tuberculosis.'

Caroline reeled back in shock. 'But he will recover?'

'Yes, yes, I should think so.' Doctor Pike sipped his tea and hid a yawn behind his hand. 'I must go. I've not been to bed since the day before yesterday. Napping all night on a chair beside a labouring woman is not very restorative.' He stood and pulled on his coat. 'I shall return tomorrow. Remember, keep both men warm, calm and plenty of water or tea, broth if you have it.'

Caroline paid him before he left, aware of how low her money supply was dropping.

Trixie watched her place the money pouch in a tin on the mantelpiece. 'We are short on money, aren't we?'

Nodding, Caroline sat back at the table. 'And another two mouths to feed won't help.'

'Why did they come to us?' Trixie asked. 'Mussy I can understand, but Jacob? Why would he not stay with Sarah and let her heal him?'

'I don't know, but we'll have those answers when they wake.' She stood and pulled on a shawl. 'I'll lock the hens up and check on the pigs.'

Trixie took the cups into the scullery. 'And I'll sit with Jacob. He's going to be in such pain when he wakes. I know only too well.'

Caroline paused by the back door. 'We need a stall at the market this week. I'll have to make some pats of butter to sell. Also, I need to start making the cheese rounds for them to mature. I thought if you could bake some cakes and bread to sell, too? We can have a stall next to Annie. We might be able to sell enough to buy more food, enough to last a little while. Our little kitchen garden isn't mature enough to harvest from yet.'

'Is money that tight we need a stall this week?'

Caroline nodded. 'I wasn't expecting to pay another doctor's bill, but if we have a stall and we sell well, we'll be fine. It just means I won't have time to help you care for Mussy and Jacob as I'll be outside all day in the dairy, and I must start ploughing the fields. I need to get the planting done.'

'Don't you worry about me. I can care for them both. You have enough to do.'

Chapter Twenty-One

In the days following, Caroline worked long hours. Waking before dawn, she saw to the animals and milked the cows and then set some of the milk aside for use in the butter and cheese making. After breakfast, she'd harness Dossy to the plough to churn up the soil in the field closest to the house.

Ploughing was hard and difficult work. Her hands blistered and her arms and shoulders ached as she fought to keep the plough down in the soil and the rows straight behind Dossy. At the end of the second day of ploughing, Caroline could have cried with exhaustion. For an experienced farmer, an acre should have been ploughed in one day, but it took Caroline three days. After ploughing each day, she then milked the cows again, worked in the dairy and fed the animals until nightfall brought her inside.

In those three days, Trixie cared for Jacob and Mussy. Caroline only saw them for a brief few minutes each evening before she fell onto the sofa and slept deeply.

By the fourth day, Trixie had baked three cakes and four loaves of bread for the market stall with help from the girls. Surplus eggs were packed in a straw-lined basket and Caroline had made several rectangle pats of butter. Trixie felt both Jacob and Mussy could be left for a few hours and told Caroline she and the girls, with Annie's help, would man the stall, leaving Caroline to start harrowing the field she'd ploughed.

Harrowing was easier than ploughing, and Caroline's back didn't ache as much as previous days, but the heat of the day tired her. She managed to finish the harrowing by late afternoon.

After settling Dossy in her stable and feeding her, Caroline went to the well and brought up the bucket. She was hot and dirty and needed a good wash. The cool water chilled her red face and soaked her bodice, but she didn't care. She scrubbed at her neck, wetting underneath her hair. She took off her bodice and stood in her corset and chemise to wash away the grime and smell of sweat.

A horse whinnied. She spun around, her bodice held up to cover her modesty. She scanned the trees lining the drive but saw nothing.

'Mrs Lawson, do not be alarmed,' called Cavendish, sat upon his horse. He rode through the hedge bordering the house field from the small woodland down by the creek.

Quickly dressing, Caroline felt ill at ease at the dishevelled state of herself. She tied on her bonnet and smoothed down her skirts. 'Mr Cavendish,' she greeted him as he dismounted.

'It is a warm day.' He smiled, looking cool and neat.

'It is, yes.' She was dismayed by the dirt stains on her skirt.

'I thought to call and see how your guests were faring?' His blue eyes were friendly, but also held a glint of interest.

'That is kind of you. They are still abed and needing a lot of care.'

'You must be finding it difficult to have so much to do and invalids to care for?'

'Trixie is their main carer. I have so much to do outside. I'm behind in the planting. But I'll get it done, do not worry on that score.'

As one, they turned and walked back towards the house with Cavendish leading his horse.

'I know you're working hard. I can see the evidence in the fields. Also, I saw Miss Wilkes and the girls at the market selling at their stall.'

'Indeed. We have only a small table of goods to sell this time but I'm hoping that will grow each week.'

He stared at the field she'd been toiling over. 'You've done well with that acre. It would have been a hard task as it hadn't been ploughed during last autumn. I would imagine the ground was thick with weed growth and old crop roots?'

'Yes, it was. Howard was too ill to till the soil. It hadn't been seen to since harvest time last year.'

'What do you plan to sow in that field?'

'Potatoes. In the next field I'll plant turnips for the animals' winter feed. I want to plough more fields ready for the autumn hay and wheat planting.' She relaxed a little talking about the farm.

'I could help with that.' He glanced at her and away.

'What do you mean?'

'Would you allow me to bring my team to plough?'

'Your team?'

'The horses belong to the estate, obviously, but I like to keep my ploughing skills honed. Sitting in an office all day or only riding about the district will soon make me fat,' he joked.

She liked that he could joke. She didn't often see that side of him. 'I doubt that, Mr Cavendish.' She glanced at his body, lithe and strong.

'Would you allow me though?'

Caroline hesitated. Did he feel sorry for her, doing it alone? Or did he think she was incapable of managing the farm without his influence and help?

They reached the house, and she stared in surprise at Mussy sitting on a chair by the back door, eyes closed. He'd not left his bed and barely been awake for three days. She ran to him. 'Mussy?'

He opened his eyes. 'I'm fine, Caro.'

'Why are you out of bed?'

'I needed to feel the sun on my face.' He closed his eyes again. 'I've been in hell for too long.'

'I'll make you some tea.'

'You're a sweet darling,' he sighed. 'I love you so...'

She turned to Cavendish. 'Would you care to stay for some tea?'

He looked quizzically at Mussy and back at her. 'No, thank you. I think I should be on my way. Good day.' He abruptly mounted his horse and rode out of the yard.

'Who was that?' Mussy muttered, eyes closed.

'Mr Maxwell Cavendish, the estate steward. He was here the day you arrived.'

'Was he? I don't remember much of that day. He's very handsome, Caro...' He opened one eye at her. 'I might like being in the country.'

'Enough of that talk.' She didn't know how to react to him when he spoke like that, knowing what she did about him.

He sat up straight, his gaunt face worried. 'You know I've been to prison, don't you? Bob told me he told you about my arrest.'

'He did, yes.'

'Am I still your friend?' his voice broke. 'Because that is who I am, Caro. That is me. If you condemn me, say it now and I'll go immediately.'

'How can I condemn what I don't fully understand?' she whispered sadly. 'Can I make us a cup of tea and you can explain it all to me?'

He nodded and sagged against the back of the chair.

'And I think you should tell me how you ended up here with Jacob Adams.'

'Has he not said?'

'He's barely been awake so Trixie tells me, and his jaw and nose is so swollen he can scarcely talk or eat.'

Mussy sighed. 'We need a *large* pot of tea, darling.'

After first checking on Jacob, who was dozing, Caroline made a tray of tea with a plate of oat cakes. Mussy had fetched another chair outside for her and a crate was used for a table.

Comfortable, tea in their hands, Caroline waited for Mussy to start.

He glanced at her. 'I don't know where to begin.'

'Tell me why you didn't come with us when we left Mrs Warburton's home. You said you would.'

'I couldn't, Caro.' He gazed down at his tea. 'You had to care for Trixie, and the girls, and you didn't need me and my problems on top of everything else.'

'How did you get arrested?'

'I had an argument with Owen, the tailor in Blake Street. Do you remember he was my friend?'

'I do remember.'

'He was the first man I'd had felt feelings for since Douglas, the first man I trusted since Douglas... But he used me and when the attention on us became too much, he tossed me aside like a used rag. He said I wasn't circumspect enough, my flamboyant manner brought us unwanted attention. Owen believed his business was suffering, the gossip, the rumours...'

'Do you think that was true?'

'I honestly don't know. Owen was ashamed of me I believe... Our relationship was beginning to flounder. We were at a private party, for men like us.' He glanced at Caroline. 'You understand?'

She nodded. A *men* only party. She'd never heard of any such thing and felt so naïve.

'Those places were called Molly houses down south, but not around here. They were safe places for us to be. Anyway, Owen and I argued, I stormed out and got drunk at some inn in a back lane near Bedern. I got friendly with a fellow. His name was Eddie... Eddie was similar to me, at least I thought he was, and I truly think he is of my persuasion, but he got scared when his friends turned up. Eddie blamed me for making advances on him and his friends knocked me about. I ran out of the inn, but Eddie followed me. I tried talking to him, but he refused to acknowledge his part in it all. Then a policeman saw us in the alley. Eddie accused me of an unnatural act. I was arrested, charged and sentenced to six months in jail.'

'Oh, Mussy.'

'Of course, Owen refused to have anything more to do with me. I managed to get word to Bob, and he wrote to my father who spoke to the right people and my sentence was reduced to three months.'

'And jail was hell,' she whispered.

'Oh, yes.' His chin wobbled with emotion. 'I cannot find the words to describe it, and I wouldn't, not to you, not to anyone. A person like me is... tortured.' His eyes filled with tears.

Caroline gripped his hands in sympathy.

'If I could have killed myself, I would have, but I had no means to do that except starve myself, but the guards would force feed me. I wrote to my father, the first time I've sent any correspondence to him in ten years, not since I left university. Father managed to have me released from prison. I don't know how, money changed hands I suspect. Father met me at the prison on the day I was released and said he was taking me away.'

'Away?'

Mussy stared across the fields. 'To an asylum to heal me, cure me.'

'Would it have worked, being at the asylum?'

He was quiet for a moment. 'As if it was that simple. I've tried to change, tried to be a proper man, whatever that is, but I can't. I don't like women in that way.' He looked at her. 'You know there have been men like me since ancient times? The Romans especially, who had the same-sex relations for power and control. I am not one man alone who feels like this!'

'But it is against the law, Mussy.'

He gave a mocking laugh. 'And that is why I must hide who I am. So, tell me, why should I continue to live? What is the point?'

'Don't say that. You are dear to me.'

'And you are the only one who cares for me.' Mussy kissed her hand.

'I know what it feels like to be alone in the world. When I first went to York, I had no one. Then you became my friend.'

'I bet you must regret that now?' He snorted. 'An unnatural!'

'I see *you*, Mussy, as my friend, nothing else.'

'How I wish others did, the world did.' He sighed heavily.

'What happened after you left prison?'

'When I refused my father's offer to go away, he told me that I was dead to him and to never contact him again. I was no longer his son. I went to Bob, who else could I go to? But I knew he didn't want me about the pub. My reputation was known, and me being at the pub would only bring trouble he didn't need when he was dealing with his grief over his mother's death. Bob told me you had gone home, and I should come and see you and get away from York. He gave me a letter from his mother, and she'd left me a hundred pounds in her will. She also named you in her will, too. She left you thirty pounds.'

Caroline's eyes widened in surprise. 'She did? I've not received a letter from her solicitor.' *Thirty pounds!* She could have cried with joy. That money would see the next quarter rent paid, and so much more. She would be forever grateful to Mrs Warburton.

'You will soon. Gordon has caused problems, contesting the will as Bob, being the eldest, received more of the inheritance than Gordon. Apparently, it all become rather undignified. It's all sorted now. Bob had my letter from his mother and the solicitor's letter with him. Naturally, Bob felt it better to hold on to such delicate information while I was in prison. I would imagine your letter from the solicitor will arrive imminently.'

'I shall go to the village tomorrow and ask at the post office. We don't get deliveries of mail out here. Howard always went into the village to collect it. That is kind of Mrs Warburton to think of me.'

'She was a good woman. Had a tongue as sharp as a boning knife, but kind-hearted underneath the brusqueness. She liked you.'

'She never once called me by my name.' Caroline chuckled.

Mussy snorted. 'A unique woman.'

'So how did you meet up with Jacob?' Caroline poured them more tea.

'Purely by chance.' Mussy sipped his tea and ate half an oat cake. 'I didn't know him, but I came across a fight late a few nights ago. I didn't want to get involved, I'd had enough beatings in my life to not go looking for them. As I was about to turn away, the thugs walked off, leaving the man on the street. I couldn't help myself and went to see if I could at least get him home or to the hospital.'

'Poor Jacob.'

'He managed to mumble the *water lanes* before he passed out. Luckily, a man he worked with came by and helped me to get him home to his sister. Jacob came around a bit and whispered something to his sister, who then asked us if we could get him away from York. I said he could come with me, I thought we could stay at an inn somewhere until he was able to look after himself and I could leave him and come to visit you. I didn't want to bring him here, to you. I didn't even know he knew you.'

'So, what happened?'

'By later that next morning, his sister found someone who said they'd give us a ride out of the city. Jacob woke up and said to me he knew some people called Caroline and Trixie and they lived in the country on a farm and might help him. I nearly fell over with shock when he mentioned your name.'

'I always hoped you'd came and visit, but I never expected you'd have Jacob with you.'

'Did we do wrong coming here?'

'No.' Caroline shook her head. 'I would never turn away a friend and Jacob was good to us when we needed him.' She stood. 'I shall go up and check on him. He needs more broth.'

Before she went inside the sound of the girls' chatter reached her. They came up the drive and seeing her, they ran the rest of the way, leaving Trixie walking behind.

'We sold everything, Caro!' Elsie blurted out before Bertha had the chance. They smiled at Mussy who they were shy of still.

'That's wonderful.' She hugged them to her. 'I'm very impressed.'

Elsie swung two empty baskets. 'The bread and cakes sold first, and then all the butter.'

'And the eggs.' Bertha added. 'I helped Annie sell her candles.'

'You both are very good to be so helpful. Now go inside and put the baskets away and have a drink.'

Mussy stood as Trixie approached.

'How are you feeling?' Trixie asked him. 'I'm pleased to see you out of bed.'

'Better. The sun is a tonic. Thank you for all your care and attention over the past few days. You have been extremely gentle and understanding towards me when I am but a stranger.'

Trixie shrugged at the praise. 'Caroline has told me a lot about you and if you're her friend, then I know you must be a good person. You must be for you brought Jacob here when he needed help.'

'I hope I can also be your friend, too?'

Nodding, Trixie gave a small smile. 'I'd like that.'

'I hear you had an excellent day,' Caroline said to her.

'I enjoyed myself.' Trixie held three empty baskets which Mussy took from her as they entered the kitchen.

Caroline made a fresh pot of tea and set a tray for Jacob. 'I'll take this up to him.'

'I can do it,' Trixie said.

'No, rest. You've just walked from the village.' Caroline took the tray up and went into the bedroom. Jacob was awake and he tried to smile with his swollen face. Every time Caroline looked at him it reminded her of Trixie's beating and how scared she was that Trixie would die.

'Tea.' She placed the tray down and poured him a cup. Then helped him to sit further up on the pillows. 'How are you feeling?'

'Fine,' he mumbled through split lips. 'Not so drowsy today.'

'That is a relief. Doctor Pike believes you had too many punches to the head, and it may have caused swelling on the brain. He says it's a wonder you survived.'

'I don't think they wanted me to...'

Caroline passed him the cup, which he held with hands bruised from fending off the attackers. 'Do you know who they were?'

'Victor Dolan's men.'

A shiver ran down her back. 'Trixie and I did wonder.'

'Dolan found out I helped you and Trixie to escape York.'

'I'm so sorry, Jacob, so very sorry.' Guilt wracked her. Because of her, two people had been close to dying. Saying sorry was inadequate.

'Not your fault.' He patted her hand. 'I made the choice to help.'

'And you could have paid for it with your life.' She rubbed a hand over her face. 'Please forgive me, Jacob.'

'Nothing to forgive.' He grimaced as the cut on his lips opened and bled. He dabbed at it with a square of cloth he held in his hand for that purpose.

Trixie came in and paused on seeing the seriousness between them. 'What is it?'

'Dolan's men did this,' Caroline told her. 'Revenge for Jacob helping us.'

Trixie lips tightened in anger. 'Will this ever be over?'

'It is,' Jacob mumbled. 'Now.'

'How can you be certain?'

'Because they are rats. Rats don't leave their own sewers.' Jacob winced as he moved. 'Dolan won't come out here. He doesn't know where you live. He has no power out here.'

Trixie turned to Caroline. 'Which is why we can never return to York.'

Caroline shook her head. 'I told you, I need to send the beasts to the market in York for Mr Bent.'

'Then I will take them.' Mussy stood in the doorway, having heard the conversation. 'Dolan doesn't know me.'

'It won't be until the end of summer though,' Caroline told him.

'So?' Mussy frowned.

Caroline blinked, stunned. 'You'll stay until the end of summer?'

'For always, if you'll have me?' Mussy grinned.

'Of course, we would be so happy if you stayed, but I thought you'd want to go to another city somewhere. You once told me you didn't like the country.'

'A man can change his mind, can't he?' Mussy tilted his head sardonically. 'Besides, I've had enough of cities, of streets full of strangers and nasty people.' He waved his hand theatrically. 'Perhaps it's time to embrace the quiet and peacefulness of the countryside, the birds and the flowers and all that?'

'Will you stay, too, Jacob?' Caroline asked. 'You would be very welcome, and I need a man's strength on the farm.'

'That's rude!' Mussy commented in mock horror. 'What am I, but a man?'

'Who's never done any manual labour in his life,' Caroline tutted with a grin.

Mussy bowed. 'That is true, my queen.'

Jacob looked at Trixie. 'I can never return to York. My sister Sarah has moved away because of the clearances, so there is nothing for me to return home to. I think I would like to stay and learn to become a farmer.'

Trixie took a deep breath, her expression soft. 'That sounds like a plan then.'

At that moment, Elsie and Bertha came in and the bedroom was full of chatter. Caroline's heart swelled. Her family was growing, and she was surrounded by good people who cared for her and she them.

The following morning, Caroline stood behind the cart ready to start Dossy off on the first row where Caroline would plant seed potatoes. Up at the house Elsie and Bertha were meant to be collecting eggs and feeding the sow and piglets but were more interested in showing Mussy around the farm.

The sound of horses and the jangle of harness broke the stillness of the early hour. Caroline turned and watched as Cavendish led a team of two shire horses up the road. He turned them into the field where Caroline worked and brought the horses to a stop beside her.

'Good morning, Mrs Lawson.'

'Good morning, Mr Cavendish.'

'I thought to make good my on promise to come and work one of your fields with my team.' His smile was tentative, waiting for her answer.

'I appreciate your help very much.' She felt nervous suddenly and shy.

His gaze was direct, but thoughtful. 'Shall I start on the next field across?'

'Yes. The plough is already at the top of the field as I was going to plough it next once I'd finished planting this field.'

'I admire your determination, Mrs Lawson. Not many women are inclined to work the fields alone as you are doing.'

'Well, I may not be alone anymore. Mussy and Jacob are going to stay and work on the farm with me.'

'Those men who turned up ill and beaten?' he asked incredulously.

'Yes. When they have recovered, they will help me.' She grabbed a handful of potatoes, careful not to knock the sprouting eyes off them.

He frowned, his blue eyes shadowed. 'Are they family?'

'They are dear friends who have become my family. And the way Jacob gazes at Trixie I wouldn't be surprised if in the future he became a sort of brother-in-law to me.' Joy enveloped her at that idea. She sincerely wished for Trixie to find love.

Cavendish kicked at the dirt with the toe of his boot. 'And the other fellow? Is he your suitor?'

'Mussy?' She laughed quietly and shook her head. 'No. Mussy isn't the marrying kind. He's come to the farm to live quietly. I see him as a sort of brother, and I am a type of sister to him. We are the very best of friends. A person can't have too many friends, don't you agree, Mr Cavendish?'

'I do, and I hope you count me as a friend and ally also, Mrs Lawson?' His dark eyebrows rose in question.

'Absolutely, Mr Cavendish, and I'm very grateful to have you in my life,' she spoke sincerely, meaning every word.

A moment passed between them, an acknowledgement of each other, a hint of something neither of them wanted to address nor deny just yet.

Abruptly, Cavendish's manner changed completely. He straightened, head high, shoulders back and his smile wide on his handsome face. 'I'd best get ploughing then.'

Caroline felt the happiest she had been in a long time. 'It's a great day for it, Mr Cavendish,' she said cheerfully.

His gaze locked with hers. 'The best day, Mrs Lawson, the best day.'

Afterword

Dear Readers,

Thank you for reading, The Winter Widow, a story I really enjoyed writing.

Once again, I have set a tale in York, a favourite place of mine that is full of history and still retains glimpses of bygone eras with its castle walls and charming streets.

The Water Lanes featured in the story have long gone. Slum clearances started in 1852 but took years to be fully demolished. Only the King's Arms public house still remains at the end of the 'First Water Lane' by the River Ouse. Although all the tenement buildings have been brought down, the lanes are still roughly in the same spot, but their names have been changed and new buildings now line each road. Using a resource of a 1853 map of York, I've been able to view where the Water Lanes were situated and other streets which are long gone. This gives me the chance to have my characters walk the original streets. I have also studied paintings of this area created before the clearances and read descriptions of the living conditions in the lanes to give me a sense of how it would look and feel.

York is a beautiful city in England, and I encourage anyone to spend a little time there and learn about its long and varied history.

I'd like to take this opportunity to thank my proofreader, Rachel Brimble, and any mistakes are mine not hers. No matter how many times we read and edit a book, it's still amazes us that some small errors get overlooked. We do our best but are, after all, only human!

I would also like to thank all those lovely readers who send me messages and emails about how much they enjoy reading my stories. I appreciate hearing from you so much. Thank you from the bottom of my heart.

Lastly, a huge thanks to my husband and family for their love and support. (They are still waiting for the Netflix deal) Haha!

Best wishes,

AnneMarie Brear

2024

About the Author

AnneMarie was born in a small town in N.S.W. Australia, to English parents from Yorkshire, and is the youngest of five children. From an early age she loved reading, working her way through the Enid Blyton stories, before moving onto Catherine Cookson's novels as a teenager.

Living in England during the 1980s and more recently, AnneMarie developed a love of history from visiting grand old English houses and this grew into a fascination with what may have happened behind their walls over their long existence. Her enjoyment of visiting old country estates and castles when travelling and, her interest in genealogy and researching her family tree, has been put to good use, providing backgrounds and names for her historical novels which are mainly set in Yorkshire or Australia between Victorian times and WWII.

A long and winding road to publication led to her first novel being published in 2006. She has now published over thirty historical family saga novels, becoming an Amazon best seller. Her novel, The Slum Angel, won a gold medal at the USA Reader's Favourite International Awards. Two of her books, The Tobacconist's Wife and The Market Stall Girl, have been nominated for the Romance Writer's Australia Ruby Award and the USA In'dtale Magazine Rone award respectively. More recently, AnneMarie's book, The Distant Horizon, was nominated as a finalist for the UK RNA RONA Awards 2022.

AnneMarie lives in the Southern Highlands of N.S.W. Australia.

If you'd like to learn more about her books, please visit her website where you can also sign up for her quarterly newsletter. http://www.annemariebrear.com

Also By

To Gain What's Lost
A Price to Pay
Isabelle's Choice
Nicola's Virtue
Aurora's Pride
Grace's Courage
Eden's Conflict
Catrina's Return
Broken Hero
The War Nurse's Diary
The Promise of Tomorrow
Beneath a Stormy Sky
The Tobacconist's Wife
The Orphan in the Peacock Shawl
The Soldier's Daughter
The Waterfront Lass

<u>Kitty McKenzie Series</u>
Kitty McKenzie

Kitty McKenzie's Land

Southern Sons

The Slum Angel Series

The Slum Angel

The Slum Angel Christmas

Marsh Saga Series

Millie

Christmas at the Chateau

Prue

Cece

Alice

The Beaumont Series

The Market Stall Girl

The Woman from Beaumont Farm

The Distant Series

A Distant Horizon

Beyond the Distant Hills

The Distant Legacy

Contemporary

Long Distance Love

Hooked on You

Printed in Great Britain
by Amazon

36871325R00189